PERFECTLY UNTRADITIONAL

PERFECTLY UNTRADITIONAL

Sweta Srivastava Vikram

NIYOGI
BOOKS

Published by
NIYOGI BOOKS
D-78, Okhla Industrial Area, Phase-I
New Delhi-110 020, INDIA
Tel: 91-11-26816301, 26813350, 51, 52
Fax: 91-11-26810483, 26813830
email: niyogibooks@gmail.com
website: www.niyogibooks.com

Editor: Gita Rajan
Layout Design: Nihar Ranjan Das
Cover Design: M/s. Seema Design

ISBN: 978-81-89738-86-0

Publication: 2011

This is a work of fiction. The names, characters and incidents portrayed in it are the work of the author's imagination. Any resemblance to actual persons, living or dead, events or localities, is entirely coincidental.

Printed at: Niyogi Offset Pvt. Ltd., New Delhi, India.

For Anudit,
my husband

ACKNOWLEDGEMENTS

Many, many, many wonderful people supported me in the writing of this book.

I thank my literary agent, Mita Kapur, at Siyahi for transforming *Perfectly Untraditional* into the book that it is today. Without her encouragement, I would never have begun *Perfectly Untraditional.* Her wisdom and vision astound me. I would also like to thank Gita Rajan, my editor at Niyogi Books, for her warmth, intuitiveness, insightfulness, timeliness, and patience. Her suggestions, both as a reader and editor, strengthened my book immeasurably. Special thanks to Mr. Bikash D. Niyogi, managing director of Niyogi Books, for his faith in my work.

Thank you also to Wendy Lee, Sumita Sheth, and my classmates at Asian American Writers' Workshop for their comments on the beginning of the book.

To find the most suitable title, I sought help from six friends, a.k.a my book-naming team: Hena Jawaid, Khurram Mirza, Samanta Batra Mehta, Shuchi Sethi, Sonal Sharma, and Sonya Choo. They analyzed every title I suggested and provided me with solid, candid feedback. Thank you, my dear friends, for your generosity and for unanimously voting *Perfectly Untraditional* as your number one choice.

I am indebted to those people, who helped me with my research about the gay community. Many of them went out of their way to assist me and shared private details of their lives. They prefer to remain anonymous, but they know who they are, and I would like to express my gratitude to them.

My warm appreciation goes to my friends, old and new, who influenced this novel: Brenna Sniderman, Deepika Mahajan, Jaya Sharan, Mayank Shahi, Vikram Anand and many others.

To my college friends from Pune—the city where I spent the most memorable years of my life—and members of my boarding school in Mussoorie, Oak Grove: You inspire me.

My deepest appreciation: my friend, Vivek Yadav, for sharing with me inimitable details about New Delhi; and his mother, Mrs. Savita Yadav, whose experiences helped inform my knowledge of the lives of Air Force officers in India over the last few decades.

I wish to note particularly two friends who encouraged my foray into fiction: Rashi Singhvi Baid and Sandhya Devanathan.

Thank you to my cousin, Nidhi Sinha, my sounding board, for loving and living the characters with me. She read multiple drafts of the novel and provided pertinent notes. I am fortunate to have you in my life.

I would like to extend my heartfelt thanks to my family, especially my father, for his gift of words and extraordinary thinking. To Diya and Sana, my nieces: You are awesome.

My husband, Anudit: For you, words can't describe what I feel. Thank you for being so supportive of your perfectly untraditional wife. You believed in me even at times when I doubted myself. May your patience remain unending.

1

While standing outside the car at Pashan Lake in Pune, India, Shaili Kapoor kept staring at the mystical, unrelenting rain imbuing her nonconformist choices. Leafing through memories and ripping out the mirage of perfect relationships from the inner layers of her belief, she conceded that the human heart was preordained to tell lies—sometimes to protect itself and at other times to shield the people it loved.

Shaili believed today was the day she had to make amends. It wouldn't be an easy task given her unpleasant past with her father, Suresh Kapoor. But it seemed the rain had washed away her animosity. Or maybe it was the fear of losing the only family member who was still alive and mattered. If Suresh Kapoor, after knowing the truth about his wife, Meena Kapoor, had somewhere in his heart forgiven her, Shaili too had to set things right. She owed it to him and her mother.

Shaili, with her long, sculpted fingers and feistiness of a solitary hunter, held Suresh Kapoor's arm and pulled at it—signaling him to step out of the car. At thirty-seven, she looked splendid and turned heads wherever she went. She looked not a day older than twenty-five: suave, svelte, fair-skinned with envious legs. In another life, Shaili could have been a super model. Suresh Kapoor's heavy lids, hidden behind his thick-rimmed glasses looked perplexed, but he stepped out. For the first time in his life, he listened to Shaili without being at loggerheads with her. It didn't go unnoticed by the two women sitting in the car: Shaili's gregarious, best friend from her childhood, her unshakable pillar of strength, Supriya Mhatre; and Persian American friend, Leila Makhmalbaf, who was visiting from New York City. The father-daughter duo looked intently at each other. The uneasiness between them was inarticulated but discernible.

"How come you are here?? I am surprised to see you." The loneliness, combined with stubborn pride was obvious in Suresh Kapoor's voice. Those were his first words all day. When the women had arrived at his house, Suresh Kapoor, a grimacer, was sitting by himself on the rocking chair, with his palms, reflective of adversity, tightly pressed together, as if latching onto a secret. He didn't haul mediocrity any better than most sixty-plus men; his face was slightly scarred by smallpox and the games of fate. Clad in a pair of white, spotless kurta-pyjama, he looked like he was in exile in his own house. Shaili hadn't seen him since her own marriage, ages ago. And she couldn't remember the last time she saw him without a glass of liquor, ever. Even after all these years, they didn't talk. Not even a hug. His conduct was almost foreseeable, like she'd never left Pune. And so was hers. He was exultant to see Shaili, but his ego didn't allow him to express elation. Shaili realized in an instant that she had inherited her pride from him.

Shaili had stared into Suresh Kapoor's eyes, like a child seeking acquiescence while owning up to something sacred, but he could not bear to look back at her. Shaili had started to walk towards the main door and like a stray, which had found a new home, Suresh Kapoor had staggered behind her. Or at least it had seemed that way. The four of them had silently entered inside the car—Supriya was behind the wheels and Mr. Kapoor sat next to her. Leila and Shaili had taken the seats in the rear of the car, which, according to Shaili, had earned them both condemning looks from Suresh Kapoor. Leila had sat behind Supriya and Shaili behind Mr. Kapoor. Logic renounced Shaili as preconceived notions and suspicion carved a temporary home on her sensitive mind. What Shaili hadn't noticed was that every now and then Suresh Kapoor would catch her reflection in the side view mirror. It was still raining heavily, but the path could be seen unmistakably. Shaili had asked Supriya to make a detour towards the lake, before they headed to the temple for the puja. Supriya, who was highly opinionated, had snapped and her faint mumbles had grown in volume and proportion. She expressed herself unreservedly and unrepressedly. She applied a sudden brake and the car screeched to a halt with a jerk.

"Okay. That's it. I have been mollycoddling you all day. The puja has to be done on time. We can go to the lake later." Supriya had thrown a fit.

"I need you to take us to Pashan Lake first. Please." Shaili was firm.

"This is outlandish."

"Don't make a big deal out of everything." Shaili tried to be patient. But she didn't enunciate why she wanted to spend a few minutes at the lake.

"I am making a big deal? I am sick of your adamancy." Supriya's language was polished, her pitch high and her fury unconstrained. "Why don't you understand? Panditji will leave for another puja in less than sixty minutes."

"It won't take long. Trust me. I promise." Against, all odds, Shaili tried to convince Supriya.

"I have reckoned with your obstinacy all afternoon. You will do what you want to do. Who will do the...?"

Shaili snapped but didn't lose control. In a gracious, even but assertive voice, she said, "I need to go *now*. But this is your car, so if you don't want to stop at the lake for a little bit, that's fine. Just stop the vehicle; I can take an autorickshaw from here." There was a deep-rooted conviction in Shaili's voice. Supriya hadn't heard it before. Something had changed about Shaili, and she couldn't dispute it. Supriya accepted defeat and took the turn towards Pashan Lake. Suresh Kapoor and Leila had sat silently.

Upon reaching Pashan Lake, Shaili asked Leila and Supriya to wait inside the car. The day seemed ideal for conversations—there was the possibility that the rain would drown out whatever was meant to go unheard. Supriya felt nervous. She knew the complexity of dealing with temperamental Suresh Kapoor. And she couldn't deny that Shaili could be overtly touchy too. But shockingly, for the first time, Supriya seemed unaware of what Shaili had in mind, which made her anxious. But she clearly understood Shaili wouldn't appreciate intrusion. Not today. Leila hadn't questioned Shaili's actions all along. She knew instinctively that with two extremely emotional people traversing through nostalgia, overwhelming challenges would surface. She could foresee a verbal bloodbath ensuing between Suresh Kapoor and Shaili once they started discussing each other's lives and unusual social choices. But she didn't lend unsolicited advice. Leila could be a persuasive talker, but if she believed it wasn't her place to interfere, she could sit as mute as a cadaver. She wasn't austere or rude, just slightly aloof, with impressively modest, deep set eyes.

When Shaili pulled Suresh Kapoor's arm, Supriya immediately realized why Shaili had insisted on making the diversion; it was Meena Kapoor's final resting place. Not just that; Pashan Lake was the epicenter of the Kapoor household. It had played a vital role in how the lives of the Kapoor family members had turned out. Supriya knew Shaili was at Pashan Lake, with her father, to bury skeletons of yesterday and consider new beginnings. A cool breeze nudged her heart. She felt hopeful for her friend. She had folded her palms and thanked the pale sky. Leila had said eight syllables to Supriya, "No wonder Shaili adores you."

"Why the hell are you here? Howcome? After all this time?" Suresh Kapoor uttered impassively.

"God, you'll never change!" Shaili rolled her eyes impatiently.

"What do you mean?"

"Your trenchant criticism."

"What criticism? I am asking a valid question." Suresh Kapoor didn't hold himself back. He wasn't an exhibitionist, so he had kept his frustrations caged in Leila and Supriya's presence. But once outside the car, with just Shaili around, he felt it was okay to let go, to convey his dissatisfaction.

"Oh really? So, you are telling me that you were not taunting me?"

"Why would I do that?" Suresh Kapoor sounded peeved.

"Can you blame me? That's what you excelled at!"

Suresh Kapoor pulled his glasses and wiped them with the corner of his kurta. His face wore no expression when he said, "Even after all these years, you are still the same—over-sensitive, full of childish outbursts."

"Don't patronize me!" Shaili's aggravation grew volumes. But in the blink of the eye, she looked sedated. She knew Suresh Kapoor wasn't off the mark, but she didn't want to admit her mistake openly. She stood silent for a few minutes and started again. "Do you understand how confused I am? I don't know where to start. What I can tell you is that I didn't think I would be here today. Less than two days ago, when Leila had suggested that we travel to Pune, I was unwilling." Her emotions were vulnerable, but her tone imperturbable.

"Why is that?" asked Suresh Kapoor with genuine curiosity.

"You hate who I am."

"Utter nonsense!" Suresh Kapoor, never of shy of exaggeration, screeched until his lungs turned pale.

"Is that so? Give me one darn second. I'll prove it to you."

"What now?"

"Since you like me and all, you should be okay with what I'm about to do next. Right? Guess what? I want you to officially meet my girlfriend. How about that? Huh? Welcome her into the family and all."

Before Suresh Kapoor could register any of the happenings, Shaili signalled Leila to get out of the car and join her and Mr. Kapoor. Leila, who was pragmatic but not meek, met Shaili's request. She had minimal tolerance for brouhaha and therefore tried to avoid it like the plague. Leila was dressed in a green salwaar kameez. The outfit fitted oddly on her robust, Persian frame though the color suited her olive skin tone. The salwaar kameez was tailor-made for Supriya who was very differently built than her. Moreover, Leila had a tomboyish taste in clothes that accentuated her cropped hair. Under different circumstances, Shaili would have teased and called her, "GI Jane," but today Shaili's sense of humor was buried under a torrent of distraught sentiments.

Upon reaching the spot where the duo was arguing, Leila stood unobtrusively but confidently, like the moonless night. Shaili introduced Suresh Kapoor to Leila in a melodramatic fashion. Leila, calmly, extended her right hand towards Suresh Kapoor and said a hello, but he averted his face and ignored her gesture. His eyes, flooded with copious amounts of humiliation, couldn't deal with the way Shaili had handled the situation. He felt her behavior reflected poorly on her upbringing. Leila stood calmly, but Shaili took offence. She glared at him and said, "Why? What happened now?"

"There is a time and place for everything, which of course you won't understand."

"Admit it. You didn't want me here and neither did Tanisha." Shaili retorted insistent on marking her point.

"You will believe what you want to," said Suresh Kapoor in a matter-of-fact manner.

"Oh really! When you found out the truth about me, didn't you yell at Ma, *'Meena, you named her Shaili. It means tradition. This is tradition? Loving another woman? This is from all the sick American movies she watches and from you. Both of you are characterless. You made your daughter like you. She will never set foot in this house ever again! Tell her that!'* God, you thought of me as some lawless rebel. And not just you; Tanisha was all riled up as well! *'What will my in-laws say, Ma? Loving another woman? Chheecheee. I can't keep up relations with her. I don't want my children to think what Shaili is doing is okay. I don't know about you, but we still have to live in this society. We are in India and not her New York.'* Just like that my own sister broke off ties with me—the same sister, for whom I went out on a limb, so she could marry a Muslim. You had threatened to disown her. Her in-laws took a long time to come around as well—not until the grandchildren were born. Abdul and Tanisha of course had no money. I was the one who took care of everything even though I could barely make ends meet. I didn't go out, for months, so I could send her money for the start of her new life."

Shaili's cheeks were tear-stained with disappointment as she regurgitated the venom her own sister had lashed at her. She decoded Tanisha's conceited personality better than everyone else. Tanisha had her father's face and hairy body and her mother's short stature. Her studious glasses were noticeable from a kilometer away along with the vindictive burst of acne, which made Tanisha covetous of Shaili's flawless beauty and the attention she got. While she spent her teenage years dabbing *Clearasil* on her face, Shaili remained unconcerned about her own beauty. However, Tanisha also had her father's pride inscribed in her genetic structure. She would never tell Shaili how much she admired her. She was surreptitiously thrilled to find out that Shaili was gay. The disclosure had made her father even more spiteful towards Shaili and Tanisha felt that she could finally win all the brownie points in his books and gain her mother's attention. Eloping and marrying Abdul had not earned her any credit but she was hoping Shaili's pronouncement finally would.

"It's complicated," said Suresh Kapoor in a crisp but committed tone.

"Try me." Shaili said hastily.

Leila sensed, in her presence, Suresh Kapoor was holding himself back. She decided to leave the two alone, again. But before excusing herself, she asked Shaili to step aside. She whispered, "Remember the pitfall of excessive pride," in Shaili's unyielding ears. Leila, in contrast to Shaili and especially Supriya, was economical with words. They were like bullets out of a gun; headed towards a precise point. Shaili didn't respond but mellowed down, even if for a few seconds.

"Is she the one who broke up your marriage?" Suresh Kapoor asked with cavalier curiosity in his eyes just when Leila reached the car.

"What are you talking about?" Shaili replied while stifling her sniffles.

Suresh Kapoor pointed in Leila's direction. "Her. Was she the reason for your break-up?"

"God, is that what you think? Geez, you are petty!" Shaili squealed.

"You made all the decisions yourself after you moved away. I don't remember being involved. And then you show up for your mother's last rites, with her, so am I wrong in assuming? Tell me!" Suresh Kapoor seemed as impenetrable as a rock.

"You are so clueless!" Shaili was horror-struck.

"Then answer my question!"

"Geez, small-mindedness is your forte, isn't it? Everything is one-track. You can't, just can't, think beyond your…"

"I should never have let you move to America. You got it from there." Suresh Kapoor's tone was terse as he interrupted Shaili.

"Homosexuality is not a disease!" Shaili fought back like a warrior. Disgust blew bubbles from her nostrils as her eyelids, exhausted from old bitterness, pleaded for mercy.

"*Battameez*! Do you, in your impudence, even remember how to talk to your elders? Or what to say to them? In India, we don't have any such nonsense." Suresh Kapoor spoke with the stubbornness of a teenager who expects to be reprimanded.

"How naïve is that! What makes you think gays don't exist in India? You are a toad in a well! Nauseating! What limited perspective!" Shaili was bleeding fury. "Are you even aware of the statistics of people leading dual lives in India? Living in denial isn't the solution to problems. Trust me."

"You were normal so long as you lived in Pune." Suresh Kapoor dismissed Shaili's remarks and continued to put forth his point.

"And normal to you would be an irate, self-loathing girl who excelled at academics and sports but barely spoke with anyone or had any friends. Sure, then I could be called out-of-the-league normal."

"I know the liberal culture in that country gave you all those horrible ideas. Look at yourself."

"Like I said, you are prejudiced!"

"Why? Because I'm old-fashioned? Believe marriage is a union between a man and a woman? Because I follow our culture? Indian culture!"

Suresh Kapoor, known for his acerbic utterances, spoke with poise. His disposition, at the time, placated Shaili. She said softly, "If I had forgotten Indian culture, I wouldn't be talking to you right now."

Suresh Kapoor tried to mask his self-consciousness when he sprung back and huffily said, "Tell me. Where did I go wrong? When you were in Pune, I did not even allow you to date anyone."

"And how do you think that worked out?"

"You were on the right path. Focused. You went to college and spent time at home. I made sure."

"Don't you think you did me a disservice by forbidding me from mixing with boys while I was growing up?"

"What rubbish!" Suresh Kapoor declared vehemently.

"If you hadn't coerced me into implicitly submitting to your insistence, who knows what today would have brought. If you'd permitted me to socialize with guys in college and in my MBA program, my instinctive reaction might have introduced me to my true self. If I, maybe, had a boyfriend when I was younger, I might have known sooner than later that I didn't like men. Not that way at least. Maybe we would all have diagnosed that I was not your typical, perfectly traditional, Indian girl."

Shaili wasn't even allowed to look at boys just as her mother wasn't permitted to look at other men. Shaili was admitted into an all-girl convent right from when she was in kindergarten. If it were left to Suresh Kapoor, Shaili would wear a sari or a burkha to school even though the school had zero presence of any Y chromosome in a five-kilometer radius. Suresh Kapoor gave consent to playdates on the condition that Shaili played with just the girls in her neighborhood. Shaili wasn't allowed to go for sleepovers if her friend had a brother. Mrs. Meena Kapoor didn't agree with her husband's whimsical stance on his kids' upbringing, but she chose to keep quiet for the sake of sanity and peace at home. She had enough problems to reckon with everyday. And deep down she knew why he acted like a stubborn mule. After all, Suresh Kapoor wasn't always a harsh man.

Shaili wanted to say so much more to him, but she let the thunderous downpour do the talking until they reached the abyss, so the dead too could overhear their long overdue tête-à-tête. She picked up a twig, absentmindedly, but just as she was about to maul the waters with it, something stopped her. Her mother, Meena Kapoor, would never allow Shaili to throw stones in the lake. She believed it disrupted the concealed life underneath the unseen depths. She compared it to disrespecting the dead using an Ouija Board. Shaili didn't fully comprehend her mother's point of view, but she didn't care to question her reasons. At that instant, she knew she would require the strength and support of everyone in her universe.

Shaili turned to Suresh Kapoor, "I will regard all your assumptions and queries, but I too have a question or two for you."

"What?" He sounded feeble. You could tell fate had defeated him but pride kept him afloat. Even the air around the two sounded incensed, trapped rage that could have been cut with a knife.

"To be fair, let's play rock-paper-scissors. Whoever wins goes first."

"I am not here to have casual talks! And what is this rock?" Suresh Kapoor grappled with the name. Shaili explained to him that it was a game often used as a selection method—similar to coin flipping. Suresh Kapoor breathed loudly from his nose but indulged Shaili. After a few rounds, they figured he won and would therefore get to ask the questions first.

"My turn?" Suresh Kapoor asked. Shaili nodded. He said plainly, "Everything is just a big game to you, isn't it? Regardless of whom it hurts, you play along."

"I don't believe that's a question." Shaili ignored Suresh Kapoor's multi-layered rumble.

"*Fine*! You want to play question game? My first question: Who is Leila? How did she find you?"

"Find me?! What was I, a three-year old lost in a fancy fair? Geez!" Shaili rolled her eyes. "You might want to rephrase your question." She spoke firmly.

Suresh Kapoor cleared his throat, indignantly, a few times. "What is this Leila's good name?" Shaili caught the condescending undertone but didn't say anything. She was surprised they were finally having a real conversation instead of lashing out at each other. She thought of Ma's words, *"Two angry people can't make a conversation, only chaos,"* and, in her head, decided to take the higher road.

"Well, Leila's last name is Makhmalbaf."

"That's all?"

"She is of Persian ethnicity. She is a famous artist who likes to read poetry. What else? Let's see. She grew up in Tehran with her parents and studied there until she moved to New York. That's pretty much what would interest you about her." Shaili withheld a significant amount of information about Leila's past. Though Leila's life was an open book uncaring about the details enclosed in its chapters, Shaili felt it was a little too soon to disclose all the contents to Suresh Kapoor.

2

Shaili didn't tell Suresh Kapoor that, at a very young age, Leila knew she was different from her peers in many ways. She was an individual with absolute certainty about what she wanted: A name for herself as an artist and not babies with a man. At the time when her friends were rebelling against the fundamentalist government that castigated meeting members of the opposite sex in public in Iran, she was secretly fighting a crush on her art professor, Dr. Mehnouz, a married woman. Dr. Mehnouz eventually became Leila's first kiss, first passionate hug, her first lascivious affair. She recognized the look in Leila's eyes—the familiar misplaced gaze. She had been there at one time. She still had that look. It was just not apparent to her husband or in-laws or children. Dr. Mehnouz couldn't openly admit who she was, so she hid under the societal pretenses of marriage and children. They grew up in times where an exposed strand of hair could put women behind bars for indecent exposure. Headscarves were mandatory. Women weren't even allowed to sing in public. So, openly admitting that one was gay was close to hara-kiri. Of course, there was no support from the families either. Women were supposed to be objects that satisfied man's needs and gave them offspring.

Dr. Mehnouz introduced Leila to a secret society in Tehran that catered to women like them. It was an underground civilization, not an open movement, which worked both as a matchmaking portal and as a counseling center. After all, all the women, whom Leila met there, led double lives. It wasn't easy renouncing the reality about their identity, but they did that to stay alive. What option did they have? If found out, lesbians could have earned retribution—ranging from between hundred lashes to death by stoning, or worse.

Leila didn't want to lie about who she was, but she realized that neither did the other women. She wasn't looking to be a martyr on a mission, so she had to be sensible about picking her battles. She wanted to satiate her artistic appetite. That's it. She accepted that she needed to be a part of the system before she could fight it.

She and Dr. Mehnouz found an easy way to spend time together. Leila asked her parents if she could take extra art lessons, a few times a week, at Dr. Mehnouz's residence after college. Dr. Mehnouz's family wasn't back until later in the evening, and they had the house to themselves, so Leila wasn't intruding. Ironically, it was acceptable for people of the same sex to personally tutor their students at home, locked inside the four walls. Leila had chuckled at the logic of the society, but it worked for her, so she didn't criticize it. The unsuspecting parents were elated because Leila wasn't boy-crazy as her other peers and wanted to focus on what she liked. She hadn't, not even once, argued with them about meeting a mixed group of classmates for coffee and pastry or sneaked out for a forbidden get-together. She met with the members of the underground society in the middle of the day, without her parents' knowledge. Even when at home, she chose to spend her free time drawing and sketching. Her parents couldn't have been happier with Leila. She was the epitome of obedience in her community. Or so they thought. They let her pursue art thinking she could teach those skills to her future children—something that would keep her busy while she swam through multiple pregnancies.

Leila and Dr. Mehnouz met twice a week. Leila later accepted that their alliance was more than experimenting and expressing their physical desires. They discerned each other's thoughts in an unsaid way. Their challenges were the same. Leila found a friend in Dr. Mehnouz—someone who appreciated her and didn't judge the commonsensical but invisible layers in her personality. Thanks to Dr. Mehnouz, Leila never lost sight of her ambition. In fact, Dr. Mehnouz continued to inspire Leila.

Leila wanted to become a professional artist, display her work globally, and hold art exhibitions. Her pieces in Tehran weren't an accurate reflection of her. How could they be? Her life there was a farce, so nothing she produced was from the soul. She considered fleeing Iran, but she knew that was a risky choice. She knew America was the answer to her prayers—a place that would allow her to openly acknowledge her true self and in turn produce pieces that represented her individuality. If the need be, she was determined to dig a tunnel to America.

Her next-door neighbor, Ariana, had started her own label of clothing in New York. She didn't wear a hijab or a burkha. Her skin saw the sunlight and soaked it like the parched earth consumes the monsoon. She spoke her mind and lived on her terms. Granted her husband, Amin, had been her biggest supporter in her entrepreneurial voyage, but the pursuit was her own. Ariana joked about how she made up for twenty years of not drinking by consuming a bottle of wine every night with Amin and their friends. Of course, Leila's parents didn't want her socializing with Ariana lest she exert a bad influence on their daughter. The community had ostracized Ariana for turning "American." But she was truly blissful. She had never once looked back and regretted her decisions. That's what Leila wanted—contentment, vision, and desire to take fruition.

So, when Soroush Firozi's family asked for Leila's hand in marriage, despite no feelings for him, she agreed. Practicality was Leila's favorite accessory. Staying detached helped because her opinion wouldn't have mattered much. She knew he was her passport to independence. Leila's parents too thought Soroush was the key to their daughter's freedom. He would take her away from the mayhem in Tehran to the land of opportunity where the Firozi clan was well settled.

Soroush's two older brothers had a carpet business in Queens, New York, which is where he would work. The family stayed together in Great Neck, out in Long Island along with a few dozen Iranian families. The sense of community was necessary to keep the women tame and prohibit them from turning Western. All the women spent the afternoon together preparing Chelo-Kebab or Khoresht, without ever discarding their headscarf or the traditions they'd brought, in their memory, from their birthplace.

Soroush and Leila's marriage didn't last long. He was a reasonable man, but Leila couldn't bear him any children. What he didn't know was that Leila didn't want any kids and she'd made sure of that. After years of faking her sexuality and suppressing herself, Leila drove him to a point where he settled to file for divorce. As part of the divorce settlement, Leila got an apartment in Tribeca, which is where Shaili and she would eventually live. This was the apartment where Soroush spent the night if he was working late. Leila didn't ask for alimony; she was relieved to bid adieu to her phony life and everything that reminded her of it, but her Persian, female lawyer, made sure she was well taken care of. Soroush was foolish enough to state his grounds for divorce as "Can't bear children." Leila's lawyer had referred to Soroush as stupid. Luck was on Leila's side; the judge who was to decide the case was a female.

Leila joined Pratt School for a Bachelor's degree in Visual Arts. Ariana and Amin provided her with meals in exchange for her babysitting services and few hours a day of minding the cash register at *Khubz*. It's not like she needed their help; the divorce settlement assured she would lead a comfortable life as long as she lived. But she wanted friends who accepted her even though she was "nonconforming" compared to most of her contemporaries back home.

Her parents had threatened to disown Leila upon hearing the news of the disintegration of her marriage especially when she told them that the breakup was her idea. Her mother was livid when she found that her daughter was barren. She had recommended that Leila ask for Soroush's mercy, for being infertile, and suggest that he marry another woman while Leila spent her life atoning in a deserted corner of his house. The other woman could have his heirs, and this way, Leila would not be stigmatized as a sterile woman or, worse still, a divorcee. With the charade, she could continue to live within the confines of the community in Great Neck.

But Leila was sick to her bones of subterfuge. She decided to tell her parents the reality about her marriage; the haunting darkness of her desires; the travesty of her life. They were of the notion, as a woman and that too an unproductive divorcée, she had no right to desires. But they were disgusted to learn that their only daughter had become a fraudulent Westerner and had chosen a lifestyle condemned by their religious faith.

But Ariana and Amin understood Leila implicitly. The three shared an unspoken bond. They were cognizant why deception was incumbent upon them to survive given where they came from. After all, Ariana and Amin had staged their marriage to be arranged; the two of them were dating even before their parents ever met. But neither of them breathed a word about it. They had told Amin's aunt, who had draped the relationship in the preferred communal garb and suggested the alliance to the parents.

In New York, Leila took great pleasure in School. It was everything she'd ever imagined it to be. Or maybe it was the autonomy of choice that made her treasure her experience more. She took classes in the evening and worked various jobs across multiple studios in Manhattan and Brooklyn. She did several art residencies in Europe, Asia and South America and finally a Master of Arts in Visual Arts Administration from New York University. After numerous rejections, one of the contemporary art galleries in Chelsea signed up Leila for a solo show. The event won several accolades and tremendous press coverage. Soon her flight to success commenced, and she never looked back.

3

Shaili's mind was still on Leila's journey from Tehran to New York City when Suresh Kapoor broke up her thoughts by repeatedly asking, "What about her parents? Leila's? Are they okay with all this you both are doing?" He spoke roughly, as he sensed Shaili was being stingy. He yearned for more information about his daughter's life. Shaili, blinded by experiences of her past, assumed he was looking for a way to blame her arrangement on someone else.

"Her parents still live in Tehran. And no, they aren't ecstatic about Leila's arrangements. Just like you, right?" Shaili gauged that Suresh Kapoor looked affronted with her bluntness. But before he could say anything further, Shaili said, "Hold on. You had your chance. It's my turn now to ask a question."

"Bolo."

"I have been meaning to ask you something."

"Come on, say what you want."

"How should I address you?"

"What kind of a stupid question is that?" The banality of Shaili's query confounded Suresh Kapoor. He felt she was making extra efforts to be unreasonable.

"I called you Daddy growing up, but Ma is no more. What does that make us? How would you define our relationship?" Shaili's intentions in posing those questions weren't as simple as her dialogue delivery.

Suresh Kapoor sermonized. "I don't know what you think, but to me, you will always be my daughter. My first child. No one can change that! But you are an adult and it is apparent no one can tell you what to do, so *you* make the judgment!" Rue and woe flirted with his eyes as he spoke. The same eyes that had demanded compliance and respect.

Shaili knew that his response was unpretentious, which left her feeling aghast. She remembered him as a man who loved and hated her simultaneously, which always left her wondering. He never truly shared his caring side with his elder daughter.

Suresh Kapoor was a narcissist who never missed an opportunity to abandon Shaili. She was a precocious child who earned good marks throughout her school and college life. Her performance was exemplary even when it came to extracurricular activities. She made her mother, Meena Kapoor, very proud. And secretly, Suresh Kapoor too. He would gloat about Shaili at work, but Suresh Kapoor never once said anything affectionate or encouraging to her face. He would smile, internally, when the teachers called Shaili a gifted child. Every semester, when Shaili brought home her honor student report card, Mrs. Kapoor would embrace her. Five *Five Star* chocolates were what she would give her daughter as a reward for her academic excellence; but Suresh Kapoor would remain mum. But after Shaili had left the room, he would wrestle his superciliousness and celebrate his daughter's brilliance. He would twirl his moustache upwards in approval.

But today, she got the feeling that he meant what he said. Something *was* different.

"This is the first time in over a decade that I have heard your voice." Suresh Kapoor said prosaically. His body language had altered, slightly, like Shaili's, but his style of conveying his thoughts remained unchanged—combative.

"You were the one who decided to cut off all relations." Shaili spoke haughtily to disguise her wounds, still fresh and raw. On some level, she couldn't believe the words escaping her mouth. Never in a million years had she imagined having a heart-to-heart with the man she had grown up to hate, curse, and wish death upon. She had made her peace with fate, but finding out that there might be a reason justifying his actions hurt a lot more.

"What did you expect, Shaili?" Suresh Kapoor tried to enter Shaili's world.

"Did you just call me by my name?!"

"Now, why is that so shocking?" Suresh Kapoor, understandably so, was piqued. Shaili kept throwing darts of insolence at him.

"Do you recall the last time you called me Shaili? Frankly, I don't. I was always a pronoun or a bad adjective to you." The anguish in Shaili's tone was evident.

"Are you telling me that I never said anything good about you or taught you anything good in your life?" Suresh Kapoor didn't appreciate the serrated allegations nibbling at him. He stood his ground. "You weren't the easiest child to deal with! Unpredictable, moody, and so different from everyone else. And you accuse me of not being good to you?!"

"Don't act hurt! I regard you as my mentor." Even an infant could have detected the disdain in Shaili's voice. She continued, "After all, you get all the credit for teaching me about resentment and abhorrence. You were my coach for personal failures, *Daddy*." Shaili, dramatically, bowed down to Suresh Kapoor.

"But…" Suresh Kapoor stood cemented when Shaili interrupted him, again, with tears burning her clothes. "You always hated me. Didn't you? Why *did* you hate me? C'mon, say something!"

"Shaili, behave yourself!" Suresh Kapoor was appalled at Shaili's appetite for hatred. And somewhere he began to realize that nothing could erase the bitterness inside her. Her perspective on her past was biased.

"C'mon! Everyone knew you had it in for me. Spit out the reason."

Shaili's intrepidness made Suresh Kapoor uncomfortable. He felt cornered and screamed, "Because you lied."

Shaili responded simultaneously. "I *never* lied!" She was displeased with Mr. Kapoor's disclosure. She was the kind of person who didn't resort to guile even if her life depended on it. And he had blatantly called her a liar.

"You lied to your parents even though a family is the most important thing. You had no regard for anybody. Not even your mother—the one family member you loved! You never once thought what people would say to us or how Tanisha's marriage would be arranged or how your mother could show her face in the society. You did what suited you best, and we faced the brunt of it all. Even today you complain about the ties I broke up with you. Do you have any idea what damage you caused us?" Suresh Kapoor's tone was frank, wounded, and intimidating, but Shaili didn't fear him. She felt a wave of self-realization consume her. She accepted that in battling her quagmire, she had never once asked her ma or Supriya if and how her decision had affected their lives. She felt remorseful.

Suresh Kapoor's pent-up rage lashed out unrestrainedly. He said, "You say that you don't lie? What did you do with Sadhil Sethi? Why did you leave him?"

4

Sadhil's name paralyzed Shaili. The name echoed for a few seconds. Pashan Lake had never seemed eerier. She'd been there innumerable times. Up until Shaili got married, her mother loved taking her down to the lake without telling Suresh Kapoor or Tanisha. Her mother insisted they admire the migratory birds together. Shaili wasn't exactly into ornithology, but the place had a tranquil effect on her mother so she was only too thrilled to accompany her. And like a faithful dog she never said a word to anyone about those outings. Trips to Pashan Lake were amongst their own little clandestine moments. Shaili treasured those lone times with Ma, the goddess she worshipped. But today, the breeze had a different essence to it. It seemed thick with the secrets nestling within its folds, ready to mingle with the downpour, whisper into unwilling ears.

Shaili had come prepared to answer many questions. But she didn't think it would start with the first relationship she ended fifteen years ago. Shaili's mind went to the fateful day that brewed up the unanticipated marital talks in the Kapoor household and eventually led to the meeting with Sadhil.

When Shaili was barely twenty-one or twenty-two and still pursuing an MBA from *Symbiosis*, Mr. Kapoor decided it was time for her to tie the knot. He gave no reason, no explanation, whatsoever. They argued one morning and the following week, he made up his mind to marry her off.

"But, I don't want to. I haven't even completed my MBA," Shaili tried to give her reasoning.

"Who asked you? You have a sharp tongue. You dare argue with me? All your time is spent with those boys. I told you I don't want you going out with them. I never should have bought you that damned *Kinetic Honda*. Loose cha…" Mr. Kapoor held himself back.

"What boys?" Shaili was unsure where the conversation was headed. She didn't know what or who her father was referring to.

"Lying to me!" Mr. Kapoor growled, threatening to slap her.

Shaili could feel the nerves around her neck tighten. "He wouldn't dare. He better not," she hissed to herself.

"I will shoot you and that boy! Is that why I am sending you to an MBA program? So you can make boyfriends and have fun with them? How many times in a day does he call! Does he have nothing better to do? That Deepak boy."

"Deepak is just a friend, Daddy." The revulsion in Shaili's tone was obvious. Suresh Kapoor had made a ridiculous allegation when she had followed his rules for over two decades now. She didn't socialize with boys. Granted, it made her gauche around them, but she didn't go behind his back to speak to boys. Unlike her sister, who had more boyfriends than clothes in her wardrobe.

"He was just calling to ask about an assignment. He isn't my boyfriend," Shaili sounded irritated.

"Don't argue! I won't tolerate it! Your mother has taught you nothing. You are just like her! Wearing short skirts and talking to men. I must end this nonsense or else you will become like your mother and..." He paused for a second and swallowed his fury.

"Huh? I will become like my mother? What did you mean by that? What about Ma? Tell me!" Shaili looked perplexed by the last few sentences uttered by Suresh Kapoor.

Mr. Kapoor caught his breath, then screamed, again, "I have found a boy for you in America. He and his parents are coming to see you. I am warning you, I don't want any drama! You meet him!"

"But…" Shaili tried to protest, but it was of no use.

Mr. Kapoor clenched his teeth and yelled, "Out of my sight."

Shaili had dreamed of chopping off her father's tongue and arms one night when he was asleep. She stormed out of the living room and sat on her bed grumbling. Mrs. Kapoor followed her inside while Tanisha stood uninterestedly in the kitchen speculating if her arms needed waxing.

"Brilliant! I have no say in my own life! First that man didn't let me study journalism. Why? Because he feared I would speak my mind? Yeah, like not studying it is going to stop me? Then, he believed I would share rooms with men and spend too much time with them when away on assignments. Really? Sick! Sick! Sick! What does he think, Ma? Every woman, who has a mind of her own, is a slut? Why is he so mistrusting of men and women as friends? Just what does he think?" Shaili squealed with blood in her eyes. She stood up and started pacing across the room restlessly.

Mrs. Kapoor tried to pacify her. "*Beta*, try to understand."

"I am trying, Ma, but I don't get him." Shaili continued pacing agitatedly. "He forced me to go to business school, so I could be financially independent. Aha, but he doesn't want me to have an opinion, so no journalism. What kind of logic is that??"

"Shaili, listen to me. It's not like that."

Shaili looked at her mother in disbelief. She put her hands on her hips and continued, "Really? 'Not like that?' What do you mean? He expects me to not talk to boys even though ninety five percent of my classmates are males. Should I wear a sack to college and demand an all female section? *Haan*? Or maybe your husband can create a country where only women live. Tanisha and I can be shipped there, and we'll kill anyone who even dreams about a man." Shaili was furious.

"Which world does he live in, Ma? Your times were different when women spoke only to four males—their fathers, brothers, husbands and sons. In fact not even to husbands or fathers come to think of it. I mean, I don't even know how to feel around men because I have never really had a *conversation* with one. 'Deepak, I don't think Professor Patil wanted you to reiterate what Kotler said' doesn't count for talking to men. Deepak talks to me *only* because we were teamed together, in the same group, for an assignment: I work hard for the two of us and get high marks; and he hangs out in the canteen with his posse and his lame girlfriend."

Shaili looked for an answer in her mother's eyes. "And why does he drag your name into everything? He said something about me becoming like you. What did he mean by that?" Meena Kapoor didn't respond. "Ma, why won't you say something? Ughh." Shaili threw her arms in the air and rolled her eyes. "I hope he dies. Stupid ass!"

"Shaili! *Stop That*! *Now*! This is not how you speak about your elders. He's your father!" Mrs. Kapoor said sternly.

Shaili wanted to run away. She knew, with age, Suresh Kapoor's drinking and abusing of his wife had increased. No one had told her that, but she had often seen indentations on her mother's body. What made Shaili feel pathetic and furious was when Mrs. Kapoor would try to cover the bruises with *Vicco Turmeric* and lie to her when she questioned the cut on her lips and the bruises around her eyes. Everyone knew what was happening, but it was never discussed. Mrs. Kapoor would say to her girls, "He never touches you girls. Sometimes, to maintain happiness in the family, a woman has to put up with certain things. It doesn't mean anything bad. That's why God made us stronger than men."

Tanisha, unlike Shaili, would never say much. She didn't care about Suresh Kapoor's threats. She was self-centered and did things behind her parents' back. But Shaili couldn't deal with her mother's excuses for her conflicted husband. "Stop it, Ma. I am not gullible. I am *not* a child anymore, please."

Quite honestly, Shaili never understood either of her parents. Her mother, whom she loved, put up with the abuse and defended her malevolent husband. A masochist! While her father, whom she reviled, though he despised Shaili's guts, wanted her to get educated and become successful. He forced her to study for an MBA. Not because she wanted to but because he thought it was the right choice. Shaili believed it was so he could kick her out at the soonest! Confused male chauvinist!

Mrs. Kapoor recognized that pursuing an MBA degree from *Symbiosis* had opened up her daughter's world. She met smart men and women in class, whom she liked, and they had changed her perception of the world. She said, "He doesn't hate me; sometimes when he gets angry he loses control. It happens in a family. He sometimes says sorry too. Listen to me. I am…"

"Please stop justifying his actions, Ma. It belittles you. Like the Stockholm Syndrome victims who can't stop defending their abductor!" Shaili said haughtily. "And what is this deal with my marriage? How did that come up? I am barely twenty-two. I have yet to complete my studies. Tell me something. Why does he want to arrange my marriage? How ridiculous is that!"

"But we know what is best for you," Mrs. Kapoor said in an unsure manner, almost avoiding eye contact with her daughter.

"I thought at least you were on my side. You and Old Man Suresh married for love, while I have to marry someone he approves? You guys are such hypocrites!"

Shaili looked out the window hoping the myna would understand her point of view. Her world seemed jarring.

"Beta, one day you will understand why I want you married."

Shaili drew in a deep breath and said, "Fine. I will try to *understand* the marriage bit, but why can't I marry someone I like? I want to live my life and not exist. Ma, I know perfectly nice Punjabi people. They would befit your husband's requirements. All I am saying is that I can't spend my life with a stranger! It won't be good." Until much later in her life, Shaili didn't acknowledge that that evening, Suresh Kapoor asked her to meet the boy; it was Meena Kapoor who persuaded her to consider the proposal.

Mrs. Kapoor didn't approve of Shaili addressing Mr. Kapoor as "Old Man Suresh" or "your husband." She grew up in times where women were considered inferior to men. The husband was treated as God. She conceded that Suresh was severe with Shaili, but she also knew why her husband was despicable towards her.

Suresh Kapoor wasn't always a bitter man. At one time, he had fought the world to marry Meena Kapoor. He had worshipped her. Sadly, Mrs. Kapoor couldn't tell Shaili about the dark secret that had morphed Suresh Kapoor from a devoted, loving man into the alcoholic monster Shaili had seen growing up. She didn't think her daughter was ready to deal with the truth. She hoped once Shaili was married and emotionally more settled, she could finally share the burden of her past. But in the interim, the guilt of not revealing the truth ate away at Mrs. Kapoor. That's why she justified her husband's idiosyncrasies.

Shaili saw the sadness in her mother's eyes and faked calming down. "What are you thinking? *Accha*, tell me again, how did you and Old…

okay, sorry. How did you and Daddy meet? Let me rephrase that. *Why* did you meet?" She winked at her mother.

Shaili's remarks brought a smile to her mother's forlorn eyes.

"Don't change the subject. Meet this boy once. Maybe you will want to marry him," pleaded Mrs. Kapoor.

"Don't start again, Ma. I want to marry for love. I don't want some random person selected by my parents. You don't get it. None of you understand!"

"See what love got me!" Meena Kapoor exclaimed loudly.

It was too late to retract her words, so Meena Kapoor looked away. Shaili sensed desperation in her mother's voice even though she and Meena Kapoor never delved into what those five words meant. In more than twenty years of her existence, Shaili had never once heard her mother say anything negative about love or her father. Her marital misery was obvious but never verbalized. That's what good Indian women did—kept their dirty laundry at home.

Shaili lay on her bed, looking for answers in her mother's face. Mrs. Kapoor knew how her older daughter's brain worked. Before Shaili could interrogate her, Meena had to think of something, quickly. Correcting her earlier confession, Mrs. Kapoor said, "All I am saying is keep an open mind. Who knows? You might actually like Sadhil. He is a good catch. He will keep you like a princess in America." Shaili tried to ignore her mother's explanation. She hid her face in a large pillow. Even the light in her bedroom bothered her.

Mrs. Kapoor patted Shaili's back affectionately. Shaili averted her face and hid her tears. She felt that even the person she loved the most didn't seem to empathize with her. It broke her heart. Adjusting the dupatta on her head, Mrs. Kapoor started to walk out of the room. She paused for a second and then turned around and said to Shaili, "Beta, do it for me. And to keep harmony in this house. Also, for your own self."

Shaili didn't say anything. She looked up at her mother and saw the raw bruises on her face. The impressions left behind by drunken Old Man Suresh. Her heart cringed, and she nodded. Shaili closed the door shut. She hoped the agonies would stay outside her room along with her family members.

Shaili picked up the cordless and called Supriya, who was the queen in her relationships and felt more positively towards men than did Shaili. Her boyfriend, Professor Mhatre, taught Mathematics at Pune University. He was a hardworking man with a good heart and undying love for his lady. With her wavy hair, petite frame, hazel eyes and soft skin, Supriya knew men found her attractive. She was quite the heartthrob at Fergusson College in Pune. It was no shock that Supriya smote Mhatre—from the day she set foot in his class. In the process of studying calculus, she too had fallen in love with him—the instructor teaching the class. Supriya knew how to make Mhatre dance to her tunes but not in a treacherous way. She was nothing if not transparent. She loved Mhatre tremendously but without compromising her sense of self. She wasn't the type of person, like most girls her age, who became oblivious to the world just because they had a boyfriend. The loyalist in her made sure that Shaili too always remained a big part of her life.

On one of the Rose Days, the annual, official, I-like-you day in Pune colleges, Supriya gave Mhatre a red rose and professed her love for him. He was embarrassed but also secretly relieved. He knew he would never have had the guts to propose to "The Supriya." Most male students in the college ogled at her and so did the other younger professors. Did he even stand a chance? Mhatre had always liked her but he was also conscious of his economic background in comparison to Supriya's family. In the beginning, their relationship met with some resistance from both sets of parents. Mhatre was eight years older than Supriya. However, the age gap wasn't the only problem; Supriya Agarkar was a high caste Konkanastha Brahmin while Professor Mhatre was a non-Brahmin. The Agarkars didn't like the idea of their only daughter marrying into lower caste and swarthiness. Two years of determined pleading from Mhatre and suicide threats and bold declarations from Supriya paid off. The parents eventually reconciled. Supriya's parents accepted that Mhatre, though an average looking professor below their caste, had a "secure future." Mhatre's parents were thrilled that their son still lived with them in Pune. He was, at least, marrying within the state of Maharashtra, unlike some of their friends' sons, who had migrated to the U.S. and came back with American wives.

Shaili narrated the events of the evening to her friend, amid tears and bursts of anger. Shaili knew Supriya would never have let anyone force her into anything, let alone a commitment of a lifetime. Shaili, the more reticent of the two, had always envied that about Supriya and secretly wished she could imbibe those qualities from her.

"So yeah, I have no say! It's my life. But no, no one cares what I think or…or…or…what I feel. Like I have no desires. Did I tell you? I have to meet this guy tomorrow to…"

"What? Really? No way!" Supriya jumped off her bed. "Some boy is coming to see you tomorrow and you are telling me now? Idiot! You couldn't have told me in the beginning?"

"I just found out. I am nervous. And who cares about some guy!" Shaili confessed.

"I care. And why are you tense? You are a smart and confident woman, no? And no one is forcing you to marry him. If you don't like him, just let him know." Supriya tried to comfort Shaili.

"I don't know. You know how things are at my place, right?"

"This is the biggest decision of your life. Don't let anyone tell you what to do." Supriya spoke her mind without mincing words.

"Why do I feel the verdict has been passed?" Supriya knew what Shaili meant. "Su, can you come over when the boy is here?" Shaili almost begged softly.

"Of course. I was going to come over whether or not you invited me. I have to approve him before anyone else, no? Let's see if he can guess what my favorite coffee shop in Pune is. If he can't take care of your best friend, then sorry, he has no chance with you."

Shaili found solace in Supriya's assurance. Supriya continued with her banter, "But tell me something about him. What does he do? Where does he live? What does he look like?"

"I don't know and quite frankly, I don't give a f...."

"Oh, stop with your pessimism. Keep an open mind."

Shaili was tired of people asking her to keep an "open mind," even though she knew they meant well.

"Listen, I am going to call up your mom and get the details from her. I can't wait to find out more about this boy." Supriya hung up and dialed Mrs. Kapoor even before Shaili could say anything.

"Namaste Aunty. Supriya here."

"Bolo beta. Do you want to chat with Shaili?"

"No, actually, I called to talk to you about the boy. Tell me more na, Aunty." Supriya spoke in a high-spirited voice.

"I am so glad you called. Shaili is very upset with us. Beta, make her understand. I know what she is probably thinking, but I know what I am doing. I mean, your uncle and I aren't her enemies. And she just has to meet him once. Not marry him that instant."

"Haan, haan. Yes, I'll talk to her. Don't worry." Supriya guaranteed Mrs. Kapoor.

"She's very stubborn at times. I just don't know what to do." Mrs. Kapoor shared her fears with Supriya, which she never would with her own husband lest he judge Shaili and go on a verbal tirade.

There was enough drama brewing up at home in any case, on a daily basis.

"Don't worry. I will be there tomorrow, Aunty." Supriya felt sorry for Mrs. Kapoor and her friend.

"Thank you, beta. Shaili too will appreciate it if you were with her when the groom's side is here tomorrow."

Mrs. Kapoor went on to share all the details about the prospective groom, Sadhil Sethi, with Supriya. Supriya heard everything with keen interest. Though she would miss Shaili, Supriya felt Sadhil might just be Shaili's ticket to a life of bliss—away from the trauma she grew up with to a life of fulfillment. After a brief conversation with Mrs. Kapoor, Supriya called Shaili back.

"Okay, so Sadhil Sethi sounds like a good catch."

Shaili was irked by the clichéd phrase describing this man she'd never met. "Will you and Ma stop saying that? You make him sound like a fish or something."

"Ufff, already possessive and all, haan?"

"Shut up!"

"Stop getting mad at me and start listening to tales about the boy from Chandigarh-Delhi." Supriya was unaffected by Shaili's reaction and went on.

"Sadhil Sethi is a thirty-two year old New York-based investment banker who works for *Goldman Sachs*. Listen, he is as Punjabi as one could get—over six feet tall, fair-complexioned, chiseled body, head full of hair, and dimpled smile. Right cheek, I think. Anyway, you know what his aunt said to your mother?"

There was no response from Shaili's end. Supriya waited for thirty seconds. And then she got agitated. Her outbursts were normally followed by a high-pitched conversation and often times, profound vocabulary.

"Shails, would you mind not turning a deaf ear?"

Shaili's mind was elsewhere. She was uninterested in updates on Sadhil or anyone else. But she did care about her friend, so she accommodated her excitement. "Sorry, Su. Yes. Go ahead. You were saying?"

"His masi said, 'What a good boy Sadhil is, you know. After living in America, he's still willing to marry someone his parents like, Meena. This is a cultured boy. Children these days don't think. They fall in love and get married, all on their own.' Your ma agreed with her."

"Okay." Shaili conceded or so thought Supriya.

Supriya continued in an animated voice, "Sadhil lives in Manhattan on the Upper East Side—75th street and 3rd avenue, to be exact. His masi said to your mother, 'It's a rich neighborhood, Meena. People with old money live there. But they accepted Sadhil too.' Anyway, Sadhil Sethi is from New Delhi—the hip, chic South Extension part. It's comparable to Koregaon Park in Pune. He also lived in Chandigarh or something like that."

Shaili responded with an, "Uh-huh. Okay."

"After completing his Bachelors in Electronic Engineering from IIT Delhi, Sadhil moved to New York City where he got an MS and MBA from Columbia University. Great na? He interned with *Morgan Stanley*, in London, for two summers, when he was in business school. He was the top of the echelon. *Goldman Sachs* snagged him in his second year." Supriya paused to breathe for a moment. She sounded like a tape recorder replaying someone's resume. Well, she did take down notes when Mrs. Kapoor shared Sadhil's biodata. She hoped Shaili was making mental observations too.

A voice, her mother's to be precise, called out to Supriya in Marathi. Supriya rolled her eyes and responded "*Aai*, I am talking to Shaili. What do you want?" Her mother informed her that the meal was getting cold. Supriya didn't want to be disturbed so she asked her mother to wait while she wrapped up the juicy chatter with her friend.

"Sorry, that was Mother. Accha, Shails, if you marry Sadhil, you could live Sarah Jessica Parker's life! A closet full of *Jimmy Choo* footwear and *Chanel* bags. The real drink, *Cosmopolitan*, every night followed by shopping every morning." Supriya believed she knew a lot about American culture courtesy of *Sex & The City* and Hollywood movies.

Shaili didn't care about Sadhil's address. She couldn't get the conversation, from earlier that day, out of her head. Other vagrant thoughts chagrined her mind. Some she could explain, others eluded her. The songs of praises for the boy made her wonder about Sadhil, the suitable boy.

"Su, don't you think it's weird?" Shaili interrupted Supriya.

"What now, Miss Negativity?" Supriya sighed in her iconic high-pitched voice.

"I mean, there have to be a lot of good girls in New York, right?"

"So?"

"Then why hasn't this well-off and good-looking financial genius settled down with anyone? Doesn't anyone care he is a lot older than me?"

"Shails, Mhatre is older than me, and he is still single. Granted, he's hooked, and I am going to book and cook him once we get married." Supriya gurgled at her own ingeniousness but couldn't manage to evoke any reaction from Shaili. She lay on her bed, facing the ceiling fan, with the phone stuck to her ears and continued, "Some people, like my parents for instance, prefer arranged marriages. Maybe Sadhil is ready only now to settle down with an Indian girl who knows his traditions. Lots of boys from the U.S. and U.K. come to India to marry, no? Maybe you are destined to be his Carrie Bradshaw!" Supriya took a deep breath after sharing her wisdom.

Both Shaili and Supriya knew that the love marriage in the Kapoor household was a failure while the traditional, arranged marriage in the Agarkar family had lasted happily ever after. "Just focus on the good things, *yaar*. He'll take you away from this mess. Pune has been wretched for…to… you." Supriya realized that she'd said too much. She quickly chuckled. "No in-laws to worry about and no interference from anyone. Every day will be like a honeymoon for you both. You can do it in the car, on the dining table, in the drawing room. Oh sorry. In America, 'drawing room' is called 'living room.' I have seen their *Victoria's Secret* catalogue. Neenu, my cousin, who sends me tapes of *Sex & The City*, had brought it when she was here last month on a visit from Chicago. What stuff they have! You can bring me new lingerie."

Supriya sounded pleased by just talking salaciously. Few more tokens of pleasantries were exchanged over the telephone. Shaili was thankful for Supriya's support. She always relied on it.

As Supriya wove hopes and dreams for her friend, she recognized unintended jealousy in her own voice because of what Sadhil had to offer. Supriya loved her beau, Mhatre, but given his profession, he didn't have the resources for many things that she aspired to own. In her heart she knew that a professor's salary could earn them a vacation in Lonavla but definitely not a fancy *Prada* handbag. The only way she would see America was through Shaili's eyes. The only way she would experience the lives of the wealthy and the famous would be through Shaili's wardrobe. She was euphoric for Shaili but a little sad for herself. And then a little mad at herself for her immature feelings towards her best friend in the world.

Shaili read Supriya's thoughts, and she implicitly deciphered them. After all, between the two girls, Supriya was the brand-conscious, fashion-savvy diva, who prized the idea of a luxurious life. All Shaili ever sought was a day in her life when there were no taunts hurled her way. Just one day when she could interpret her desires.

"Shails, I have to go now. Aai and Baba are waiting for dinner. But I'll be there tomorrow. Just sleep tight. Everything will be fine. Not every man is a pervert like Humbert Humbert. Mark my words; not every man is out to mar and molest women. Have a little faith." Supriya finally spoke the language that Shaili understood best—her favorite book, *Lolita*.

They hung up the phone. Shaili wanted to say so much more. Unspoken words and unheard feelings occupied her mind like ghosts in a cemetery. No one would comprehend her dilemma. She herself wasn't clear about her apprehensions. Shaili picked a cotton swab and wiped away the kohl from under her eyes, brushed her teeth, and gargled out those puzzling thoughts. She decided to spend the remainder of the evening curled up inside her bed, read *Lolita*, and wonder about Sadhil Sethi.

5

Even in the present day, Shaili's mind was wrapped around memories from the past involving Sadhil Sethi and the days preceding their wedding. Suresh Kapoor broke her reverie with his incredulous words. "You could have told us the truth the day when you both met. But you didn't. You chose to hide information from all of us! You know what I think? I think you were angry with me, so you chose to ruin our family's name. Just to get back at me!" Shaili looked astounded as tears from her eyes flowed impetuously along with Suresh Kapoor's questions.

"But..." The kohl staining Shaili's cheeks tried to testify, but Suresh Kapoor was unstoppable. Whatever Shaili tried to say didn't permeate into his ears.

"If I'd kept you back in India, things would have been different."

"How so?" Shaili asked, wiping her tears.

"You would have stayed married and had two children by now. End of story!"

"The way you did?"

"Shaili!" Suresh Kapoor raised his voice, but Shaili was unafraid.

"What happened? Did I touch some 'forbidden wounds'?"

"Keep quiet!" Suresh Kapoor fought the urge to smack Shaili.

"Let's say you are right. My husband could have forced me into procreation, which is statutory rape. But then what? Could I have loved these children who I saw as the reason I had to deny myself true contentment and companionship? So what would the outcome be? Another generation of unloved and unwanted family would roam this planet! Would you want me to treat them the way you dealt with me? Huh?"

Suresh Kapoor deliberately ignored Shaili's last two statements and said, "Whatever you say or don't, that country changed you. You were happily doing an MBA here. All of a sudden you wanted to become a journalist after you moved there. Then you divorced your husband. Now you love women. I see a pattern."

"Are you kidding me? I never wanted to pursue an MBA."

"I didn't force you to study anything. I might have strongly suggested what I thought of an MBA degree but that was about it. It is not like I took any entrance exams for you. Or filled out university forms. You did them yourself. I wanted you to become independent. Earn a living, so it helped you with your future. So you didn't have to depend on anyone. MBA would have given you that security."

"You never asked me what *I* wanted." Shaili cupped both her ears. They were burning up. "Pursuing an MBA was your Draconian law. Just as my marriage to Sadhil Sethi was."

"Now you are saying that you married Sadhil because of me? Will you ever take responsibility for your actions?" The parent in Suresh Kapoor wanted to shake Shaili up, but the grieving widower in him stopped him from doing so. He continued, "I still remember that evening when Sadhil, his parents, and his aunt were over to see you or as you describe in your first book, *Am I a Defiant Girl?*, 'The vulnerable ritual of seeing a girl over high tea is a part of the decrepit, traditional arranged marriage scenario in India.' You did all the drama of wearing a sari and jewelry and chitchat. I didn't ask you to. Not once…"

"You read my book?" Shaili cried out in disbelief. The astonishment in her voice competed against the sound of rain beating against the rocks. Learning Suresh Kapoor had read her book almost had the same impact on Shaili as finding out about her mother's secret and the clarification for Suresh Kapoor's eccentric behavior all these years.

Suresh Kapoor chose to remain oblivious to Shaili's inquiry and said gruffly, "Do you recall, Shaili?"

"I have retained a lot of things and some I have chosen to block out. What are you referring to?"

"The first time Sadhil came home. Much to my surprise, you showed up like a willing bride in a sari. Remember? It was raining like it is today."

Shaili nodded. On several occasions she'd said to Leila, "If only I could go back in time and change those weeks of my life, just for Sadhil. Even if inadvertently, I did him wrong."

Shaili called to mind the day Sadhil Sethi and his family visited the Kapoors and the incidents following that day. The memories were permanently imprinted on Shaili's conscience.

The Kapoor household was abuzz with preparations for the Sethi family's visit. No stone was left unturned when it came to the preparations. There were *Kayani's* Shrewsbury biscuits and Mawa cake along with sweets and snacks from *Chitale Bandhu Mithaiwale*. The fine silverware and crockery was brought out for the guests. Meena Kapoor inspected each corner of the house until she was satisfied. But Tanisha pushed up her glasses with her index finger and drew her eyebrows in a furrow. She despised all this extra attention being showered on Shaili.

But that day, Shaili was exasperated at her mother. She had never seen her so in charge. Mrs. Kapoor was an unstoppable ball of verve rolling from one corner of the house to the other. Despite the thunderstorms and rains, the Sethis arrived on time. The family was nicely dressed. They'd brought three boxes of gift-wrapped Indian sweets, two boxes of savories, two baskets of fruits and a box of dry fruits for the occasion. Sadhil Sethi wore an *Armani* suit with a yellow *Hermes* tie. He looked breathtakingly handsome. His mother wore a chiffon sari with light embroidery and in-your-face diamonds while his aunt wore a silk sari with pearl jewelry. You could see his father's relaxed personality through his casual cotton shirt and trousers.

The Sethi family, Suresh Kapoor and Meena Kapoor exchanged hellos, namastes, and thank-yous. The Sethis marveled at the Kapoor mansion. After the pleasantries were over, Suresh Kapoor, at his best behavior, asked the guests to sit down and make themselves comfortable. Meena Kapoor excused herself saying, "I will just check on Shaili."

She walked up to Shaili's room and was astounded by what she saw. Much against her wishes, Shaili had worn a burgundy *Kanjivaram* silk sari. Supriya, dressed in a fancy salwaar kameez, had helped Shaili drape the sari. "No loud jewelry or any of that garish stuff, Ma," Shaili had told her mother. The six yards of cloth was wrapped elegantly around Shaili's slender frame. Shaili didn't make an effort, but even then her bare midriff looked sensual. Her hair, tied in a casual knot, accentuated her perfect cheekbones. She looked like a stewardess of *Indian Airlines*. At her mother's behest, Shaili wore a bindi on her forehead and four golden bangles on her right wrist. Her long fingers looked eager to wear a ring. Her thin lips looked delicate with a natural shade of *Revlon* lipstick. Shaili always wore a thick layer of black kohl under her almond-shaped eyes, maybe because they disguised the pain in them. That evening Shaili looked exceptionally beautiful, and the mole on her cheek stood out rebelliously. But on the inside, Shaili felt like a mutilated deer caught in the hands of the society dressed as a hungry lion.

Mrs. Kapoor stared at her first-born in awe. She put a thin chain with a small diamond pendant around Shaili's neck. "You look like a queen. May you always live like one." She planted a soft kiss on her daughter's forehead and one on the mole on her cheek. Before Shaili could walk towards the door, Mrs. Kapoor asked her to wait. She took the black kohl pencil and put a dot behind Shaili's ears, said, "May no one cast an evil eye on you," and then spat softly on the side.

Mrs. Kapoor went back into the living room to socialize with the groom's family; Supriya followed her; Shaili went into the kitchen to perform the first step of the arranged marriage ritual—check how everything was panning out in the kitchen.

"Shaili, you look so nice! My God. So beautiful. You should always wear saris. Sexy *ekdum.* Like a Cinestar;" Tanisha screamed. Though envious of Shaili's beauty, she was also in awe of her that evening. It was hard not to be.

Tanisha's voice was heard in the living room by the Sethis and the Kapoors. Sadhil smiled. His anticipation grew. Mrs. Kapoor looked at Supriya and said, "Beta, can you ask Shaili to come here?"

"Sure Aunty." Supriya caught Mrs. Kapoor's signal, which meant to ask Tanisha and the maid Gita to lower their voices and for Shaili to bring the tray of steaming tea along with platters of goodies. The display was against everything Shaili believed in but she did it nevertheless. She reminded herself that she was doing it for her mother.

When Supriya got to the kitchen, Gita pounced on her. "Didiji, what does he look like? What did he say? Did he ask about Shaili didiji? What has he worn?"

"Baggy pants and combed back hair like all those Delhi boys?" Though Tanisha tried being funny, the viciousness in her voice was obvious. But everyone disregarded her childishness. The evening was about Shaili.

"Relax ladies. I will tell you." Supriya cleared her throat, acting pretentious and pricey.

She then nudged Shaili's right arm. "Quite an item this Sadhil Sethi is. He's clean shaven like Mr. Big!" Supriya almost squealed. "Body like Salman Khan's; eyes like Shah Rukh Khan; dressing sense like Feroz Khan; warmth like Aamir Khan. And voice? Hmmm. Thankfully not like Saif Ali Khan." The three women sniggered as Supriya filled them up on the details. Shaili looked blankly at the trio. She heard snippets of the conversation and the word "Armani" was repeated several times.

"Accha, you both need to keep your voices down. You can be heard in the drawing room." Supriya pointed her finger at Tanisha and the maid.

And she told Shaili, "Shails, Aunty wants you outside."

Shaili felt powerless, but she wanted to keep her promise to her mother. Supriya looked at Shaili and said, "Remember what Carrie Bradshaw once said, 'As we drive along this road called life, occasionally a gal will find herself a little lost. And when that happens, I guess she has to let go of the coulda, shoulda, woulda, buckle up and just keep going.' I just want you to remember that." Shaili hugged Supriya tightly.

As Shaili entered the living room with the tray of goodies, all eyes turned to her. "Come. Sit with us," Mrs. Sethi suggested as she surveyed Shaili. She stroked Shaili's hands, shook her head, like a pendulum, in acknowledgement, and said, "You are very beautiful." Shaili was unsure how to respond. No one ever told her what the expected norm for marriage-related conversation was.

Fortunately, Mrs. Kapoor read her daughter's mind and came to her rescue. Or so Shaili thought. "Shaili prepared all these delicacies." Mrs. Kapoor bragged. She continued with false "Shaili-promotion." Shaili shot a maddened look at her mother for fabricating lies. Forget samosas, Shaili could barely make cucumber sandwiches, and she had no inclination to learn to cook roti and daal or any of the family's secret recipes. She spent her free time reading, secretly writing, playing sports, or working in her father's garage. Her father had criticized her on several occasions for her lack of involvement in household chores, but her mother had always protected her until now. And today her mother was saying untrue things. Shaili felt her heart ache. Shaili wondered if her mother felt humiliated because Shaili wasn't the consummate homemaker-material.

Mrs. Sethi exclaimed loudly, "*Bhai*, I am impressed. She will keep my Sadhil very happy in New York. You get Indian food, but it's not like India." The layers of fat over her abdomen reverberated listening to her food tales from her New York trips. *Curry Hill, Little India,* and *Jackson Heights* were repeated incessantly. Mrs. Sethi, if she had her way, would have Shaili fill out a questionnaire and write a blurb testifying to her culinary talents.

The evening was far more draining than Shaili would have ever anticipated. She was perplexed that this modern family judged a woman's abilities by the culinary skills she exhibited at home. Or at least the fat woman, Mrs. Sethi, did. Mrs. Sethi further said, "Girls today can seldom manage the house front." Shaili lowered her eyes and continued to look fixedly at the tea in the silver tea set, which was now getting cold—the opposite of Shaili's body temperature. She didn't want anyone to see the abomination in her eyes. Shaili's brain was wired with an overflow of feelings, half of which she didn't know what to make of.

After a few, trivial verbal exchanges, the families decided to leave Shaili and Sadhil alone. Mr. Sethi suggested, "Let them chat and get to know each other. What are we doing with these youngsters anyway?" Sadhil looked up at his father and mouthed a thank-you. He wasn't pleased with his mother's behavior that evening. He knew his mother would continue to ask daft questions about things that didn't matter to him and that would only make the process uncomfortable for everyone.

"Haan, haan. They are the ones who have to live together, if Sadhil likes her." Mrs. Sethi, satisfied with her own suggestion, got up from the sofa. She acted important because her only son lived in America and earned an outstanding salary. She turned to Shaili, "Come and sit next to Sadhil. Let us see how you both look together. Both of you are so fair complexioned. That's good."

Shaili looked at her mother and then at Mrs. Sethi. Disgust was oozing out of her eyes. Sadhil sensed Shaili's apprehensions. He knew how obsessed his mother was with getting a fair bride. Sadhil knew the only reason she wanted Shaili to sit next to him was to see how Shaili's skin color measured up against his own. He was revolted.

Sadhil came to Shaili's rescue. "Let it be, Mom. You are making it awkward." Mrs. Sethi glared at her son. He completed the sentence with, "For me, Mom." Sadhil's tactfulness wove a temporary web of muteness on Mrs. Sethi's lips. Shaili's heart felt ripples of relief and she thanked her stars. She wanted to say, "Well played." The smile echoed in Mrs. Kapoor's heart. Sadhil had handled the situation very well without letting his mother down. He had sided with Shaili but acted like he had requested a favor from his mom. She was convinced Sadhil was the apt choice for her daughter. She believed his Chandigarh upbringing had something to do with his polite demeanor.

Mrs. Sethi picked up her *Pierre Cardin* handbag, with the logo facing everyone, and said with one raised eyebrow, "Fine. What do we care? Youngsters these days have a mind of their own." Then she said some more incomprehensible words. Mr. Sethi, a light-hearted man, jokingly asked her to relax, have a drink, and maybe a smoke.

"Thank God. All the old skeletons are gone. I was beginning to feel like a geriatric patient with all those oldies around." Supriya squealed as the parental generation of the Kapoors and Sethis left the living room. She had a gift for putting people at ease. She sank on the sofa with her right leg folded and tucked under the left. Shaili and Sadhil, both shocked at Supriya's forthrightness, laughed.

Supriya got up suddenly and said, "All right, my work here is done. Enjoy, you two." She saluted Shaili and Sadhil and turned to walk away. As Supriya started to leave, Shaili gently pulled her dupatta. She didn't want to be left alone with a stranger and his questions. She was uneasy. Though Sadhil had evaded his mother's request, she didn't know if Sadhil would ask her about her rajma-chaawal cooking skills or if the dining table's cover was embroidered by her fair hands. After all, that's what the entire evening had been about. Up until now, no one had asked her what she did, what she liked, or what she wanted to do with her life. Did she even want to accept this role of a prudish, domesticated woman existing with the sole ambition of keeping her husband happy? Did no one care that she didn't know how to act around the opposite sex?

Supriya gave Shaili a dirty look but stayed back. Much to Shaili's surprise, Sadhil was exceptionally bashful. He didn't say much even after the elders left. He smiled every time Supriya made a silly comment. Shaili tried not to like him, but she had mixed feelings. Somewhere she felt nauseous. She tried to unravel her angst but in vain. What she didn't know was that the whole evening had panned out exactly the way Sadhil didn't want it to either.

Sadhil didn't share the same ideas as his mother about the criteria that made any woman qualify for a "good wife." He didn't care about marrying a fair-complexioned super model, or a trophy wife, with no brains or opinions of her own, to decorate his apartment. He wanted a partner in every sense of the word. The girl's competence in the kitchen or at household chores was of no significance to him because he wasn't looking to marry a woman so she could "take care" of him. He had help for cleaning and take-out arrangement for food in New York. In addition, he was quite the food connoisseur and gourmet chef himself, something his mother had deliberately not mentioned, as she believed cooking and related chores were beneath her son.

Sadhil had wanted to meet Shaili without the parents, but to keep peace in the family, he accepted the Indian tradition of not seeing the girl unsupervised. Since he was the only child who lived far, far away, his mother felt girl-screening was her only opportunity to earn importance as the prospective groom's mother. Sadhil had then proposed meeting Shaili in a restaurant with her friends or cousins but his mother threw a fit again. She wanted her ego petted at the girl's place over high tea. His father understood Sadhil's stance, but he indulged his wife for the sake of avoiding drama.

Sadhil had always desired a marriage of equals where each pursued his or her dream while inspiring and complementing the other. The facilitator could be anyone—parents, friends, or a social gathering. It was immaterial to him. He felt that a connection between the boy and the girl was pivotal. He was of the belief that it was easy for people to be pleasant when you met them for a few hours every day or be mystified by their beauty for a few days; the true colors came out when they started to live under the same roof. At least that's what had happened to his parents. So, he was willing to wait until the right girl came along.

To some, Sadhil might have seemed too good to be true with his benevolence and handsome looks. But what most people didn't know was that Sadhil had fought hard, his entire life, to not be like his parents. He disliked their equation with each other and never wanted those things from his own relationship. Though fond of his father's congenial nature, Sadhil never understood his timidness. His father had swallowed his dreams to keep his wife happy. Sadhil would often think, "They had a love marriage. What did they have in common?" Mr. Sethi, on one of his foreign trips, smitten by his wife's beauty, had proposed to her. Even after marriage, he had pampered her until she misplaced good sense along with her chin. By the time he realized his mistake, it was too late and Mrs. Sethi's crudeness, weight, and adamancy had mutated. Mr. Sethi reconciled with fate and never honestly told his wife what he thought of her. He used humor to disguise their personal failures.

He wanted to be accommodating, unlike his mother, without being a wuss, like his father. Maybe his efforts made him, almost, cordial to a fault. Without over-exaggerating, one could say that Sadhil turning out sane was nothing short of a miracle.

Shaili wanted to ask him so many questions, but her inexperience with men held her back. The cynic in her contemplated if Sadhil was meeting her of his own free will. She wasn't meeting him out of her own choice. She had heard of Indian men who had live-in relationships with American women in the United States but didn't tell their parents about them. When the parents insisted they get married to an Indian girl of their choice, the plan would be met with initial resistance. Soon the parents' coercion and emotional blackmails, made the sons vacillate. The boys would hop on to the first flight available to India. Before reaching the airport, they would make a pit stop at *Costco* to buy a generic diamond engagement ring for some woman they would eventually marry on the trip. The parents would greet their sons with a bunch of photographs at the airport, in order of their own preference. A 16-hour flight, twenty photographs, ten high teas with samosas and burfis at several girls' houses later, they would narrow down their choice to five Indian girls. Before the end of the two-week vacation, the marriage deal would be signed, rings exchanged, dowry collected, the marriage consummated, and the girl's dependent visa application submitted.

Supriya knew Shaili's mind could be antagonistic. After all, she had not nicknamed her "Miss Negativity" for nothing. She couldn't blame Shaili for it after what the poor girl had been through. She sensed awkwardness between Shaili and Sadhil and decided to break the ice. "Okay, if you two don't start talking, maybe I will. I will start asking Sadhil questions and maybe marry him? You can keep Mhatre, and I will fly to New York. Sadhil, if you promise a ride in stretch limousines and shopping on Fifth Avenue, I'll dump Mhatre in a second. What say?" Her humor worked and both Sadhil and Shaili grinned, again.

"Since Shails won't ask you, would you like a samosa?" Supriya asked Sadhil courteously.

"No thanks. I am good. I am badly jet-lagged, so pardon my lack of appetite," said Sadhil with a classy accent—erudite with a mix of American, Indian, and British enunciation.

"Do you have American friends? Whites? Blacks? Or only Indians?" Supriya's eyes sparkled as she poured him a cup of tea. She couldn't curtail herself on hearing his diction. Supriya was in awe of Sadhil's Americanism and worldliness. She secretly wished the two would get married, just the way a five-year old wants to marry her Barbie doll to Ken. To her, Sadhil was everything a woman could ask for in a man.

"Both, actually." Sadhil wasn't into hanging out with people based on their ethnicity or skin color. He was neither into India bashing nor was he obsessed with a perpetual nostalgia of his motherland. He liked people for who they were and not where they came from. It was the wavelength and the goodness of the heart that he cared about. Sadhil turned to Shaili. "Shaili is a beautiful name. What does it mean?"

"It means tradition," Shaili said tepidly.

"Nice! I have never heard it."

Sadhil waited for a moment, but Shaili didn't respond to his kind comment.

"Would you call yourself traditional?" Sadhil took a sip of tea.

Shaili felt judged by Sadhil's questioning. She cringed. She wanted to say, "I am sitting here and following a traditional ritual, aren't I, idiot?" But she chose to be civil. "I suppose so, but it depends on how one defines tradition."

"Fair enough." Sadhil was delighted with Shaili's ingeniousness. He had a hunch Shaili wasn't a meek woman trying to please him. She had a mind of her own, and he valued that.

"What does Sadhil mean?" she asked with reprisal.

"Believe it or not, it's a sanctimonious name with a relative meaning." Sadhil smiled as he said this.

"Pardon me?" Both Shaili and Supriya spoke at the same time.

"Sorry. Sadhil means *perfection*."

"Why do you say it has a relative meaning?" asked Shaili.

"Well, I might be perfect in my parents' eyes but not in your friend's or yours."

Shaili pondered if Sadhil was trying to tell her something. Was he imperfect, and if yes, how so?

"So, you are from New Delhi?" Supriya had a Hercule Poirot look on her face. "But you live in New York, right?" She paused to solve the puzzle in her head. Sadhil and Shaili waited for Supriya to convey her remaining thoughts. Supriya smacked her right temple with her palm and said, "Oh, that's why."

"I am not sure I understand." Sadhil looked bewildered.

"I mean that is why you don't have that Delhi style."

"Delhi style?"

"*Yaar*, that typical style of talking and mannerisms."

"Is that a good or a bad thing?" Sadhil was baffled. He didn't know what to expect next.

"Superb, wonderful. We Bombay-Pune people are not in love with Delhi folks."

"Okay. But why?"

"Forget it. Some other time."

Shaili was beginning to feel furious with Supriya for making a fool of herself in front of an outsider. But Supriya continued with her mockery. She wanted to know which of the two cities did Sadhil like more: New York or New Delhi.

Sadhil read the earnestness in Supriya's endeavors. He didn't need to mull over his response about which of the two cities he liked more. Though brought up in New Delhi, he had never felt like he belonged there. He did his middle and senior schooling from Delhi Public School (DPS), after spending the first ten years of his life in Chandigarh. His father was at a high post in the Indian Foreign Services. But his successful career meant that he and his wife lived a globally transient life every few years. Sadhil needed permanence. It was decided that he would live with his *nani,* his maternal grandmother, in Chandigarh, temporarily until his father got a permanent job in India. Once his parents settled down in the Indian capital, Sadhil went to school in New Delhi.

Sadhil was miserable in New Delhi. He missed the simplicity of Chandigarh and his nani. He felt discomfited with the crowd at DPS and the unintellectual, shallow atmosphere at home. He felt several of his classmates flaunted immodesty, just like his mother. When Sadhil refused to smoke or drink or exploit women, his peers ostracized him. They called him names like "fag," "*chhakka,*" and "*lalloo*".

Sadhil was anything but settled in New Delhi. He didn't have anything against the city, but he recognized that he wasn't cut out for it. Maybe because Sadhil hated pretenses or maybe he tried too hard to not imbibe his mother's genes of ostentatiousness; in the process of fighting his inner battles, Sadhil alienated himself at school.

Sadhil often wondered if spending his childhood with his nani had made him a different man. She was firm but even-tempered, genteel, well read, pragmatic, strict, and loving with a heart of gold. These weren't qualities Sadhil had seen in his own mother. He was surprised how the "classy" genes had skipped a generation. His own mother, despite world travels and all the exposure, turned out to be an abominable, loud-mouthed bigot while her mother, despite living in Chandigarh her entire life, was cultured, and sophisticated.

"Arrey, Sadhilji, tell me. How do you like New York? Do you want to settle there? Big apartment, cars, and all." Supriya asked.

"Su!" Shaili's eyes spitted fury.

"That's quite alright." Sadhil told Shaili. He then turned to Supriya. "So far so good. I mean, I miss India, especially my nani. But to be frank, I love my life in the Big Apple. It allows me to be what New Delhi didn't."

New York and Sadhil were made for each other. He was astounded by how unpretentious the city was, or at least he felt that way. He could be himself without questioning his actions or worrying about what the neighbor's mother or aunt had to say. The societal pressures didn't bury him. Even when alone, he was never lonely. He loved to cook and took Italian cooking lessons. *Formaggi* sounded so eloquent when Sadhil pronounced it. He was a worldly man living in one of world's most cosmopolitan cities.

"But I haven't really decided where I want to be twenty years from now. I mean, it has to depend on the person I marry. We will both figure it out as a couple."

Shaili was astonished by Sadhil's progressiveness. He wasn't like the typical stuck-up, Ivy-league educated, haughty investment banker from New York. But her ego wouldn't let her show that. Her pessimist mind was stuck on Sadhil's words. Shaili speculated what was it in New York that "allowed" Sadhil to be, and Delhi didn't?

Sadhil broke up her train of thought. "What do you do, Shaili? Mom mentioned you are getting an MBA from *Symbiosis*. That's awesome!"

"Yes." Shaili's response was a three-letter monosyllable.

"Do you know what you want to specialize in?"

"Not yet."

"Do you work part-time?"

"No. Unless you count repairing cars."

"Do you plan to have a career once you are done? As in, do you want to work?"

"Haven't yet decided what I'll do after graduation. Like I am allowed to…" Shaili stopped and didn't complete her sentence.

Shaili's answer annoyed Supriya. She wondered why Shaili was acting like a self-indulgent fool. Sadhil was a nice guy who was legitimately interested in hearing about Shaili from both her and Supriya. He was decent enough to ask her the "right" questions.

"Do you have a problem with working women or housewives?" Shaili asked as she petulantly crossed her legs.

"I don't care one way or the other. I would want my future wife to be independent."

Shaili's eyebrows were raised. Sadhil continued, "Life in New York can get lonely if one doesn't have a day commitment especially because I keep long hours. But if she prefers to not have a career, it's her call." Sadhil was unruffled. Shaili felt bad for judging him midway through the conversation.

Sadhil was at ease talking to both Supriya and Shaili. The couple found out a lot about each other, through Supriya, and things in common. Minutes turned into an hour. That's when the parents showed up again. "Gup-shup ho gayi?" asked Mrs. Sethi.

Sadhil nodded his head in the affirmative. So did Shaili. Sadhil said, "Nice meeting you both," to Shaili and Supriya.

"They look very happy together. Don't you think? Sadhil is getting a package deal after all. Supriya along with Shaili. Haaaaa." Mrs. Sethi proceeded to talk and laugh at her own inanity. Silence was a concept that eluded her.

"Thank you for your hospitality. We'll take your leave now, but latest by tomorrow morning, we will get back to you with whatever these children have decided. Don't want to leave you hanging." Mr. Sethi said in an affable voice, with his hands folded. As Shaili joined her hands to say "Namaste," Sadhil's father said, "May you live a long and happy life, my child. God bless you!"

After Sadhil and his family left, Shaili ruminated over the proceedings of the evening. She felt muddled. Shockingly, she'd enjoyed Sadhil's presence, yet detested the possibility of a nuptial arrangement. She tried to figure out what was it about the evening that irked her the most. Sadhil was attractive, gracious, polished, and unprejudiced. He indulged her eccentricity, but she hadn't felt any butterflies at the pit of her stomach. She had been exceptionally cruel to him, but he survived each attempt of hers to discountenance him. Despite all that, she couldn't point her finger to that one thing that stood out—the core reason why she disliked the idea of liking him.

As she brushed her hair, she remembered, they had several things in common. Pizza and Indian Chinese were their favorite foods and Charades, their choice game, which they discovered due to Supriya's chattiness. They were both unobvious romantics. Shaili had thrown in some alcohol-indulgence information into the conversation to throw off Sadhil's game. Supriya was annoyed by it, but he was fine. He didn't care she drank. Shaili was astounded to discover that, like her, Sadhil too was a big fan of Rabindra Nath Tagore's literature, Nabokov's works, Mozart's musical composition, coffee, and *Sex & The City*.

Shaili reminisced about how she got her first taste of New York. It was through *Sex & The City*. She and Supriya were hooked to the show because of Supriya's cousin Neenu, who would send her recorded tapes. The two would rewind and watch the episodes repeatedly until they had all the dialogues memorized.

Shaili and Supriya, on several occasions, had sneaked into bars on the other side of town in Koregaon Park & Camp. They wanted to feel hip and liberated like the women in their favorite television show. They wanted to order *Cosmopolitans* because that's what Carrie Bradshaw drank, but since the cocktail wasn't available, they would add cherry-colored sweet *Rasna* or *Rooh Afza*, which they would carry in six-ounce bottles from home, to gin and tonic, so it looked like a cosmo. Pune wasn't like New York then, so their clothes were a little more conservative along with their student budget, but their attitude was comparable to the television stars. Shaili didn't care for the attention she got from men at bars. If anything, the flirtatious lines made something inside her squirm. Supriya always joked that it was the fear of a tight slap from Old Man Suresh that freaked Shaili out.

Supriya would loosen up and swing a little after her first drink. Shaili thought Supriya had a vixen nymph, like Samantha, inside of her, which was brought out by a few fake cosmos. With lowered inhibitions, Supriya would insist on purchasing a few smokes and singing Bollywood songs on the streets. If Shaili suggested that her actions might get them into trouble, Supriya would be dismissive. This side of Supriya wasn't hidden from Mhatre. She never lied to him about it, but he preferred to deny it existed.

It was different for Shaili. She didn't enjoy cocktails, for the taste, as much as Supriya did. It was one of those things she did to keep Supriya happy. Growing up with an inebriated father, she knew the effect alcohol could have, so she never would allow herself to be wasted, irrespective of the quantity consumed. And maybe her subconscious mind was paranoid that her true desires would become visible, to her, in an intoxicated state. Three drinks down, she could still stand up straight, drive her *Kinetic Honda*, drop Supriya home after stuffing her with burgers and fries at *King Burger*, and have dinner with her family. She could function like the queen of sobriety even when saturated with multiple drinks.

Both Shaili and Supriya imitated the Carrie Bradshaw laugh and walk and repeated her dialogues.

"Stop this 'Currie' walk, you crazy girls," Mrs. Kapoor would shout at the two of them.

"Ma, it's not 'Currie.' It's Carrie." Shaili had laughed at her mother's sputtering. "You have to see this show. It's cool. These women do what they want. They eat all their meals out and enjoy life. You don't even let me eat breakfast in my college canteen," Shaili would rag her mother.

"Beta, their culture is different. They have no mothers to cook for them. Look, how the poor things live alone. They clean and cook themselves. So thin. Our maid looks fresher than them. They need a few aloo parathas for breakfast. Eating only greens, like they were cows or something. Imagine living only on salad."

Shaili would make a face. A moment later, Mrs. Kapoor would throw in some drama into the conversation. "Wait, you don't like my food? Fine, I won't cook for you. I will marry you off to someone who lives in New York like your Currie. Then you will understand."

"Ma, you are too sentimental and if I may say so, a little too hopeful. See, I am not marrying anyone and definitely not leaving Pune." Shaili would end the conversation with a big hug and Mrs. Kapoor would plant a million kisses on her daughter.

"Shailu. Shailu," a familiar voice called out and broke her reverie. It was her mother. "He is a nice boy, no? We like him. Do you like him too?"

"Does it matter, Ma? You guys have made up your mind in any case!" Shaili wanted to say those exact words, but she decided to eat them up instead. She remained silent.

"What happened? He wasn't nice to you? Will you say something? Will you say a yes?" Mrs. Kapoor sounded desperate.

"Nothing. He's all right. He was nice to me. Happy?" Shaili continued to comb her hair.

Before Shaili could say anything else, or her mother could ask any further questions, the phone rang. Mrs. Kapoor answered it.

"Helloji, Mrs. Kapoor. Raj Sethi here." It was Sadhil's father.

"Helloji, you all reached okay, no?" Mrs. Kapoor enquired.

"Haanji. Sorry to call so late, but we didn't want to wait until tomorrow morning. We have some good news; we like the girl..."

Mrs. Kapoor didn't hear the rest of the conversation and almost jumped with exhilaration. She lunged across the bed and gave Shaili a kiss on her cheek—right on the mole. It took her a second to catch her breath.

"How very kind of you. Thank youji. Congratulations." Mrs. Kapoor said, sounding excited & breathless.

"But, there is one thing," said Mr. Sethi, interrupting Mrs. Kapoor.

Mrs. Kapoor went numb. She knew this was all too good to be true. Good things didn't happen to her. But why shouldn't they happen to her daughter? *She* hadn't done anything to deserve misery.

"Mrs. Kapoor, are you there?"

"Yesji."

"Sadhil wants to meet Shaili once again without us adults. Don't get me wrong; consider everything final and yes from our end. But the children need to understand each other. If it's okay with you, can they meet tomorrow during the day?"

Sadhil had convinced his father that he wanted to clarify a few things with Shaili. Moving to New York would be a huge decision for her and he wanted to be sure she was okay with it and not being forced into anything. She had seemed reserved when they'd met. Mr. Raj Sethi agreed with his son's point of view and approved the meeting. For once, they ignored Mrs. Sethi's opinion.

"Yes. Yes. Shaili also likes Sadhil. She would be glad to meet him. Tomorrow at 11 a.m. at *Pune Coffee House*?"

It was decided. For once, Mrs. Kapoor didn't think about confirming anything with her husband. She was animated. She took upon herself to make sure Shaili was settled in her lifetime.

Shaili stood chagrined. Another decision was made about her life, and she wasn't involved. What was the point in meeting Sadhil again? Did she have a say in anything? At least she didn't think she did. True, Shaili wanted to ask him several questions like why, at thirty-two, an accomplished and forbearing man like him was still searching for a wife. Living in America, how could he think of having an arranged marriage? What was he hiding from her? Did he lead a dual life? How many relationships had he had? Shaili didn't believe men could be as good. Or at least, she hadn't met one yet. She felt her emotions were tied in knots and now her mother wanted to put her through the agony all over again.

"This is my point." Suresh Kapoor's index finger was thrust in Shaili's face.

"What are you talking about?" Shaili looked irritated.

"Why did you agree to meet Sadhil at *Pune Coffee House*?"

"Because you and Ma insisted."

"I never told you anything! If you didn't like him, you should have said a no."

"But…"

"No, but you had to go for coffee. Why? To spite me?" Suresh Kapoor's hands were turned inside, mocking and asking questions.

"That's not what happened." Shaili took a deep breath and revisited that day she'd had tried to forget over the years, but the memory of Sadhil's generosity wouldn't allow her to. Until she'd met Sadhil, Shaili believed all men were conceited despots. But Sadhil was different from everybody else—kind, caring, and simple.

Even as a teenager, Sadhil was lonely because his ideologies didn't mesh with his fellow classmates at DPS. He didn't see any purpose in writing letters dipped in blood or keeping filthy nicknames for the girls in his class just because everyone was doing it. Sadhil wasn't opposed to dating, but he didn't like anyone in particular in his school. But the boys in Sadhil's class expected Sadhil too to go to second base, especially with girls suffering from low self-esteem, because he was at an advantage point with his extraordinary looks. But Sadhil didn't budge. He was nothing if not honest and respectful.

What Shaili and her family didn't know was that on their way back home, after meeting with Shaili and her family, Sadhil's mother had suggested that he meet four other women the same week. This way, he would have a list of the best, eligible women in Pune ready by the weekend. Sadhil was appalled at her ludicrous suggestion. He knew of cases where the girl was asked to sing and walk in front of the groom's side, with a tray of tea in her hand, so they could determine she didn't have a limp. His mother knew him too well and didn't suggest the absurd idea when they decided to meet Shaili, but he knew the scheme did cross her mind. Much to his mother's dislike, Sadhil condemned the idea of putting Shaili or any girl or her family under the ordeal of "I like you; I like you not" and then sucking them dry.

Upon reaching home, he'd expressed his desire to meet Shaili at *Pune Coffee House.*

The next morning Supriya was asked to accompany Shaili to *Pune Coffee House*. She didn't want to go, but the Kapoors and Shaili needed her. Shaili, much against her mother's wishes, had worn a pair of Levis and cotton shirt and her hair was tied into a ponytail. Mrs. Kapoor wanted her daughter to wear a salwaar kameez. "Like a sweet little Punjabi girl," she had said.

Upon hearing the suggestion, Shaili had shot rebelliousness out of her eyes and said, "Ma, this is who I am. Take it or leave it." Mrs. Kapoor knew it was time she backed off. But all this while, Mr. Kapoor hadn't said a word to his wife or daughter. A hesitant, warm smile lurked around the crack of his lips, but he chose for it to be unseen. For once, neither women paid heed to him as each had a lot on her mind. For once, he wasn't the center of attention. For once, there was a shimmer of hope in the Kapoor household. For once, Mr. Kapoor made an effort to not be nasty and spoil everything.

Sadhil showed up five minutes before the women. He was dressed in a blue and white check cotton shirt and a nice pair of jeans. His *Florsheim* shoes looked expensive, and his square rimmed glasses made him look like an intellectual. Even his hair was perfectly set without any discernible display of hair products. Pune weather had done no damage to his crisp ensemble. When Supriya and Shaili entered, he waved out to them. Supriya gaped at him and whispered in Shaili's ears, "God really took a lot of time and trouble creating this one." Shaili ignored her.

Sadhil wasn't surprised to see Supriya. In fact, he had expected it. He could tell that Supriya meant a lot to Shaili. And he didn't mind Supriya's company at all. But, somewhere in the corner of his heart he'd hoped Shaili would have met him alone. She seemed so modern in every other way. He wondered if she was meeting him out of compulsion. "That's why I'm here. To find out if she has someone else on her mind," he thought to himself.

"Hi." Sadhil extended his arm to shake hands first with Shaili and then Supriya.

"Hello." Shaili responded in a semi-stern tone.

"Good morning Romeo." Supriya addressed Sadhil mellifluously. She then broke into a hit Bollywood song from the nineties as she nudged Sadhil, "*Dekha hai pehli baar, sajan ke aankhon mein pyaar.*" She greeted Sadhil with a wink. Both Shaili and Sadhil's face changed colors. Hers turned crimson with anger; his showed a tinge of pink, as if blushing from the comment.

"Sorry I rushed you guys in the morning. The Wimbledon finals are tonight. Pete Sampras is playing." Sadhil admitted sheepishly.

"That's okay." Shaili said condescendingly. As a tennis fan herself, she didn't want to miss out either on the historical match. She thought, "Another thing in common—love for tennis." But she didn't say it out loud because the other side of her brain said, "So what? Are you sure this is what you want—love for pizza and tennis in common?"

"Don't you worry, bhai! Shaili is the same way. She can miss meals and classes to watch tennis. She can kill you if you make her miss recordings of Martina Navratilova or Pete Sampras's play."

Sadhil was elated and exclaimed, "We'll get along just fine." His dimple looked seductively deeper when he smiled.

Supriya plopped down next to Shaili. The two were seated across the table from Sadhil—Shaili in front of him and Supriya diagonally opposite.

Supriya played music, on the table, with her nails, as if it were a tabla. She stopped suddenly and in her light-hearted chitchat said, "I hear you are like in love and all with Shails." Her volume was distinctly audible.

"Shut up, Su!" Shaili retorted with fury in her eyes.

"Fine. Fine. I will keep quiet but only after Sadhil treats me to a cold coffee and chicken dosa." She turned to Sadhil. "Specialty here. It's my favoritest coffee house in Pune." Sadhil had passed the first test in Supriya's books.

Sadhil liked Supriya's outspokenness. He grinned. He almost wished Shaili would be at ease with him the way Supriya was. But he also respected the lucidity in Shaili's personality. She seemed true to herself and the people around her. She was anxious meeting him, a random guy and had no qualms showing it. That's what had attracted him to her in the first place—her loyalty to emotions. Something Simran didn't have. That's what had started the end of it all.

He called the waiter and ordered two dosas, two cold coffees, and three waters. Shaili didn't want anything. She wanted to be left alone, and Sadhil could sense she was being somewhat indignant.

Supriya looked at Sadhil. "Did you know Shaili writes really well? *Amazing*! In fact, she's won so many awards too."

Sadhil turned to Shaili. "That's wonderful. How come you didn't decide to study journalism or creative writing?"

Shaili wanted to claw his eyes out. "Dad didn't let me."

Sadhil knew he had touched a raw nerve. He felt awful. "I am sorry. I didn't mean to pry. New York has incredible writing programs, should you choose to…Anyway, what kind of writing do you do?"

"Life."

"Care to explain?"

"I write about life." Shaili said, in a flat, emotionless tone, as she played with the straws. Sadhil was caught unawares by her brusqueness.

Supriya realized Shaili was being unnecessarily terse. She believed that there was a time for being direct and then there was a time for being what the society needed you to be. She said to Sadhil, "Since you guys are all about boring talks, can I tell you a funny story? How Mhatre and I got engaged? You want to hear?"

"No he doesn't." Shaili was abrupt, again.

"Sure. Tell me about it." Sadhil said to Supriya, ignoring Shaili.

Supriya told Sadhil about the time she was doing her undergraduate degree from Fergusson College. She and Mhatre were in love. Of course, it was against the institution's policy for a professor to date his student because of which Mhatre changed his job. But, a few complications happened right after he moved.

"I had an Analytical Chemistry professor called Ahmad Khan. He was the only one who knew Mhatre and I were dating. They were good friends. Anyway, when Mhatre moved to Pune University, I was a little lost. Plus, Shaili and I were in different classes. And I hated interacting with those oil-in-their-hair and glasses types. But I like your glasses, Sadhil. You look *smart*!"

Sadhil's dimples stood out again.

"Anyway, Ahmad felt that I was feeling lonesome or something, which was true. He suggested we go out to lunch. Over lunch, we spoke about college, his wife and kids, and Mhatre. But as soon as I got up to use the loo, he made a pass at me."

"No way, dude!" Sadhil shouted. "You are making this up."

"Tell Sadhil that I am not lying." Supriya looked at Shaili.

"Yes. True story." Shaili didn't think there was a need to share this story, but she rolled her eyes and shrugged her shoulders.

"He squeezed my waist." Supriya, with reminiscence in her eyes, turned to Sadhil. "I was shocked. I didn't know how to respond. I continued to walk to the bathroom. In there, I looked at myself in the mirror and contemplated the various ways in which I could handle the precarious situation. Tell him off or twist his arm? Punch him in his face? I knew those tactics wouldn't work. He was my professor and Mhatre's friend. I had to handle the situation with diplomacy. And mind you, subtlety is not my forte. So, I decided to…"

"What did you do?" Sadhil couldn't contain himself and interrupted Supriya mid-sentence.

"I walked back to the table like nothing had happened. But that idiot wouldn't stop! He stroked the tip of my feet from under the table. I ended up saying, 'This has to stop. I can't do it.' Ahmad Khan looked bewildered. He asked 'Why? Haven't you felt this breeze of carnal desires around us?' I didn't know how to react, yet again."

Right when Supriya was going to delve into the juicier details, the waiter brought their order. Shaili looked at the waiter and said sheepishly, "Could I get a cup of coffee please?" Both Sadhil and Supriya exchanged looks. Shaili was, maybe, just maybe, having a change of heart and allowing herself to have a good time.

Supriya took a big sip of her coffee and said, "So, where was I?"

Sadhil said, "Ahmad Khan asked you for a reason why you couldn't go out with him."

Supriya said with a smug look, "I like it that you were paying attention. He's worth keeping, Shails. Men don't listen normally." Before Shaili could reply, Supriya continued with her saga. "Anyway, I said to him, 'Because this can't go anywhere. You are married with children. And I have a boyfriend. And you teach me. This will only break homes.' I threw in a few Bollywood dialogues, yaar."

"Then?" Sadhil was engrossed in Supriya's story. He took a sip of his cold coffee and continued to listen intently.

"Then what. Ahmad sat with a content look on his face. I felt stupid about making up those dumb reasons and every time I did, I yelled at myself internally. I swear I was talking to myself while listening to Ahmad Khan's nonsense."

"You don't say," Sadhil teased Supriya.

By now, Shaili was tired of the day and felt a little sickened. She asked Supriya to finish the story. But Supriya was on a roll. "That jerk said to me, 'I understand. But, maybe we can get a quickie for this one time? Just once—to remember each other by. We both agree that we have something going here. My wife is out of town too.' I was frantic. I said to him, 'I am hopelessly and madly in love with you. One time won't do it for me. It's too painful to bear. Never mention a word of it. Not to Mhatre or your wife. We will have to sacrifice our needs for the sake of others.' Ahmad Khan, with a self-satisfied look on his face and falsely disproportionate sense of self, paid the bill and never spoke of this incident again."

Supriya, tickled with her story, said, "Of course, I told Mhatre about the incident. He got hysterical, and I got a ring on my finger." She thrust her engagement ring in Sadhil's face.

Sadhil couldn't stop laughing and applauding Supriya for her presence of mind and of course, wit. Shaili felt a little envious of Supriya right now because of all the attention she was getting from Sadhil. And she wasn't even sure why she cared about Sadhil focusing on Supriya instead of her. Supriya read Shaili's mind and was ecstatic, for her. "Maybe she's beginning to like Sadhil? Laaa laaaaa." She hummed to herself.

"Anyway I know when to leave." Supriya abruptly picked up her purse after eating half her dosa and drinking a quarter of her cold coffee.

Sadhil was happy in a way. He had enjoyed Supriya's banter and informality but he would finally get to be by himself with Shaili. Now that she had begun to warm up a little, he felt hopeful. Shaili felt betrayed and excited in the same breath. She was finally going to have to be alone with Sadhil. But the unavailability of choice bothered her.

Supriya waved at the couple. "Lovebirds, I'll see you both by 12:30 p.m. when I come back to pick up Shails. Don't do anything that I wouldn't. Well that doesn't leave much to be desired, now does it?"

"Where are you going?" Shaili cut her off.

"I am meeting up with Mhatre near Hong Kong Market."

"Well, you can ask him to join us. Kind of like a double date? Just like old times." Shaili was being sarcastic. Both Supriya and Sadhil understood. Supriya ignored the inane proposition and asked Shaili to step outside for a minute.

"Only if it's okay with you, Sadhil." She fluttered her eyelids.

"By all means." Sadhil smiled as he took a sip of his cold coffee.

The two women walked towards the ladies room. Supriya's demeanor and language changed drastically in those few steps. Her friendly voice got replaced with exasperated high-pitched screeches. She held Shaili by her shoulders and shook her up. "Look here, Shails. I don't know what you are trying to do but stop being puerile! Sadhil has been amiable and solicitous and benevolent and tolerant. So far. Don't push it! He argued with his mother for you. He's put up with my load of hogwash since last evening. Why? Only because he likes you and anyone who might be important to you. And you have been mean and insolent. Why do you have this bitterness towards him? Your altercation is with your father. Not every man is like that fiend. Stop comparing every man to Humbert Humbert! Why persecute this poor guy? It's not Sadhil's fault that your family..." Supriya looked at the floor and stopped herself. Though angry at Shaili, she felt sad for her. She thought of another way of reaching out to her friend.

She pleaded. "I know you. Stop hurting him because you are hurting yourself in the process! Walk away if you'd prefer, but don't behave like a bitch when you are not one. And sometimes it's not okay to be that naively obvious! Especially when there are lives at stake. You should know that better than anyone!"

Shaili stood stunned by Supriya's audacity. She was unsure what to make of the different dimensions to Supriya's accusations. What did Supriya know? She didn't respond. A lot of what Supriya had said was austere but it was also true. She knew Supriya cared for her. More than her sister or father ever could. Moreover, she saw Supriya's eyes were deluged with tears. Supriya didn't cry so easily; it melted Shaili and made her think that she must have done something terribly wrong.

They walked back to where Sadhil was sitting. Supriya was back to being vivacious and charming. She said a bye while passing out flying kisses to Sadhil. She didn't even look at Shaili. Shaili noticed the cold energy. It didn't escape Sadhil either.

Sadhil dug into the melted ice cream inside his cold coffee and asked Shaili. "Are you okay?"

"How do you mean?"

"Overall."

"Yes."

"And with this marital arrangement?"

Shaili was taken by surprise by Sadhil's openness. "You seemed really quiet, so I didn't know what to make of it." He admitted frankly.

"I am sorry if I offended you. I am fine." Shaili said detachedly.

"Shaili, there is nothing to be sorry about. You have every right to feel and think the way you do. I mean, I know how unnecessary this system is, you know, of 'checking out a prospect.' And, I am not here to act like God and decide our destinies. We both are entitled to our own opinions." Sadhil meant well, but he rambled on. He had wanted the interaction to be perfect, but Shaili's languid behavior didn't make the situation any easier. Out of nervousness, he filled the room with words.

All this while, Shaili didn't say anything because she couldn't accept a man could be so understanding. Sadhil continued, "That's why I wanted to meet you by yourself. I don't want you to feel harried into making any decision just because of your parents or mine. It's your life. You should have a say in it."

Shaili gave him a half-hearted smile. Sadhil touched Shaili's left hand and lightly caressed her ring finger. It was a subtle hint. He patted her hand, trying to make her feel relaxed. Her skin was soft and untainted. Their hands fit perfectly in each others. They looked a pair of Greek gods in conjugal bliss; but only for a few seconds. Shaili withdrew her hand with a jerk as if Sadhil were a leper. She didn't know what to do with her free hands, so she grabbed her coffee, took a sip, and almost burnt her tongue. She didn't know why she had acted like that. Maybe it was a reflex reaction. No guy had ever touched her before. Her father had always damned contact with the other gender. She wondered if she was scared of being reprimanded or if she truly disliked his touch—Sadhil's touch, a man's touch. Shaili felt scared even contemplating the latter. Supriya had always told her that the first touch was special. But Shaili felt sick. Too many tortuous thoughts crossed her mind.

Sadhil was taken aback by her reaction. But he assumed the newness of the situation must have made Shaili act that way. He gave her the benefit of the doubt. It dawned onto him that Shaili didn't know that he was going to propose to her and that's why he had held that particular finger. He contemplated if he liked her "rude-honest-shyness." It was definitely refreshing, and he felt his heart leaning towards a yes. He too wasn't a sucker for unabashed romance. He saw that softness in Shaili. Her genuineness enhanced her beauty, at least in his eyes. He didn't want to but couldn't help compare Shaili to Simran, in his head. Simran had wanted to go to bed with him on their third date. And Shaili was ill at ease even when he touched her ring finger. But Sadhil wondered why Shaili never asked him any questions about him or his life in New York. He would have told her what she would have wanted to know. Like why he hadn't married anyone yet. To him, a spiritual, emotional, physical, and intellectual connection is what mattered. Up until Sadhil met Shaili, he hadn't felt that compatible-sensation with anyone. His instincts told him this was it. That Shaili was the right person for him.

"Shaili, I really like you. I promise to keep you happy. Is there anything you want to ask me?"

Shaili was a bucket of emotions waiting to overflow. She was unsure how to ask what. Shaili couldn't interpret what thoughts were permissible. Her feelings towards Sadhil were presented to her as coded messages from her brain and heart. She was perplexed. She appreciated his sensitivity, and he definitely wasn't full of himself. Then there was this overarching responsibility of keeping her mother safe. Her refusal to this proposal might earn her mother more colorful dents from her father's handiwork or so she assumed. She was sick of her family situation. She was exhausted from trying to figure it all. In some ways, Shaili wasn't even thinking about her own self when she said, "It's a yes from me."

Sadhil heard no happiness in Shaili's voice. He felt sad. That's not how he'd envisioned this morning. Or this occasion when he and his future wife would decide to spend their lives together. He had waited a long time for this day.

Men like Sadhil didn't exist, normally, but it was the imperfections of his parents' marriage that had turned Sadhil into who he was—an idealist who desired, what many would call, the nonexistent. He saw Utopian dreams even with his eyes open. He was one of those sensitive guys who wanted to marry the "right" girl, settle down, and have children. He fantasized about cooking Saturday brunch and serving it, for his wife, in bed. Reading the *New York Times* in his lounge pants, with the family sprawled over the king size bed, was his idea of a perfect Sunday morning.

Sadhil, like many rich, single men, had a line of women desperate to sleep with him in New York, but he wasn't a one-night-stand kind of guy. While significant number of men his age and with his affluence would go through women like a packet of cheap cigarettes, Sadhil was a low maintenance Platonist. He had dated just one girl in his entire life, Simran.

Sadhil and Simran were classmates at IIT Delhi. They broke up after three years of being together. He didn't hate her even today, but he always disliked one thing about Simran; she had lied. Lies were unacceptable in Sadhil's idealistic world. If only she had told him what was wrong. Even if they couldn't have fixed it, they could have parted amicably. But to do things behind his back when there was no reason, he was revolted by it. He never wanted to see her again.

After his break up with Simran, Sadhil was even more convinced that New Delhi wasn't for him. He always remembered his nani's words, "Delhi is about extremes. Extreme love, extreme hate, extreme holi, extreme diwali, extreme winter, extreme summer, extreme temperament, extreme passion, and extreme people. If you aren't extreme or don't like extremes, Dilli won't agree with you." Was she right!

His manipulated heart ached for a change in place and gave him the ideal excuse to leave the capital. That's when he moved to the U.S. for further studies. Sadhil finally made real friends in New York with compatible people—well-read men and women, who didn't chastise him for not being a bully or a Casanova. They liked him for who he was.

With his New York friends, Sadhil traveled around the globe, went wine tasting in small villages in Italy, and hiking in Peru. But Paris was a city Sadhil had never traveled to, and he intended to keep it that way until he could go with the love of his life. He wanted to attend the opera, spend the day at the Louvre, take her shopping at quaint French boutiques, relish coffee and beignets at a street side café, munch on ham and cheese baguettes over wine, walk by Champs Elysée at night, do a romantic dinner for two on a rented boat sailing through the Seine, followed by hours of passionate lovemaking. Not sex. Not lust. Not the mundane routine. But adoring each other under the moonlit night and a soft silk sheet while serenading the stars until the crack of dawn—that's what he had in mind. All of a sudden, he saw Shaili's face in Paris, in bed, in theatres, with him—a vision he wanted to behold.

"Haylo sweethearts." Supriya broke Sadhil's daydream as she returned to the restaurant at 12:30 p.m. to pick Shaili up. Sadhil didn't realize that he and Shaili had sat in silence for more than fifteen minutes. Mhatre was with Supriya. She introduced the two men. Sadhil shared the news with Supriya, who gave him a big hug. Shaili didn't say a word.

"Do you ladies want to stay on for lunch?" Sadhil suggested.

"No. We have to leave now. It's getting late. Ma must be waiting," said Shaili. Sadhil was hoping Shaili would have agreed to stay back, but he understood her hesitation. On some level, he felt reassured by Shaili's response. To him, it meant, unlike Simran who had slept with half of IIT Delhi and then lied to him about it, Shaili was not a fake, promiscuous woman. But Supriya and Mhatre, who knew Shaili, were shocked by her tone. It was tired, sad, and curt. She had just accepted a proposal, but she sounded like she had agreed to a life sentence.

The ladies then bid adieu to Mhatre and Sadhil and drove back to the Kapoor residence. Supriya was greatly piqued by Shaili's unsuitable behavior. Neither of them clearly knew what had prompted Shaili to act that way though Supriya tried probing innumerable times. When Shaili didn't respond, Supriya sat in the driver's seat of the *Kinetic Honda* and despite a simple, self-start button that she could have pressed to get the two-wheeler moving, she insisted on kick starting it while grumbling. Even the dust around her feet and face pleaded for mercy. She screamed, "Go to hell! Don't ever talk to me!" Shaili stayed silent because somewhere she knew she had been iniquitous.

Mrs. Kapoor was literally parading up and down when Shaili and Supriya got home.

"Where were you? You are ten minutes late!"

"Aunty, we stopped to fill petrol."

"Never mind. So, what happened? What did Sadhil have to say? What did you say, Shailu? Will someone tell me what happened?" She went on a rant without noticing that Supriya was trying to mouth something.

Supriya rested both her arms on Mrs. Kapoor's shoulders and said to her in a comforting voice, "All is well, Aunty. Congratulations. They have both 'officially' said a yes. Let's celebrate." Supriya broke her unsanctioned vow of silence around Shaili. She was still disappointed in her but she didn't want Mrs. Kapoor to see her disapproval.

Mrs. Kapoor blinked at a feverish pace. She was numb from delirium. She asked Supriya to repeat the news. She couldn't believe her daughter was getting married. She asked Tanisha to bring burfi from the refrigerator. By the time everyone ate a piece of burfi and soaked in the good news, the phone rang. Mrs. Kapoor answered the phone in her state of exuberation. It was Mr. Sethi. Mrs. Kapoor said, "Haanji" every few seconds. Then she yelled, "Wedding in two weeks from now? But, how will we prepare? Cards have to be printed, guests have to be invited, shopping has to be done, food has to be arranged, and…" Mr. Sethi gave a reason, which Shaili or Supriya couldn't hear except for a few "Haans" from Mrs. Kapoor. She finally said, "Noji. I understand. If Sadhil has to go back, and you don't want to wait for the marriage until his next trip, then it has to be now. Even we will be more relaxed if the children are together." Mr. Sethi asked a few more questions to which Mrs. Kapoor replied, "No, Shaili doesn't have a passport. Uh-huh. Uh-huh. Okayji? Really? You are too kind." Mrs. Kapoor put the phone down.

Shaili had never seen her mother more in control. She turned to the girls and Suresh Kapoor, "Sethi Sahib's brother works in the foreign ministry. He will get Shaili's passport ready in three days. The Hindu ceremony will take place in two weeks, but the court marriage will happen next week so Shailu can get the visa. Sadhil wants to take her along with him to America. He leaves in three weeks. He is a good boy. I am happy, but all this is too quick. It is wonderful, but how will we manage everything? I am not complaining. Thank you God!" She joined her hands and looked at the ceiling, as if thanking the Omnipresent.

She gave Shaili a big squeeze and planted innumerable kisses on her forehead and her cheeks. Meena Kapoor started crying and wiping her tears. But the torrent of salty water was symbolic of bliss. For the first time in twenty-two years, Shaili saw Suresh Kapoor wipe his wife's eyes. His eyes too looked overwhelmed. Mr. and Mrs. Kapoor briefly hugged each other, and Mr. Kapoor assured his wife that all would be taken care of. Their interaction felt unnatural to Shaili, Supriya, and Tanisha. A smile seeped onto everyone's face and flooded the house with laughter when Mrs. Kapoor mispronounced "tension" and said, "*Bahut taen-shun ho rahee hai.*" Tanisha, as always, volunteered to correct her mother's intonation. But instead of rebuking her, Mrs. Kapoor held her close to her chest. The Kapoor household had never heard such quantities of gurgles and glee. There was harmony in the house. But Shaili noticed that amidst all the merriment, no one asked her what she thought of the alliance. Or the move to a new country. Why did she sense that her parents wanted to get rid of her?

Shaili and Sadhil both watched Pete Sampras win the Wimbledon finals that year but from the security and solace of their own homes. Little did they know, like Sampras the following year, the result of their match would be completely unexpected.

6

Shaili stared into Suresh Kapoor's eyes and said "I swear, I wish I could have prevented the whole Sadhil-episode in my life." Her eyes looked apologetic.

"Prevented? Neither were you tied to a pole nor did I put a gun to your head. You married him out of your own free will." Suresh Kapoor refused to hear Shaili out when she tried to justify her side of the story. But he couldn't be blamed. He had no idea Meena Kapoor had pleaded with Shaili to consider the alliance. He wasn't privy to the conversations between his dead wife and daughter. He believed he had coerced Shaili to meet with Sadhil, not marry him.

"We gave you education, house, and a good life. What more did you want? Haan? You got everything too easily but had appreciation for nothing! You are an ingrate!" The tension escalated when Suresh Kapoor bellowed, "I should have guessed that treachery wouldn't skip a generation."

"Where are you going with this?"

"You cheated on Sadhil! Just like your mother did on..." Suresh Kapoor bit his lip. His eyes spitting filth and fury, he gulped down his anger along with his unfinished sentence.

Shaili lowered her eyes and said, "I did not betray Sadhil. I shattered his trust but not intentionally. If I had clearly known certain facts about myself, I would have never married him. Or any other man." The mere mention of Sadhil's name softened Shaili. She said with humility, "I owe Sadhil so much. No one can feel worse than I do about what transpired between us. Not a single day goes by when I don't think of him and how I wronged him."

"Are you telling me that even after marrying Sadhil, you did not know you were abnormal? Lies, again!"

"Again, by 'abnormal' if you mean gay, then no. I did not know that right away. I wish I had, but I wasn't that fortunate."

"And Sadhil encouraged your foolishness? He couldn't be man enough to teach his untruthful wife a lesson?"

"He was very considerate." Shaili spoke in measured tones.

"Considerate? What do you mean? How could he not know? As a man, he didn't do anything?"

"If you are asking whether or not Sadhil abused and violated me, then the answer is *No*! He was no ordinary person. It was Sadhil who made me believe that not every man was a monster!" Shaili's last sentence was shot from her eyes and hit Suresh Kapoor on the right spot. He backed down, momentarily. His tune changed, like he understood her viewpoint, even if a little bit, or maybe because he felt mortified. He knew Shaili was alluding to him and to one particular incident when she used the word "monster." By now Shaili was breathing hard. She was reminded of the time she accidentally walked in on her parents. She must have been seven or eight. That was the day she officially began to resent Suresh Kapoor and hate men overall.

Suresh was discreet about abusing Meena. It was always after Shaili was asleep. In a sick, twisted sort of way, he tried to protect Shaili. His issue was with his wife, not the child. On some levels, he didn't hate Shaili. That evening too, Shaili was supposed to be in bed. But she woke up after a nightmare where a monster was trying to kill her mother. Even years after this occurrence, no one could tell if it was telepathy between the mother and daughter that had led Shaili to dream about the events and then run to protect her mother. Anyway, the frightened child, Shaili, wanted her mother. She ran crying into Meena and Suresh's room only to see Suresh mounted on top of Meena, throwing profanities at her. One of his hands was inside her kurta aggressively rubbing her breasts; his other arm was pinned against her left thigh. He was pounding her like meat. Meena was lying in bed with her pajamas down to her knee. She looked still as a corpse. Even the tears were frozen around the corner of her eyes.

Suresh was shocked to see Shaili. He didn't welcome the uninvited intrusion, more so because he had never wanted Shaili to ever be exposed to what happened between him and his wife. He stopped raping Meena and started staring into his daughter's naïve eyes, trying to mask his overpowering guilt. He felt enraged at himself for having forgotten to bolt the bedroom door from the inside. For a brief moment, he loathed himself for what his daughter had witnessed. The silence in the room was unnerving. All this while, Meena continued to lie down like a cadaver. It was Suresh, who brusquely pulled up her pajama while he pulled down his lungi. He regained his mental strength, and his anger got misdirected towards Shaili. He screamed at her for barging into their room unannounced.

At her age, Shaili didn't understand the meaning of those multi-syllabled, impudent terms oozing out of Suresh Kapoor's mouth, aside from kutti meaning bitch and gadhi implying ass. She didn't realise that her mother was being raped until she reached her teens and was taught about reproduction in her biology class. The bestial movements on the bed were alien to her, but they nauseated her. And she would always remember that sight. She was cognizant that tears represented pain. And the distress in her ma's eyes, even as a child, the fierce loyalist in Shaili couldn't bear. That was enough. Shaili caught Suresh's lungi and began to cry, "*Chod do*! Stop. *Ma ko chod do.* Leave Ma alone!" She might have thrown in a few baby punches at Suresh's belly as she wailed and called him a monster.

Suresh pulled his lungi out of Shaili's clutches. He picked Shaili by the collar in her nightdress. Just as he was about to fling her against the cupboard, Meena snapped out of her trance and begged him to put her down. It took him more than two minutes to make up his mind. He eventually put Shaili down but not because Meena pleaded. The mole on Shaili's right cheek stopped him. It stared, indignantly, at him. Also because Shaili wet her pants and his half-naked body, but her eyes remained dry. After throwing Shaili on the bed, right next to his wife, he screamed, his eyes bloodshot.

"You tell this mongrel to behave. This is my house, Meena. My rules. If she doesn't like it, she can leave!"

Equations changed that night onwards in the Kapoor household. Shaili saw her father in a different light. To her, he was an ogre, not just an authoritarian parent. He was a demon who wanted to kill her and hit her ma. She went from pleasing her father to loathing him. She said to her mother, for the first time, "*I Hate Men! I Hate Daddy*. I never want to get married."As she thought back now, she wondered if things between Suresh Kapoor and herself would have been different had her mother revealed chapters from her past, once she was grown up. Maybe things would have been different. Maybe the Sadhil episode might not have happened. Just maybe her life in India would not have been entangled around doubt and loathing.

"I can't do this!" Shaili threw up her arms in desperation.

"What did I do now?" Suresh Kapoor felt betrayed. Shaili had chosen to blame her entire life on him.

"Don't you see it? We may have both grown older, but mentally we are still the same—incompatible. Even after all these years, we are hurling hurt and insults at each other, not talking things through."

"Shaili, what do you want? You want me to apologize, is that so? Should I go down on my knees and beg your forgiveness for my *unruly tongue and wayward mind*? Haan?"

"I never wanted that."

"Then what? You don't know what you want? That's always been your problem."

"How easy it is for you to blame me? To look at me like I am some imbecile. But have you asked me how I have been? My life in New York? The first few weeks of marriage? What agonies I went through!" Shaili articulated earnestly without any pause between sentences.

"You know the problem with your generation?" Suresh Kapoor stamped his foot until the ground shuddered. He pulled his glasses, like a cannibal tears flesh, and said, "When we show interest, you push us away suspiciously; when we let you do things your way, you say we ignored you."

"When did you ask me anything?"

"Why would I be inflicting this harsh downpour on my aging body if I wasn't interested in listening to you?"

"Are you ready for my story?"

"No one is ever prepared for bad news, but you learn to cope with it. I am ready to hear whatever you have to say. Talk away."

Shaili knew that patience was never one of Suresh Kapoor's virtues. She stroked her left elbow with her right palm and said, "Sadhil was always generous and caring, but I was miserable from day one."

"Why? Because of her?"

"Why am I wasting my breath when you have already made up your mind??" Shaili muttered with frustration.

"Okay. Okay. Carry on."

"Right from day one of our marriage, I felt like unrest brewing inside me. I was consumed by limitless anger I could not comprehend. But I didn't know that my inner turmoil would wreak havoc on Sadhil's life too."

"So, your friend Leila makes you happy?"

Suresh Kapoor asked unexpectedly or so Shaili thought. She didn't realize it was awkward for him to discuss his daughter's love life let alone an unconventional one.

"Yes, she does."

"She takes care of you?"

"Uh-huh."

"But why her?"

"I don't understand." Shaili said with a quizzical look.

"Were there no Indian women in New York?"

"You are not serious, right?"

"Your Mother would have thrown a fit—a foreigner and that too a Muslim at that?"

"Hypocrisy thy name is my parents. You and Ma were of different religious faiths, and yet you ask me why I couldn't date a Hindu or at least an Indian?" Shaili's tone was sarcastic, again.

"Clearly I can't ask you why you won't date a man, so I thought I would pick my battles."

"What do you want from me?" Shaili showed her resentment openly, her old rebellion flaring up.

Suresh Kapoor looked at Shaili quirking his left eyebrow, a puzzled glint in both his eyes. He spoke in a domineering voice, reminiscent of landlords in pre-independence India, "Would you like some Pune-style coffee?" Shaili was flabbergasted. Here she was pouring out her heart, amidst all the stress, and all he was thinking was about coffee. Shaili chose to be deliberately blind. She didn't want to see why he'd made the offer. It was her comfort-beverage, one that always managed to soothe her nerves. This particular coffee was a Kapoor family favorite. Suresh Kapoor had inferred that it wasn't easy for Shaili to have this conversation with him without her mother present. Maybe the hot drink would give her the strength and create the illusion of her mother's presence. He was too proud, as always, to show his caring side. And she was too skeptical, as always, to acknowledge even remote traces of goodness in him.

"You remembered? Well, that's a surprise." The smugness on Shaili's face was evident.

"I am your father. You like it especially when it rains." Suresh Kapoor's statement was bland, blunt, masking the latent concern.

Both Shaili and Suresh Kapoor thought of Meena Kapoor at this instant. Shaili said, "Ma would make this for us every morning. Even if I were running late, she would make me drink a cup. I could escape the five-almond rule but not her coffee. She was of the notion that her coffee was the cure, the panacea for everything in the world—cold, measles, mumps, or a bad day at school." She was silent for a while. Looking at Suresh Kapoor she added, "I have to say it was particularly wonderful around the monsoons. Sometimes Ma would make onion bhajiyas along with her exceptional coffee. Nothing could beat that combination. The smell of oil would cling to our hair and clothes. Back then, I didn't mind it."

"You don't like Indian food any longer?"

"I did not say that!"

"Do you like anything Indian anymore?"

"Of all the things I said, that's all you chose to deduce? Seriously? How can I not love Indian cuisine? It is my food!"

"I don't know. You don't like other things Indian." Suresh Kapoor was defiant. Shaili couldn't interpret the message hidden in the saliva bubbles around the corner of his mouth.

"I was talking about the unmistakable smell associated with it," Shaili continued.

"Now you find that smell repulsive?"

"God, talking to you is draining—like explaining the relationship between candy and cavities to a three-year old."

"You didn't answer my question."

"Geez, I do not find the aroma repulsive! Happy? It's just a joke between us."

"Who? What joke?"

"Leila and I." Suresh Kapoor didn't take too well to Shaili's referral to Leila and her own self as a couple. "Every time we cook Indian food, I get paranoid about the odor. I frantically open all windows and burn incense and candles. The wooden flooring absorbs the smell of curry and transports it to our jackets. It's not very appetizing. Leila always rags me that I am a coconut—brown from the outside but white from the inside." Shaili couldn't help but smile, slightly. Suresh Kapoor tried not to look upset or befuddled. He didn't get the joke, but it didn't seem like he minded not knowing.

Shaili continued, "Anyway, where were we? Oh yeah. Tanisha and I would open the living room windows and Ma would yell, 'Idiots, water will come inside.' Instead, on Ma's suggestion, she, Tanisha, and I would stand out in the balcony; collect hailstones in a round, copper-bottomed vessel; get soaking wet until one of us started shivering and then run inside the kitchen to enjoy the remainder of the 'monsoon-food,' as we called it." For a few minutes, Shaili held her anguish in abeyance. She sighed loudly. "There is something magical about Pune rains. It gives you a perspective on life, right?"

Suresh Kapoor both did and didn't want to ask what Shaili meant by that. On the one hand, he didn't think it was an opportune time for palavering. He belonged to a school of thought where parents and children didn't break into casual conversations midway through arguments. Or even have heated arguments to begin with. On the other, he felt responsible for her. He was the one who had introduced coffee in the conversation to change Shaili's mood. He found it as erratic as the tropical winds.

"What was that music countdown show on TV with this lame anchor mom loved?"

"There were so many of them." He replied apathetically. He remembered the name, but he didn't want to let his guard down. By now he was beginning to get really annoyed.

"No, there was one in particular. It was Ma's favorite. She was like an encyclopedia of old songs. She would dance to the Bollywood actress Helen's hits. She was a different person, you know, when you weren't around. She taught Tanisha and me to jive. Boy, could she dip!" Shaili ran her fingers through her wet hair, gently massaged her scalp, and continued to remember her mother fondly. "She would fight with us over playing cards and cheated and threw tantrums like a five-year old. She also loved pillow fights. But the energy and her demeanor would change once it was time for you to return home." Shaili spoke with a hint of both melancholy and abhorrence in her voice.

Suresh Kapoor consciously let her comment slide by. He knew Shaili was telling the truth. Tanisha, in one of her attempts to win the "favorite daughter contest," had told him about the things the three women did in his absence. He knew Meena Kapoor had saved some of her beautiful dresses and blouses from when she was still a Goan. She, Shaili, and Tanisha would try them on and parade around with exaggerated British accents. Even though Meena Kapoor was born and raised a Catholic, Suresh Kapoor didn't allow anything 'Crristan'—his Punjabi style of pronouncing Christian—in the house. The family had to pray to Hanumanji and turn vegetarian on Tuesdays. That was the day Tanisha and Shaili would chew Meena Kapoor's brains to sneak an egg into their lunch boxes. The atmosphere at home would be convivial. Tanisha, surreptitiously, had told her father that her Ma didn't fit into most of the items aside from the long skirts with elastic.

"What is the point in talking about irrelevant things?" Suresh Kapoor demanded. From his standpoint, Shaili was delaying everyone and every unsaid word.

Shaili retracted herself from her past and said, "I digress. Anyway, where will you find Pune-style coffee here?" The sudden softness in her voice, occasioned by reminiscing about her mother, was noticeable.

"There is a tiny teastall right on the mainroad. I'll get it from there." Suresh Kapoor was relieved the conversation had changed course.

"And you know about it how?"

"How does it matter?"

"Because I want to know."

"You might have gotten older, but I'm still your father. And if I don't feel the need to share everything with you, I won't."

Shaili gulped her irritation and said, "I think you make a persuasive case, so I can manage to curtail my curiosity, for now."

Suresh Kapoor didn't tell Shaili what had transpired between him and Meena Kapoor right around the time she died. He had found out that Meena Kapoor would secretly visit the lake even after all these years. He quietly followed her on a few occasions but didn't say a word. He would drink coffee at the teastall and watch his wife pour her tears into the lake or talk to it. Of course he lashed out at her in other abusive ways when she was home. Two days before her death, he had confronted his wife about the lake. It was his birthday, and instead of visiting the temple to pray for her own husband's long life, he saw her offering flowers to the lake. That was the day he demanded to know what was special about that place. Meena Kapoor was stumped. She felt reprehensible. Despite everything, Suresh Kapoor had accepted her as his wife. Granted they didn't have the healthiest of relationships, but she knew it was mostly because of her. She couldn't deal with the humiliation all over again, so Meena Kapoor decided to end her life in the lake where it all began. She left her husband the diamond pendant for Shaili and a letter apologizing for her past. She begged for his forgiveness and pleaded with him to accept Shaili for who she was. She told him in the letter that if he did choose to forgive his daughter, he should give her the pendant. That Shaili would understand the significance. Meena Kapoor ended the letter with a question: she asked Suresh Kapoor if their mistakes were the cause for Shaili's woes and unconventional choice.

Suresh Kapoor's eyes were moist. He was unable to brush aside his wife's question from the letter. So Shaili didn't see his overwhelmed eyes, he said, "I will first use the toilet and be back. Meanwhile, check if Supriya and your umm…friend…would like to have some coffee."

"Her name is Leila. You can ask her yourself. She won't bite." Bitchiness came to rest on Shaili's tongue, yet again.

"You ask her. She might not understand what Pune-style coffee is."

"A decade and more of living with me has made her part Indian. She can make coffee, the Indian way, just how I like it. One teaspoon of instant coffee with two teaspoons of sugar in three quarters cup of milk and a quarter cup of water and then heat it for a minute and a half. And, she is the one who cooks at home, including Indian food. Remember, I always hated cooking!"

"Listen, Shaili. I am trying to get to know you. It's new to me—your life, your attitude, you altogether. Don't expect changes overnight. There will be bumps along the way." Suresh Kapoor squirmed with mild annoyance. Shaili didn't want to get into another argument now that they both seemed to be making an effort to understand each other. No one could tell if she had come to terms with the fact that it was never easy for a parent to accept that his or her child was so different from the societal standards of normalcy.

Shaili walked back to the car and asked Supriya and Leila if they wanted coffee. They both replied in the affirmative. Shaili briefly updated the two women on the happenings so far. Supriya threw a volley of questions at Shaili while Leila asked, "Is this the place you dreamt about?" Shaili nodded.

"What place? What dream? Why didn't you tell me?" Supriya asked deafeningly. The protectiveness and jealousy in her tone was evident.

"I had this recurring nightmare for the last two months where I saw myself locked inside a glass box with my wrists and ankles bound with iron shackles. The box had no lid. I screamed for help, but in vain. I saw vague faces pointing fingers and yelling, *"You maligned tradition. You brought us disgrace. You must die."* I had had the same dream every single night—same people, same place, same voices, same allegations. But couple of nights ago was the first time I identified the waters. It was this—Pashan Lake. The next thing I knew, my limp body inside the glass box was at the bottom of the lake. My hair flowed waywardly, covering my eyes and blinding me temporarily. It blocked my nose making every breath even more difficult than the one before. There was a spurt of blood mixed with water and saliva. It was surreal.

"It sounds like telepathy." Supriya spoke with her eyes wide open.

"What are you saying?" Shaili asked in a soft voice. Talking about how her mother's life ended made her emotional, even today. She sobbed softly.

"Meaning, this is where Aunty died." Supriya pointed towards the water. "In Pashan Lake. You kept dreaming about what was going to happen, but you didn't know it was going to happen to Aunty. Like she was communicating with you. And finally the day you recognized the location, that was the day the tragic incident occurred."

Supriya, for a brief moment, looked content despite the gravity of the news she imparted, the sombre surroundings. She liked knowing that she still knew her best friend better than anyone, even Leila. Leila understood Supriya's sentiments, so she kept quiet. It was evident to her that Supriya felt Leila had taken her place. Both Leila and Supriya got along fairly well, but Leila knew it was time she left the two friends alone. Just as she was about to leave, Shaili's angst gained volume. Leila, hurriedly, stepped out of the car, hugged Shaili and stroked her hair urging her to calm down. Supriya sat quietly in the driver's seat, her feet between the accelerator and brake, a million thoughts racing through her mind. She wasn't sure how to respond. She caught glimpses of the two women in the rear view mirror. This was the first time she had actually seen Shaili or any other unconventional couple so closely. They seemed so similar, in their expression of affection and concern, to her and Mhatre, yet so very different.

As Shaili began to calm down, her mind kept going back to the night when she saw the nightmare for the last time, when she was in New York—the one that opened a vacuity of emotions and distorted truth as she knew it.

Just when Shaili thought of giving up and embracing death, in her dreams, the alarm rang. She woke up with a fright, panting for breath. Her hair covered her face partially. With half-closed eyes, she glanced at the world around her. Though her body was wet from fear-induced perspiration, she recognized her surroundings. It was her loft apartment in Tribeca, New York. Shaili vaguely touched her nose and eyes and was relieved to feel no blood. She looked down at her feet and was relieved to see that her long legs were freely resting next to her better half. A white satin sheet covered their bodies. The large, French windows allowed a few reckless rays of sunlight to tease the tips of their feet. Shaili pulled the covers over them.

"You okay?" asked Leila from inside the covers.

"I'm fine. It was the same nightmare, again. Go back to sleep."

Shaili got out of the bed feeling a little worn-out and more perplexed. She wore a pink, silk robe over her flawless skin. A creature of habit, every morning, she brushed her teeth and then combed her naturally straight auburn hair, always in that order. She tied her hair in a knot and walked down the stairs of her duplex apartment to make coffee.

Her apartment was an architectural marvel. Her friends called her place the "Esoteric Mahal." Each nook and corner had mystique written on it. You could tell that an artist had designed the house. There were personalized installations, paintings, and a few other visual art pieces on the wall that matched the color of the upholstery. The basement in the apartment was a library where Shaili worked. There was a heart-shaped candle stand next to her book, *Am I a Defiant Girl?* on the coffee table. The book had won Shaili several awards but cost her more than she could ever imagine. As she flipped through the pages, her eyes fell on the foreword. It read, "This book is dedicated to Sadhil Sethi—the man who gave me my real life; taught me generosity; and, introduced me to selflessness." She thought of Sadhil and smiled. A warm, heartfelt smile. It had taken her years to get to that point where she could feel happy in her heart, while saying his name aloud. Right next to her book, was a copy of Vladimir Nabokov's *Lolita.* Shaili was always amazed how much the book had influenced her life. The book worked as a tour guide when Shaili went on an unintended self-discovery voyage.

Shaili played the *Gayatri Mantra* CD, in the background, keeping the volume low. On the shelf above the music system, there was porcelain *Ganpati*. She touched the deity's feet with her index finger, bent her head slightly, and brought the same finger to her forehead and then her lips. She then took two mugs out of the kitchen cabinet for the morning beverage. They both had identical words inscribed on them—"I BREW MY CREATIVITY IN HERE." Shaili's mind was still preoccupied with the recurring nightmare. Now that she recognized the location of her dream, she wondered about its significance. She remembered that the lake was close to the National Defence Academy.

She thought to herself, "Why Pashan Lake?" She hadn't been to India in over fifteen years so why now? Her heart ached to call home but she knew her limitations. She looked endearingly at the *Bang & Olufsen* phone, which was blinking indicating there was a message on the answering machine. The phone was a gift she bought herself when she earned the six-figure advance for her second book. After a hand-to-mouth existence as a struggling writer for several years, the substantial token was welcomed.

"Oh, it looks like we forgot to check the voicemail last night," Shaili mumbled. The night before, she was at a friend's gallery opening in Chelsea. It was a perfect Friday evening with champagne overflowing from crystal glasses and petite hors d'oeuvres being served to people discussing art. Her friend had sold three paintings priced at over $10,000 each. Once the gallery closed, a bunch of them had walked down south, in the direction of the breeze, to their favorite wine bar in the neighborhood, for congratulatory drinks followed by dinner at a newly opened Latin-Japanese fusion restaurant in the West Village. Loud music and artistic hybrid cuisine flirted with suave palates and creative hearts until the wee hours of the morning. The group didn't disperse until 3:00 a.m. Shaili, exhausted from the day's activities, must have called it a day around 3:30 a.m. without checking her emails or voicemail.

"I'll see my emails first and then listen to the messages. It must be Suzy confirming brunch plans for today." Shaili thought to herself. But as she logged into her inbox, Shaili realized there were five emails from Supriya.

Supriya's emails to Shaili that morning had a tone of urgency in them. "I left you a message on your answering machine. Call back. It is important!"

Shaili grinned as she injected words into her thoughts. "She must have fought with Mhatre again. I am sure she wants me to play mediator. Even after fourteen years of being married, he is so enamored by Su. He'll do anything to keep her happy. Lucky woman."

Shaili picked up the phone and dialed into her voice mail system. "Shails, where are you? Why are you not picking up your phone? This is Su. I have been trying to call you for so long. Phone me right away when you get this message."

The message didn't have the usual "Supriya tone." It was abrupt contrary to her regular affable and effervescent tone. Quite often, the answering machine would cut off Supriya because she would say more than what could be recorded. It was a joke between her and Shaili. But something was wrong this time around. Shaili felt a knot at the pit of her stomach. Her fingers fumbled as she nervously keyed in Supriya's number on the speed dial. After all, Supriya was her only link to her mother, to Pune, to India, to the family, to her past. Suresh Kapoor had clearly told his wife, "As far as I am concerned Shaili is dead. You are my wife so she is dead for you as well. Do you understand? You better understand!" His threats echoed in the house and no one dared go against him. He was known to rely on more than mere verbal threat to make people agree with him. Meena Kapoor and

Shaili stayed in touch without Suresh Kapoor's knowledge, and Supriya was the conduit.

Shaili heard Supriya's phone ringing and then Supriya's voice came through. Grave, sombre.

"Hi. Is that Su?" Shaili said in an anxious Indian-American accent.

"Yes. Shails?" Where were you?"

"Is all well? I got your voicemail and emails. We got home really late last night. And I didn't check my messages until now."

"I need you to sit down," Supriya interrupted her.

"What is it?"

"You have to come to Pune."

"You're scaring me. What happened?"

"Shails, I have news for you. It's not very good." Supriya's voice cracked. She choked on her words. To distract herself from the pain, she shouted at her children, using profound vocabulary, to lower the television's volume and finish their homework. Shaili knew the yelling and the eloquence was a shield Supriya used when distressed.

"Will you be more specific?" Shaili bit her lower lip. She knew something was terribly wrong.

"Umm." Supriya sniffled. "I don't think you can take it."

"What are you talking about?"

"Actually, where is Leila? Can I talk to her?"

"She is sleeping. Can you tell me *please*?"

Supriya drew a deep breath. "I am sorry to tell you this: Aunty is no more."

Supriya divulged what Shaili had least expected to hear. Or ever wanted to. Supriya went on to share some more details. There was an ominous silence for a few seconds.

"Are you there? Hello? Say something!" Supriya was nervous about the silence at the other end. She knew how attached Shaili was to her mother. She was the only family member Shaili cared about. More than anything, Supriya knew Shaili. And she feared for her friend.

The phone slipped from Shaili's hands onto the floor. The line went dead and so did her heart. She sank to the floor. On hearing the noise, Leila got out of the bed, with a start, and came running down the bedroom stairs to check on Shaili.

"Are you alright?"

Shaili looked like she had seen a ghost. She was shivering, breathless, and pale. Upon hearing the disconnected ringtone from the cordless phone lying on the floor, Leila pointed towards it and asked, "Who was that?"

Shaili didn't answer. It seemed her overpowering grief had sewed her ability to respond. Leila picked up the phone and gently shook Shaili, "Hey, what is going on?" There was no response, from Shaili. Shaili's face was blank, her eyes wore a destitute look.

"C'mon."

Maybe it was the affectionate pat on her cheek that prodded Shaili's deliberation when she finally mumbled. "It was Su."

"And?"

Shaili drowned in affliction.

"Will you say something?" Leila asked yet again. Persistence was one of Leila's most impressive strengths.

Shaili looked up at the skylight, trying to stop the crude reality from barraging her face. "It was about Ma."

"What about Mrs. Kapoor?"

" She...ummm...She, she...is dead."

"How? When?"

"She *ended her life*!" Shaili expressed with helplessness.

"*What?*" Leila went numb for a few seconds. But she collected herself as she realized the moment wasn't about giving in to her own feelings. She comforted Shaili in a genuine and discernible voice. "I am so sorry."

On hearing kind words, Shaili's sniffles gained momentum and frequency. She turned her right wrist at an angle, with the palm facing towards her, as if asking herself a question. The shock of the news had rendered her words incomprehensible. "I can't believe my ma left me. Ma would....But she was...I mean..."

"How did she die?"

Shaili wasn't paying attention. Her eyes looked vacant as if they were searching for answers from within. Finally, after the fifth attempt from Leila, Shaili spoke.

"She drowned herself in the lake."

"What lake?"

"The one that I have been dreaming about. Pashan Lake." Shaili wiped the torrent of tears from her eyes to gain clarity about her recurring nightmare.

"Are you serious?" Shaili didn't catch the quiver in Leila's voice.

"It was the same lake where she took me for twenty years. And she killed herself there?" As she explained her dream and sorrow out aloud, Shaili realized the actuality of her loss. The only person in her family who cared for her was now dead. She wailed inconsolably and lay on the floor in a fetal position. She called out to her mother like a two-year old—desperately, gibberishly.

Leila helped Shaili get up from the floor. She walked her to the couch and handed her a box of tissues. "Let me get you some coffee."

As Leila got up from the sofa, Shaili clung to her arms and said, "Can I ask you something?"

"Sure."

"But be honest."

"Do I know any other way?"

"Do you think I killed her?"

"What?"

"Am I responsible for my mother's death?"

Leila closed her eyes so Shaili couldn't read them. She couldn't muster the courage to tell her the actual truth, the real cause for her mother's act, for what could have driven her to suicide. It wasn't simple. Not yet. It was too soon.

"How many cups should I bring?" Suresh Kapoor, who had just returned from the bathroom, called out to Shaili as he straightened his white kurta. He was a few feet away from the car and Shaili's back was towards him, but he saw Leila comforting Shaili. He chose to express his unfamiliarity with the situation by physically maintaining the distance and readjusting his glasses.

Shaili moved away from Leila, wiped her remnant tears, faced Suresh Kapoor, and said, "Four cups. Should I come with you?" Suresh Kapoor gestured a no.

Before anybody could say anything else, Leila walked towards Suresh Kapoor. While rolling up the sleeves of her kurta, she said to him in a no-nonsense tone, "If it's alright, I'd like to walk with you." Suresh Kapoor didn't invite Leila, but he didn't object either. He noticed that Shaili and Leila were polar opposites. Leila seemed tougher, straightforward, independent, focused, and quieter.

7

As the pair walked towards the teastall, Shaili and Supriya watched them with their jaws dropping.

Supriya screamed, "What happened here, Shails? Just what did happen?" Supriya had gained weight over the years, but she still looked attractive dressed in a pink and beige cotton sari, her hair plaited in a braid. The sparkles in her eyes were exuberant like the galaxy of stars. Shaili remembered how the boys in college had nicknamed Supriya *pataakha,* firecracker, because of her unreserved personality. She had a response for everything under the sun.

"What do you think they are talking about?" Supriya fidgeted with her wristwatch.

"Beats me." Shaili knew that Leila, the more pragmatic of the two, always knew what she wanted, and she made sure she got it. She must have had her own reason to spend some time alone with Suresh Kapoor. No hurdle was detrimental or insurmountable for her.

"Never in a million years did I think this would have happened!" Supriya exclaimed.

"I know what you are saying, but there is a soft side to Leila, unseen by most people. She is generous and accommodating of people she cares for."

"Ya, ya. That I know. I never questioned it. It is Uncle. I am shocked Uncle didn't say anything." Supriya changed the topic. "Shails, can I ask you something?"

"Sure."

"You never really told me what happened."

"When?"

"You know, between you and Sadhil or you and Leila. I am sure it was difficult, but was it odd?" When younger, Supriya knew her friend better than Shaili could ever know herself. Years ago when Shaili and Sadhil had gone their separate ways, Supriya had asked Shaili what had transpired between the two of them. In response, Shaili had regurgitated a dialogue from their favorite TV show, "*My marriage is a fake Fendi.*" Interestingly, Supriya decoded different layers of meanings from Shaili's confession and she was the first person to ask Shaili if she'd left Sadhil for another woman. The two friends didn't talk about how Supriya knew what she did, but Shaili had always wanted to ask her. And Supriya had always wanted to know if being gay was Shaili's choice or her fate. But the friends never spoke of it.

"I wouldn't just call it *odd*. It was heart wrenching. Phone seemed impersonal and inappropriate for sharing such personal details, but I am here now. You know I am in Pune after all these years because the phantoms of my past needed burial."

"Come and sit inside first, my philosopher friend. You're soaking wet." Supriya opened the car door. Before Shaili could say anything or get inside, Supriya asked her, "Pune has changed a lot in the last decade, no?"

"Yes, it has, but not the rains. There's something furtive about the monsoon in Pune. Every drop unleashes a verdict." The teardrops in Shaili's eyes reflected the hue of the raindrops. Shaili and Supriya shared a moment where no words were uttered but the silence conveyed a more forceful message than a sentence ever could.

"So, what did you want to know, Su?"

"Your life in the past fifteen years. From the time you got married and left and never came back. Or was never permitted to return. I mean, the last time I saw you was when your house was all decorated for your wedding. Your wedding might have been hurried but the preparations were still elaborate. Uncle paid extra for those last minute bookings at *Hotel Aurora Towers*. Aunty made sure your house was adorned with vivid, long garlands of marigold and jasmine.

"Ya, Ma was insistent we hired a *shehnai* troupe, and she allotted them a permanent place at the main gate entrance for those days so that the music played on continuously. The decorative *shamiana* worked as a canopy for the luscious green garden. The strings of colorful lights elegantly covered the entire house. Caterers and guests poured in but blinded by all the festivity no one detected that you and I still weren't talking. Why were you mad at me?" Shaili asked with a sigh. Her question both pleased and surprised Supriya.

"I had a sense that something wasn't right with you. I couldn't articulate my thoughts, but I knew. I just did. I felt helpless. I am your best friend; I should have known. Seen the signs or something. But I was mostly angry because I felt that you didn't want to share those thoughts occupying your mind. You have always been so secretive, Shaili. I felt, even before you moved to America, you wanted to create a distance between us."

"My marriage to Sadhil wasn't your fault or responsibility, Su. And not share with you? Are you crazy? I was petrified thinking how I was going to manage in a new country without you. New marriage. New people. In the beginning, Leila thought I sought her out because I missed you. She wasn't totally wrong." Shaili nudged Supriya. Supriya's face beamed with delight. Shaili added, "Since I didn't have you around, I spent more time with her. She would tease me and call herself "NYC-

Supriya." On hearing "NYC-Supriya," Supriya grinned to a point where her teeth and jaws begged her to stop. Shaili continued, "Uggh. Those were terrible days." She disentangled her wet hair. "The tragedy is that around the time of my wedding, sadly, I myself didn't know what was happening. You know Su, getting cold feet before your marriage is different; I was despondent. No one saw that? You somewhat got a whiff of it. I didn't expect Dad or Tanisha to even try to comprehend my behavior. They were very happy to kick me out of the house. But I wondered how and why Ma didn't read my distress signals."

"Aunty was distracted with the preparations for your wedding and Uncle's behavior those days. I recall her going on a shopping spree for both you and Tanisha. Even Uncle didn't deplore Aunty for any extravaganza associated with the wedding arrangements contrary to his usual stingy, angry self. Every now and then he would smile and nod in appreciation, which was a shock to all of us. I remember Aunty continued to shed euphoric tears. In fact, she had mastered the art of laughing, weeping, and spending money all at one go." Shaili and Supriya giggled thinking about Meena Kapoor.

"Thanks for taking such good care of Ma."

"Shut up! You have become very American, Shails. Too many thank-yous and pleases accompany your conversation."

"Silly, because of you, I could speak with her. Calling her up, at a predetermined time, at your place, was one of the things I looked forward to. Hearing my favorite ladies cackle in the background. It was always during the workweek, when Dad was in his office, so Ma sounded less stressed. Remember the time I suggested buying her a cellphone?"

Though Shaili appreciated hearing her ma's voice during the week, with her busy schedule, she couldn't talk for very long. Weekends were when Shaili could catch up with her ma. Once, she had said, "Ma, I am sending Supriya some money. She'll buy you a cellphone. That way I can listen to your voice whenever I want."

"Beta, what's a cellphone?" Mrs. Kapoor enquired innocently.

Shaili forgot that in India the handset was called a mobile phone.

"Ma, I mean, a mobile."

"Oh, I have one already."

Shaili smote her forehead. "If you have one, why didn't you tell me? Why would you not give me the number?"

"Your father is paying the mobile bills. If he finds out I am talking to you, we both know what will happen. Supriya doesn't mind me coming to her place. Do you, beta?" Mrs. Kapoor asked Supriya while patting her left cheek.

"Of course not, Aunty," said Supriya. "Your daughter has become too American."

"You haven't changed. I am so glad." Shaili held Supriya's hands.

"Well, perfection doesn't need to change, does it, sweetheart?" Supriya fluttered her eyes.

"A decade ago you called me an American, and you did the same even today." Shaili grinned and continued.

"But you have changed, Shails." Supriya's smile metamorphosed into a gloomy look when she said, "All these years, we spoke over the phone and exchanged emails, but it wasn't the same thing. I really missed seeing you and spending time with you. It's like when you left Pune, you were somebody else; and now you have returned as a person I didn't even know existed. How do you think that makes me feel?"

"I haven't changed as much as I have learnt to embrace the reality about myself."

"I am happy for you. Believe me. I am just telling you what is in my heart, honestly."

"As always, you know how much I respect your candidness. If it helps, I purposely didn't hide anything from you. What could I have told you when I was unsure myself?"

"When we were young, there was no one? It's difficult to believe, no, don't you agree?"

"You know, at times, I found myself admiring some of the seniors in high school and college, but I didn't make much of it. Women are open about idolizing other women. I mean, you liked Julia Roberts and Sarah Jessica Parker. Thing is, I couldn't even imagine having a crush on a boy fearing Old Man would find out about it and chop me to pieces. God, I can promise you none of it was easy. My head and heart were at constant war with the nebulous known and the fear of the unknown. Su, I felt torn constantly. My vulnerability exacerbated after marriage."

"I am sorry I couldn't be there to help you."

"Thanks, Su. But no one could have helped me. I had to figure this one out without you or Ma. And I did. I just wish I could have avoided hurting Sadhil in the process."

"Gain cannot be made without some other person's loss. Didn't you tell me about this saying by Publilius Syrus? One of the very few quotes I remember. Maybe because my gain in jewelry has translated to the loss in the number of rupees in Mhatre's bank account."

Supriya, as always, managed to crack Shaili up.

"I have missed you too, Su. You have no idea how much." Shaili hugged Supriya tightly.

"I remember your wedding and vaguely recall our talk right before you left for New York. You were upset with Sadhil about something," Supriya said as she jogged down memory lane.

On the day of their wedding, all the guests thought Sadhil looked handsome in his cream colored sherwani. He had chosen to arrive on a horse with a few of his relatives. Due to short notice, none of his friends could make it to the wedding. But Shaili was convinced he had skeletons in his closet and that was why he was unaccompanied by his posse. Maybe she hoped he did. It would make her feel a little less guilty perhaps of feeling so unsure of her feelings.

Despite her bruised mind and conflicted heart, Shaili had looked resplendent as a bride. Her red lehengaa and copper dupatta contrasted well against her fair-complexion. Her Chuda, the wedding bangles adorning her fair hands, ricocheted untold tales. The ringlets, on her dainty feet, echoed the beats of her disbelieving heart. The intricate henna tattoo on her arms and legs had a vivacious orange color. On seeing the henna tattoo, Mrs. Sethi had said, "The deeper the color of the bride's henna tattoo the more her mother-in-law's love for her." Shaili wanted to ask her opinion on blood but she held her tongue. Shaili didn't smile through any of the functions. Be it the wedding in Pune, the reception in Delhi, or the second reception in Chandigarh. She sat as mute as a cadaver embalmed by grief. When the professional photographer suggested the bride and the groom both cuddle with each other, and that the bride smile with her eyes, Shaili's disobedient tears defied her. Sadhil saw that and advised the photographer against it.

On the afternoon of her departure, Shaili had called Supriya. "Su, are you still angry with me?"

Supriya had sounded placid. She looked for the right words, "Shails, you are my best friend. You know I think of you like a sister. How can I remain angry with you for so long?" Supriya had sighed loudly. "I just hope you know what you are doing. Sadhil seems like a wonderful guy."

Shaili didn't address Supriya's skepticism. She was crying quietly. "I'll miss you in New York. What will I do without you?" Shaili and Supriya were used to talking to each other every single day. The only exception was the time when Supriya was in Kolhapur and the phone lines were down due to thunderstorms. The friends didn't hear each other's voice for forty-eight hours, and it was the longest two days of their lives.

Supriya was bawling by now. "Idiot, you have to stay in touch." Wiping her tears, she repeated a Carrie Bradshaw dialogue. "I don't believe in email. I'm an old-fashioned girl. I prefer calling and hanging up."

The two friends had giggled. It felt as if they had heard each other's happy voices after ages. In all seriousness, Supriya said, "You better call me every day." She then paused for a moment and spoke again, "Okay that might be expensive. But at least a few times a week for sure you can call me. I can chat with you online. Then there is the webcam and all that. Listen, you have to come to India for my wedding. I am not getting married without you. Sadhil knows that and so does Mhatre. You don't want Mhatre to suffer, no?"

"Of course, yaar. How can I not be there for your marriage?" Shaili promised. But fate had other plans.

Shaili felt a little at peace. She had mended at least one important relationship in her life, with the one person who would support her through thick and thin at all stages of her life.

Supriya addressed Shaili in a mischievous tone. "So, how did everything work out between you and Sadhil? You are here and he is in Chandigarh. I mean, no action as newlyweds?"

Shaili was like a pressure cooker waiting to burst. "See? That's what I have been thinking. What kind of a husband is he who doesn't want to spend the first few days of marriage with his new wife? We had just one week together in India after the wedding. You know what he said, 'My nani is sick as you know. And I am very attached to her. I am not sure if I'll get to see her the next time we are in India. You saw how frail she was when we met her in Chandigarh. I'd like to spend the remaining few days of my stay in India with her. She is the one who brought me up when Dad was posted abroad.' He goes away to Chandigarh to be with his nani, and I am left alone."

"Okay. Now I am confused. I thought you didn't like Sadhil. You didn't want to marry him but you did anyway." Supriya did the fake cough and seductively uttered, "And now you have only 'crazy love' on your mind." Supriya made kissing sounds.

"Shut up! I still don't like him, I think. I mean, whatever. It's not like I hate him. But my point is—why does he not want me? He hasn't even touched me! How can a newlywed man keep his hands off his wife?" Shaili argued. Shaili didn't tell Supriya what antics she had pulled on her wedding night. And even the nights after that, like a con artist, she had faked sleep. "Feeling tired" was her excuse for getting out of everything. She and Sadhil hadn't had a real conversation, let alone a kiss. But Sadhil hadn't attempted to come near her. He could have if he'd wanted. After all, her father did so even when her ma didn't want him to.

"Wait. I don't understand. Didn't he ask you to accompany him? I thought you refused to join him. Shouldn't you be happy he's so considerate? He is giving you space and time to adjust to all the nuances of newness."

"Stop siding with him. You are my friend. It's more complicated than you know. It's just that…Umm.Umm."

"Shaili, it's time to leave. Hurry up." Mrs. Kapoor had screamed from the kitchen. "I have to go. I'll call you once I, sorry, once we, get to New York." Shaili had to end the heart-to-heart even before she could complete her statement.

"I was so enraged with my life, Su, that I treated Sadhil like he was some random weirdo mumbling on the streets. I failed or maybe chose not to hear the rest of what he had to say about visiting his nani. *But I would also like to be with you. I'd love nothing more if you would join me in Chandigarh. But I don't want to force you one way or the other. I understand that you'd probably want to spend these last few days in India with your family. It's your call. Don't feel compelled to do anything but what's in your heart. I mean it, Shaili. And in case you are wondering about my mom, don't. She'll be fine.* I misinterpreted everything he said or did. I myself don't know why I was such a bundle of contrariness. Sadhil's mother wasn't happy that, I, her daughter-in-law wasn't spending time with her side of the family. Ma, on the other hand, was elated with her new, solicitous son-in-law. I don't think she saw signs of confusion in my behavior. She probably assumed I was angry about the sudden arrangement of my marriage. Ma told me it was normal to feel anxious. I was about to start a new life with a stranger. She gave me last minute advice on how to keep Sadhil happy and make my marriage successful. She reiterated that I wasn't an exception. Boy, was she wrong or what!" Shaili chuckled sarcastically.

"I always thought about what you had wanted to say. But then you had to leave for the airport. It seemed important. I felt, it was maybe the reason why you had been antsy all along. I wondered if it was about another man. But then I also knew that I would have known if you liked another guy. I tried to analyze if it was about Sadhil. But then, I couldn't imagine Sadhil hurting you. So, what was it?"

"On that day?" Shaili chuckled. "I was uncertain what I had really wanted to declare to you. I was a multitude of unreadable emotions myself. I couldn't deny that there was something, but words eluded me."

"What about Sadhil? Did he say something?" Supriya asked in her highly energetic and caring voice.

"Sadhil didn't make much of my attitude. You know how newlywed women in India often looked sedated with kilos of jewelry and heavy saris forced upon them. He let me be. Not because he wasn't concerned, but because he felt it was only fair to be compassionate. A lot had changed in my life in two weeks. The least he could do was give me some space and time to come around. He probably hoped that things would change once it was just the two of us in New York." Shaili let out a sigh. "Between waterworks, implicit promises and affectionate kisses, I left all you guys in India. I remember Ma and I had held each other for almost twenty-five minutes at Mumbai airport. My last words to Ma were, 'Only for you. I am doing it just for you.' Ma had looked at me with contrition. Before she could say anything, Sadhil intervened to inform that it was almost time for the flight. Sadhil had suggested that Ma move in with us for a while so I would be happy. Ma hugged him for his magnanimity; I scorned at what I thought was a 'pretentious suggestion,' made by the man who had dumped his bride for his nani and acted like he cared about his mother-in-law. God, I was such an imbecile! I didn't give Sadhil the benefit of the doubt!"

"Shails, we couldn't talk then, but I am here for you now. What's on your mind? Talk to me. Tell me what happened. Every detail. And what transpired in New York?"

Shaili's mind went to the happenings on the day of her wedding and the weeks following the event. Her last, in-person words with Supriya. Her interaction with Sadhil over the first few weeks of their marriage. Her journey into discovering the truth about her own self, denying it, and then finally embracing it. The promises that were made and broken. Each incident was etched in her memory, fresh even after all these years.

8

Shaili didn't say a word to Sadhil on the flight. If he tried to talk, she pretended to be asleep or looked distressed. Every now and then, Sadhil looked at her from the corner of his eyes to see that *Lolita* and gin and tonic kept Shaili company. He hoped she didn't think of herself as a victim, like Lolita, and of him, as the abductor, Humbert.

Sadhil wasn't upset with Shaili's behavior. He knew some of his other South Asian friends had faced similar challenges. Their wives had taken their time to settle in a new country with the stranger—their husbands. One of his best friend's wives had slept in the guest bedroom for over a month. Like Shaili and Sadhil, their's too was a rushed wedding followed by multiple receptions. What made things worse for Shaili and Sadhil was that they had had no honeymoon, meaning no opportunity to get to know each other. There had been no time to think or digest any of the happenings. If anything, at this time, Shaili's uneasiness made her seem virtuous. But Sadhil pondered if Shaili was displeased about not having a honeymoon. He had promised her Paris in September, but it wasn't the same as getting away right after the wedding madness.

The couple landed at JFK airport on a Sunday evening. After a swift run through customs and immigration, they took a cab to Sadhil's apartment. Shaili noticed his accent was more American in New York than in Pune. She contemplated what else he'd been two-faced about. The city lights hurt the darkness inside Shaili. She worried her apprehensions would stand out in all the bright lights. The dreadful traffic on Queensboro Bridge gave her the opportunity to reflect upon her passage. She was still outraged with everything that had transpired over the past couple of weeks. Or was it years? She didn't know. Shaili felt vulnerable about what she wanted or who she needed and no one seemed to be bothered. She fought herself for reasons she was unconfident about. Sadhil's reticence made her think she wasn't alone in her resentment. But she was presumptuous. She gazed hopefully at the city skyline, a place she was going to fall in love with eventually.

By the time they got to Sadhil's apartment, it was close to 9:00 p.m. The uniformed doorman in his building welcomed the couple warmly. Shaili had never been to New York, but thanks to Carrie Bradshaw, she knew the top bars and best bakeries on the Upper East Side and Manhattan.

Sadhil's apartment was unlike any bachelor pad Shaili had seen on television. It was sparkling clean, the credit for which Sadhil attributed to his cleaning lady. The décor was hip and colorful and the furniture, though minimal, was trendy and contemporary. The wine rack, in the shape of a tree, looked like it was growing out of the wall. Then Shaili didn't know much about wines, but she saw a splash of branded reds hanging out from the branches as if protecting the fine variety of wine glasses underneath them. There was a wine chiller boasting few bottles that Sadhil had bought at the last wine auction.

There were two huge bedrooms, two full bathrooms, with a huge patio attached to the master bedroom. The master bedroom also came with a Jacuzzi and "His" and "Her" taps. On seeing the glass shower and the heart-shaped Jacuzzi, Shaili felt her frustration morph into anxiety. Sadhil saw that look in her eyes. His face had reddened with the anticipation of the forthcoming nights; her face was an epitome of disgust and distress. Neither said anything. They were both thinking on different levels. The second bedroom was almost unfurnished. There was nothing in the room apart from a sleek laptop, a desk and a chair, and a beanbag. This was Sadhil's work area and that was about it. The French windows enhanced the beauty of the L-shaped living room and unleashed the spectacular view of the East River. A fifty-two inch television fitted stylishly into one of the corners in the living room like a super model in a pair of slinky size zero jeans. A *Bose* music system was placed strategically right next to the refrigerator, so no corner of the house was deprived of music, especially the kitchen. Shaili had never seen so many CDs from ghazals to hard rock to Mozart to Bollywood hits.

Though Shaili didn't cook, she couldn't help but marvel at the open kitchen with an island in the center. Copper vessels were hanging from the ceiling like *mang-tikka* adorning a bride's centre parting. Sadhil liked entertaining so, to him, compromising on the kitchen would be like desecrating the shrine. A splendid host, he would go out of his way to ensure his guests had the best time.

Shaili was surprised to see his tastefully done up apartment. For a second, she wanted to believe that maybe Sadhil was into kinky associations. That's why he'd wanted a quick wedding, so a new member added to his group would bring some freshness. Maybe that's what the empty, second bedroom was for? But she then brushed aside her, preposterous theory as she admired how immaculately even the kitchen cloths, inside the kitchen drawers, were arranged—from light to dark. She was convinced; Sadhil was too kempt for a normal man.

Sadhil broke her train of thought. "You hungry?"

"What?"

"Do you want to split a pizza?" he asked.

Shaili spoke plainly, "I don't want anything."

"Are you sure? You barely ate anything on the flight."

"Yes, I am."

"Okay. I'll order some grocery from the store in the building. They deliver at home. You'll have some food for tomorrow. Do you need anything specific?"

Shaili was fuming, famished, jetlagged, petrified, and overwhelmed. She wanted to say, "How about some poison?" But instead she chose to respond politely because Sadhil was being pleasant. It seemed like the right thing to do.

"Milk, bread, and eggs will be fine. You have coffee and sugar?"

"Yes, ma'am. I do. I mean, we do." Sadhil's dimples looked like a gorge of love when he realized that it was "their" apartment and not "his," any longer. He savored the feeling. He liked the change in status.

Shaili avoided looking at his athletic body. He looked striking against the soft lights. Or was it New York that suited him? Or was it the feeling of being reunited with someone else perhaps?

As soon as Sadhil picked up the phone to order the groceries, Shaili said, "How do I ring India?"

"Glad you asked. I was going to tell you anyway. The number of MCI, the long distance carrier, is on the speed dial. Just press *1. The machine will prompt you to enter India's country code followed by the number. I'll give you a card that you can carry with you at all times and make calls from anywhere."

"No. It's okay."

"As in?"

"Can you wait a minute?" Shaili walked towards the piece of furniture where her handbag was resting. She dug out a little diary from one of the pockets and sifted through the pages until she'd reached alphabet H.

She asked Sadhil to repeat MCI's international dial number and wrote it under "Home." Sadhil saw it as an auspicious sign—Shaili thought of New York as home; but Shaili entered the number in that particular section because it was her access to home as in Pune—Ma and Supriya. Sadhil tried explaining how the speed dial offered more expediency, but she refused to accept technology or logic that evening.

Sadhil then ordered the items from the grocery store. He thanked someone by the name of José and informed him that his wife might be placing orders too in the future. He wanted Shaili's name added to his monthly account that he had with them. Shaili continued to gawk at Sadhil. How perfect his teeth were. His head full of hair looked arresting. Sadhil walked up to her. Her breathing became louder. She couldn't control it. "Am I moaning?" She wasn't sure if she wanted him to take her or go away. Sadhil walked up to her and said, "What's up?"

Shaili blabbered incoherently. Her throat felt dry. Sadhil had a cheeky smile. He had observed that Shaili was glaring at his body. "Thank you, peripheral vision," he whispered to himself. He didn't think it was proper to make any moves right away, but he felt it was not rude to rag his wife jokingly especially because she was looking at him amorously. He turned towards Shaili and said in a deep voice, "Let me show you."

"What?" Shaili spoke over him and bellowed.

"What do you think?" Sadhil raised his left eyebrow.

"I don't know." Shaili's vocal chords felt scratchy.

"How the television, taps, switches, phone, and appliances work. Make yourself at home, Shaili." For the first time, Sadhil flirted with his wife, and he enjoyed the sweet sensation. Shaili tried to feel upset. Sadhil fiddled with the remote to set it to a particular station, which he thought Shaili might like. Shaili snatched it from him. She was better at repairs and maintenance than most men she knew, and she was losing her patience watching him beat the remote against his palm. All her aggravation had crept back in. She couldn't believe she had looked at him admiringly. She didn't think she even liked him. When her fingers and thoughts lost synchronization, her hands touched Sadhil's very tenderly. Sadhil grinned because of obvious reasons—at least to him. Shaili noticed how alluring Sadhil looked even after two weeks of continuous madness, and a long Mumbai-New York flight. Then she chafed at her inability to keep her eyes off him.

"I am new at this too, so bear with me as we move along," Sadhil tried to enter Shaili's world.

Shaili didn't respond. She was caught in that uncomfortable moment. She didn't know how to make sense of what was going on. He continued, "This television is new and came with a tiny battery for the remote. You know why the remote isn't working? Because the genius in me forgot to add a battery inside it." Sadhil snickered at his own ignorance. Much against her wishes, Shaili smiled too. Sadhil was charming and had that easygoing, fuzzy energy exuding from him. Sadhil walked towards the linen closet and took out extra sheets and towels. "I have to leave for work really early tomorrow, so I am going to crash. I don't want to disturb you in the morning; I'll take the couch."

Shaili was almost relieved that once again she didn't have to sleep with Sadhil, a stranger, in a new house. Granted, they had some awkward moments today, but Shaili had felt adulation for Sadhil's body; not lust or passion. This was the first time in her life that she had seen a male physique at such close quarters. Or was it the gentleness in his personality that she was enamored of? She wasn't thinking of any chemistry between the two, like all the nights prior to this one.

On their wedding night, when Sadhil walked into the room, Shaili had faked passing out due to overtiredness. She wanted to avoid him and the matrimonial expectations. Her mother had never given her the "sex talk" and Supriya's notion of bold, raunchy romance could put Mhatre to shame, so not much help from her either. Shaili tried to recollect what she'd seen in films, and Bollywood's perception of the *suhaag raat,* the wedding night, freaked her out. Upon seeing the glass of almond milk in her room and the bed decorated with flowers and immersed in attar, perfume the Mughals were famous for, she'd felt queasy and exposed. She flushed the milk down the toilet; changed into her pajamas; and hid her face inside the covers until Sadhil entered the room, checked on her, changed out of his sherwani, and slept on the sofa.

Next morning, Sadhil had said to her, "I know this marriage was sudden and a whole lot has changed for you, me, and us together. Take your time. We have our whole lives ahead of us."

Shaili had shifted uneasily. Did Sadhil notice that she was awake when he came into the room? True to his name, he had behaved like a perfect gentleman. He could've done whatever he wanted to, but he didn't. He had respectfully wished her a good morning and left her by herself so she could get dressed for another function where they were expected to show up as a couple. He had returned after an hour with two mugs of coffee in his hands. The coffee tasted familiar, like what Mrs. Kapoor made every morning for her family. Shaili curled up like a turtle after the first sip.

When Shaili woke up the next day, in New York, Sadhil wasn't around. She intently looked at the world around her and grabbed her hair-tie from the bedside table to fix her hair in a knot. The clock on the table flashed 11:30 a.m. Shaili's eyes fell on a colorful envelope with her name on it. The note said: "Leaving for work. Didn't want to disturb you. There are a hundred dollars for you here and an extra set of house keys. Will be late. Don't wait up. If you need anything, talk to Romano, the doorman on duty. I paid him fifty bucks to help you around. Sorry, but I'll make it up to you soon."

"What the hell does he think? Leaving me hundred rupees like I am his maid? What value does hundred rupees hold? Two, maybe three chicken frankies in Bombay will cost more than that." She cursed him aloud. Shaili didn't see any difference in the value of hundred rupees versus one hundred dollars. Just the way she couldn't comprehend that Sadhil had wanted her beside him in Chandigarh and not away in Pune. She couldn't believe what Ma had got her into. She tore his note to pieces and bawled her eyes out. She muttered invectively and pulled her hair in desperation. She hit the walls with both her wrists. Shaili thought of calling her mother and Supriya, but her pride came in the way. She held them accountable for her inexplicable frame of mind. But before she knew it, she fell asleep again. The journey and the wedding had taken a bigger toll on her than she'd expected.

When Shaili woke up again, it was 6:00 p.m. but still bright outside. Though forlorn, Shaili was a city girl with confidence and she had inherited her father's hubris. She decided to venture out and discover her, no, Sadhil's neighborhood. She unpacked part of her luggage to take out clothes to wear when her eyes fell on the homemade laddoos her mother had packed for the couple. Shaili felt tears inundating her eyes on seeing the goodies made by Ma labeled "Shailu and Sadhil." She longed to hear Mrs. Kapoor's reassuring, uncomplicated voice. She thought of calling home, but it was middle of the night in Pune. Shaili knew the phone call would have to wait, so she decided to take a shower and continue with her original plan of stepping out of the apartment. Shaili avoided the bathroom in the master bedroom. After showering in the guest bathroom, she decided to go for a stroll. She wrote down Sadhil's address in her little diary, the same notebook where she'd inscribed the phone number the night before, so she wouldn't lose her way.

The previous night, between fatigue and frustration, she hadn't realized that Sadhil's apartment building was exquisite. The lobby had a tropical theme with a waterfall and a dozen Chinese good luck fishes, Koi. There were four different sets of elevators, one for each of the north, south, east, and west wings, and no thirteenth floor. The sound of water crashing against concrete was tranquil. There was a 24-hour doorman in the building, an indoor swimming pool, a fully equipped gym, a yoga studio, a grocery store, coffee shop, pizza place, dry cleaners, cleaning services, ATMs, and a play school for toddlers.

Shaili stepped outside the automated lobby doors. Right across the street, there was a Nepalese fruit vendor. He said something in Hindi, but Shaili was lost in her own world. She hadn't anticipated communicating with anyone on her first day in New York let alone anyone speak with her in Hindi. She didn't answer back. She noticed a florist, a French bakery, an Arab gourmet coffee shop called *Khubz*, and a *Starbucks* around the corner from the building. She liked the neighborhood. She walked around the area window-shopping at boutiques, wine shops, art-framing stores, and lost track of time. The weather was perfect with a temperature of 72 degrees Fahrenheit.

After a long leisurely walk, Shaili decided to turn around and get back to the apartment; Sadhil's home. She decided to stride down a different avenue and discover the area further. But there was construction work going on 2nd Avenue, which Shaili didn't know about. As she sauntered past the construction site, a few of the workers whistled at her. One said, "Hey beautiful!" Another guy joined him in Spanish, which at the time, given her unfamiliarity with the language, sounded like rambunctious commentary. Shaili faked valor but not for long. She felt a cloud of solitude engulf her. There was no one there to shield her from the goons. Just then, the third guy said something about a sewer. In her tenuous state of mind, Shaili believed he'd addressed her as a *soo-ar*, a pig. Impudent tears wet her face and stunned the construction workers as well. Shaili missed Supriya. The same Supriya who had once smacked an autorickshaw driver with her bag because he'd adjusted his rear view mirror to catch a glimpse of her underpants showing from underneath her skirt. Supriya had noted his indecent gesture when she turned her head towards him and asked him to change the song in his music system. He was leering right at that moment. Not only did she abuse and kick him, but she also got the local storeowners on MG Road to beat the guy until he addressed her as *didi,* sister, and begged her pardon.

When Shaili reached the apartment, she was starving, desolate, and drowsy. Her head hurt, and the overpowering pain made her homesick all over again. In Pune, a headache always translated into a hot oil massage by her mother. Then, she had whined about the lubricant and the stench of coconut oil in her hair; but today she pined for the maternal fingertips to gently knead her scalp and clear her head and bicker how her lustrous mane wouldn't be so bountiful had it not been for the ancient therapy of hot oil mixed with mother's love. She yearned for *adrak ki chai,* ginger tea, Ma's ideal cure for a nasty headache. Adrak ki chai served while she sat on her bed or watched television or yapped with Supriya. Savoring those memories, Shaili came to the realization that there was no one in New York to make her tea, so she gathered the strength to brew herself a cup while she watched television. She popped a laddoo in her mouth to satiate her hunger. As she opened the refrigerator to take out the milk, she found a pizza in there with a note that read, "I know pizza is your favorite food, so I ordered some from the pizzeria below. Hope you like it." There was a smiley and "S" signed underneath it.

By now Shaili felt vehemently hostile towards Sadhil. "He's not here. Leaves me all alone in a new country! With street urchins eve-teasing me and just a hundred rupees. And I don't even feel well. He doesn't know me but pretends like he gets what I am about." She put the kettle on the stove and fumbled through the kitchen drawers for spoons. As the kettle whistled, a sign that the water was ready to be poured, Shaili's tears found a vent too to flow profusely. She cried until every inch of the apartment heard her pain. She was disturbed about many things, mostly relating to inarticulate feelings. But that evening, she decided to blame it on the fact that she had to wash her own dishes even though the henna in her hands was still fresh from the wedding. Not that she cared about the fading color or the bridal symbols or anything.

She thought of her mother and Tanisha and how her mother would whip up a fresh meal the minute Shaili or Tanisha mentioned that they were hungry. She would try to overfeed them by saying, "*Koi nahin, beta.* Eat it all up. Let it stay put in your stomach." She had once said, "Ma, I can't eat anymore unless you want me to eat the spoon and the fork too. I am not a camel saving food for future reserve." Today she wished she had humps on her body where she could have stored her mother's food. Dabbing her tears and sipping her tea, she warmed up some pizza, and watched reruns of "Full House." The charming Olsen twins and Comet, the golden retriever in the show, brought respite to her vacillating heart. Before she knew, Shaili passed out on the couch with pizza crumbs stuck to the corner of her lips.

In the middle of the night, Shaili felt a warm hand touch her shoulder. She froze for a minute. She half-opened her eyes to see who it was. It was Sadhil. Her suspicious mind started working overtime. Shaili could hear her heart beat with fretfulness. She felt unwell. She picked up a cushion and put it in front of her chest with one hand; with the other, she looked for something to hit Sadhil with. "I won't let him take advantage of me. He can't touch me," she said to herself. She shifted her legs and pulled them towards her pelvis. Her discernment told her he was there to demand his rights as a husband. After all, that's what her father did to her mother. Aside from that one scarring incident from when she was seven, Shaili had never personally witnessed him violate her mother. But then Ma's body wore permanent marks of mellow cries and unutterable episodes of lacerations as if a hungry lion had mutilated a deer in the darkest hour of the night. Shaili had vowed to herself that she would never let any man do that to her. She would fight—even if it meant hurting Sadhil in his man parts or biting him with her sharp canines. If nothing else worked, she planned to run towards the door and ask for Romano. Shaili clung to the cushion tighter as she deliberated the perfect getaway.

"Hey, it's me." Sadhil spoke lovingly with his hand still on her shoulder.

"What am I? Blind?" That's what Shaili wanted to say but was too shaken up to sound bitchy. She just looked at him hoping he wouldn't sniff her trepidation.

"Did I startle you?" He sounded sincerely apologetic.

Shaili wondered if Sadhil was going to force himself on her. Before she could say anything, Sadhil moved his hand from her shoulder and said, "By the way, how was day one in New York?"

By now, Shaili was trembling with embarrassment. She had misjudged Sadhil yet again.

"It was okay." She didn't mention the encounter on 2nd Avenue.

"Are you okay? You look pale?"

"Yes."

Sadhil touched Shaili's forehead to gauge if she had a fever. Her body temperature felt normal. He expressed relief that she wasn't burning up and concluded it was the jetlag acting up. He asked if she wanted any decaffeinated honey tea. Shaili replied in the negative.

"Did you eat anything?"

"Yes."

"Did Romano show you around?"

"Uh-huh." Shaili flinched.

"Did you talk to anyone in India?"

"Uh-huh." Shaili wasn't sure what Sadhil implied. His parents or hers? But she didn't care.

"Sorry, I didn't have much cash on me so left just a hundred bucks. Let's open your bank account this Saturday and get you a cellphone."

"I am sleepy," Shaili said abruptly. She couldn't stand to be in the same room as Sadhil. Or was she mortified about miscomprehending his decent intentions? Years later, Shaili would discern that her demeanor that evening was the first insight into her complicated and closed-minded upbringing. And Sadhil would concede that evening was filled with clues hinting the truth about Shaili. He just hadn't seen them. Or did he choose to be oblivious to them?

Sadhil was taken aback but quickly regained his composure. "I didn't mean to disturb you. Why don't you go inside and sleep? I have some work to finish and have to leave early again tomorrow."

"Good night." Shaili tucked her chin under the cushion and left the room.

"Good night, babe." Sadhil didn't say the adjective out loud.

Once Shaili plunked on the bed, she could barely sleep. She felt edgy. A part of her was amazed by how concerned Sadhil was but the other half thought it was bizarre that Sadhil still hadn't tried to touch her. Did he even want to? They had been married for over ten days. She wondered if he was impotent or if he had a girlfriend hidden somewhere. Sadhil had said to her in India, "I owe you a honeymoon. I promise, once we are back in the U.S., anyplace you want to go. Just name it." He'd hinted at Paris, but he hadn't repeated his offer in the past 48 hours. She wasn't longing to consummate their marriage, but in her mind, Sadhil was abstaining from fornication, and it was unbearable.

Shaili didn't want to accept that every opportunity that Sadhil got, he tried to get close to her, both physically and emotionally. But he wasn't the type of person to flaunt his desires or impose himself on her. She wasn't aware that Sadhil had witnessed two of his classmates from business school undergo a bitter divorce because the husband raped the wife every night. Theirs was an arranged marriage too. Both the boy and the girl were accepted in the same school and moved to New York together, which at the time seemed like a good thing. But soon the abuse started and by the time they graduated from school, the couple went their separate ways. Sadhil was both a sensitive and a sensible man. He wanted to win Shaili's love, not steal it.

The next morning, Shaili woke up late again feeling a lot more rested. In some ways, she felt she had never slept better before. She couldn't figure out if it was the mattress or no taunts from her father or visible discomfiture in her mother's persona.

Sadhil had left for work. She had woken up, thanks to the jetlag, at an unearthly hour when he was getting dressed and eating his breakfast and reading his paper; but she had chosen not to grace him with her presence and avoid the morning awkwardness of beguiling small talk. She had lazed around for some time, counted backwards from one to thousand, a tactic she and Supriya diligently followed when they were kids and were offered a *Cadbury* for taking an afternoon nap during their summer holidays and gone back to sleep. Sleeping in late was another luxury, which her father wouldn't allow if he were home as he considered it a trait for idlers. Of course, his children weren't permitted to be lazy.

When Shaili woke up, Sadhil was obviously not in the apartment. With no one around, Shaili slipped into a T-shirt, barely covering her hips, and no pants. As she made coffee and strut her long legs in the apartment, looking for the phone, she valued the privacy that New

York offered. In Pune, with the constant entry-exit of the maid and the chauffeur and her father's clients, she and Tanisha were expected to be well dressed at all times, or at least fully dressed. But in New York, the zero possibility of guests showing up unannounced allowed Shaili a completely new wardrobe-freedom. She decided to call Supriya and tell her about it. But Supriya's number was busy, so Shaili decided to call her mother.

"Hello. Suresh Kapoor speaking." Shaili's heart popped out, almost. She didn't know what to say. She'd hoped her mother would have answered her call. Or even Tanisha but not her father. She considered hanging up but she couldn't bring herself to. He would have known she'd called and then disconnected. The Indian phone system had distinguishable ring tones for incoming domestic and international phone calls.

"Hello. It's me. Shaili," she answered hesitantly.

"I know. How are you?"

"Um. Okay."

"How is Sadhil?"

"Okay."

"Do you need anything?"

"No."

"Money?"

"No…Is Ma there?"

"She has gone to the grocery store. She should be back any minute now."

Shaili was at a loss of words but her father wasn't. He continued to enquire about her well being, but Shaili insisted on following the trail of monologues. The exchange became dolorous when Suresh Kapoor exclaimed, "I miss you. I mean, we all miss you. Both of you."

Shaili was dumbstruck. Every inch of her wanted to believe it was a slip of tongue from the man she'd grown to detest. But it wasn't.

She waited for him to retract his kindness but he didn't. Shaili was doubtful if there was room in her heart to accommodate any more confusion. As she fought her inner battles with articulation, Mrs. Kapoor was back from grocery shopping. Suresh Kapoor's tone was back to being austere. "Meena, it's her." He handed the phone to Mrs. Kapoor and walked away. Shaili became cognizant, for the first time, that her father's spitefulness got exacerbated when her mother was around. Shaili brushed aside the uncomfortable moment, and the mother-daughter duo continued with their light-hearted banter. Shaili decided not to disclose the chats she had with Suresh Kapoor, and her postulation on his temperament, to her mother. In her own way, Shaili was trying to protect her mother.

After having updated her mother on New York weather, her milk-inclusive diet, Sadhil, and people, Shaili decided to hang up and breathe in some fresh air. She got dressed and decided to amble around town, cautiously avoiding 2nd Avenue, and get a sense of the neighborhood. She passed by *Khubz* again and was intrigued by the décor of the café that boasted exotic, surreal paintings and visual art pieces highlighting a conflux of Eastern and Western culture.

"Miss, you lost?" a female voice in a husky tone called out.

Shaili clung to her bag and said, "No. I am fine. Thank you."

Shaili increased her pace and before she realized, she had walked down ten blocks. Her experience from the day before had traumatized her. She kept turning around to see if she could still see who had called out to her. There was no one, but something about *Khubz* haunted her. Or was it the accent? The smell of coffee? Shaili longed to speak to Supriya. She was used to spending most of her free time talking to her while drinking coffee, reading and writing, discussing world politics and literature, watching TV, but certainly not being chased on Manhattan streets. All of a sudden she felt deserted without her best friend's company. She was shocked to see New Yorkers eat alone and read alone. She recalled people in Pune always hung out in groups, and the memories made her nostalgic.

Lost in her thoughts, she turned around on 65th street and headed back in the direction of Sadhil's apartment. An old, grey bookstore caught her eye—the kind she'd read about in books about England. She stopped at the charming bookstore, near Hunter College, and venerated the rare collection of books. She didn't want to spend a lot since she didn't earn and Sadhil's money was still foreign. What she'd brought from India could only last her so long, and she didn't want to ask her father for more even though he'd generously offered. But the bibliophile in her promised herself that she would return one day. After all, she was drunk on the offerings of this bookstore. Little did she know that her self-determination would bring her back to the same doorstep; not to make a purchase but when one of her first few readings, of her own book, would happen in this store.

Shaili felt reassured in the company of wrinkled, aged paper with that defining scent, and it changed the tune of her mood. Once she got close to her building, a hand touched her shoulder. Shaili was stunned. Who in New York knew her? Was it that ominous voice again? Those prurient construction workers? Someone trying to mug her? Then she heard a "boo" in her ears in an identifiable voice, but by then Shaili had screamed and dropped her bag. As she bent down to pick it up, their heads clashed. It was Sadhil.

"That wasn't funny." Shaili roared.

"I am sorry." Sadhil stood beautifully tall in his *Brooks Brothers* formal business wear. Shaili didn't say anything. Sadhil pleaded with her.

"Won't you ask me what I am doing here in the middle of the afternoon on a busy working day?"

"What?"

"Going to eat lunch with my beloved."

Shaili felt an ache in her heart. She always knew that Sadhil was too good to be true. She wanted to call up her ma and Supriya and ask them if this is why they wanted her to keep an "open mind." Not only did he have a girlfriend in New York but to meet her, in the middle of the afternoon, was reprehensible. Then he was openly telling his wife about it. Yes, wife. Shaili had abhorrence written all over her face; Sadhil was oblivious to the reason for it.

"So, should we?" Sadhil asked pointing towards a cab.

"What?" Shaili didn't want to cry in public for the second time in two days.

"Don't you want to come along?"

Shaili didn't want to be a part of his lunchtime instant gratification. She didn't move.

"Shaili?"

"*What?*"

"Let's go."

"Go where?"

"Ummm. Lunch, Madame? I thought I'd take you out for a meal. Indian Chinese?"

"Me? Lunch?"

"Who else?"

"I thought..."

"I have been waiting for over twenty minutes outside the building. Romano said he saw you walk out, so I figured I'd catch you here on your way back home for lunch." Sadhil interrupted her.

"Oh. I assumed..."

"What did you assume?"

"Never mind."

Shaili didn't say anything further. She felt odd about what had just transpired and somewhat petty. She was aggrieved about a non-existent person, a creation of her own insecure, wild imagination. To her, it was a clear sign that she needed to do something productive with her time. Sadhil continued to tell her about a few Indian Chinese restaurants in Murray Hill, forty blocks south from where they lived. He promised her India-style sweet corn soup, American chopsuey, and chicken manchurian. Shaili salivated at the mere mention of the entrees. They were her favorites. Supriya and she would bike to the University Circle every Sunday evening and eat those same dishes from the street carts. She was amazed how much Sadhil knew about her likes and dislikes. He remembered the minutest details like how she liked inordinate amounts of "*schezuan* sauce" in her sweet corn soup and added it until it turned red in color, so he'd asked the waiter to bring extra. She wondered if Sadhil had retained all the information from their tête-à-tête in Pune, thanks to Supriya's sharing nature, or if he'd called and asked her. Either way, she was touched; to her, men weren't thoughtful creatures. After all, her father would forget her birthdays ever since she was a little girl, but Sadhil seemed different.

Once they got to the restaurant, Shaili was flabbergasted to see the menu. It was like *Ying Yang* and most other Chinese restaurants in Pune. She was shocked to see white and black people sitting in the restaurant and licking their fingers over chicken lollipops. Some men and women, dressed in their work clothes, were drinking. A new life and freedom beckoned her.

Sadhil asked Shaili about the first half of her day. She responded using a few more words than the day before. He asked her if she had spoken with her family and Supriya. She nodded her head as she slurped the soup. He told her that he too had called up her mother and informed her that they had reached safely and that week one was coming along fine.

Shaili was mildly irked; Sadhil confounded her. Sadhil had made an effort to reach out to her family when he hadn't once directly suggested that she call up his parents. She decided that maybe he wasn't so bad after all as she gormandized on chicken manchurian. Sadhil was delighted to see Shaili was having a good time. He was kind but not dumb. He was satisfied that at least the food did the magic of bringing them closer. Shaili looked relatively more content. In fact, this was the happiest he had ever seen her. He'd muttered to himself that perhaps New York was suiting her. After lunch, Sadhil put Shaili in a cab and caught a train back to work. He'd kissed her on the cheek, a soft "see you in a little bit" peck, before she got into the cab. Shaili was shocked. Her body language had clearly indicated "Don't you come near me," and Sadhil had respected it. He didn't hug her. But overall, it had been a lovely afternoon. In those sixty minutes, Shaili hadn't once thought of failed marriages or discredited Sadhil's generosity.

On her way back, Shaili felt like drinking a cup of coffee. She decided that she would stop at the *Starbucks* close to Sadhil's place and pick it up from there. But due to an emergency, *Starbucks* was closed and the French bakery was overcrowded. Shaili toyed with the idea of purchasing coffee from *Khubz*, but out of edginess, her feet stood planted outside the entrance. Thankfully, *Khubz* had a take-out window. Once Shaili spotted it, she went directly to it. The female, who had called out to her earlier that day, was nowhere to be seen. Shaili let her guard down. She looked at the menu and decided to order an espresso. It was the only item that sounded familiar in the cornucopia of choices from the beverage world. That's what Supriya and she always drank at *Radhika's* in Pune. The sweet froth would touch the tip of their nose and Supriya would talk incessantly about her love life. Sometimes Mhatre would join them, on the sly, and Supriya would force him to treat the ladies. At *Khubz*, when the server handed Shaili her order of caffeine, Shaili looked baffled. It was in a short glass, the size in which instant *Nescafe* coffee was served at airports and railway stations in India. And there was no milk or sugar in it. It smelt horrifically strong. She took a sip, and her insides were jolted. Shaili felt remnants of coarse coffee on her tongue like sediments at the bottom of a riverbed. She didn't know who to ask about the untried beverage. She didn't like it but certainly wasn't going to toss the drink. Her mother had never allowed her and Tanisha to waste even a single morsel of food. She believed that the "Food Gods" would curse them. And then, she had just spent four dollars, which in rupees would have bought her four espressos in Pune. With her dignity intact, Shaili took the cup of espresso home and hid it in the refrigerator.

When Sadhil returned that evening, Shaili generally asked him about the different kinds of coffees served in New York. Sadhil, unsuspectingly, told her that she would probably enjoy cappuccino, the lathered, steaming hot beverage or café au lait, a lighter coffee with chicory in it—a lot like the filter coffee in India. He casually educated her that espresso in Pune was the same as cappuccino in New York and that she might want to avoid espresso shots until she developed a taste for American coffee. It all made sense to Shaili, but she refused to waste her wrong order of coffee. Over the next four days, she would add milk and sugar to it, to make it lighter and tolerable in taste. She was pleased with herself in the end. Looking at the new math, she had spent four dollars on four cups of coffee, which was a dollar a cup, which was again comparable to prices in Pune. In some ways, it made her feel less incongruous.

The routine didn't change much in the Sethi household over the course of the first week. Sadhil worked late and Shaili, full of conflicted feelings, spent her days walking around the neighborhood and fighting jetlag. She spoke often with her mother and Supriya but didn't tell them anything about her inner turmoil. Supriya's first question was always if Shaili had tried drinking the "real thing"—a *Cosmopolitan.* She was thwarted that Shaili hadn't been to a bar in her first week in New York. When Shaili told Supriya about the "pleasant" conversation with her father from a few days ago, Supriya had literally jumped off her bed and said, "New York holds a lot of surprises for you. Be prepared. Your horoscope for the week says that you should expect change."

On the Friday afternoon of her first week in New York, Shaili decided to go back to *Khubz*. But this time, she went inside the main café and not the take-out window. By now, the espresso at home was over too and so was her phobia of the "voice." She was curious to see what the coffee bar was all about since she'd walked past it the last week.

The entrance had a chime attached to it, and the music playing in the background was a melodious blend of Middle Eastern and Western. The place had an erudite yet chic feel to it, and Shaili liked the vibe. The lower level had friendly energy and looked appealing with low seating chairs and tables with intricate work. She noticed a spiral staircase leading to an upper floor. Before she could gaze any further, someone addressed her.

"It's you," the female husky voice, the one she had heard a few days before and felt scared of, said loudly.

Shaili looked startled. How did the woman recognize her? She held on to her handbag.

"Why don't you come on in for a cuppa Joe?" the lady said in a naturally gruff but courteous tone. She came up from behind the counter. She was a dark-haired beauty with olive skin and deep black eyes. She was rebelliously Bohemian in her appearance—shocking pink lipstick, artistic pants, five metallic perforations in her ears, and cropped hair with gel in it. Shaili thought for a moment, *"Long hair would have looked nice on her. What a beautiful face for a bag-snatcher?"*

"Huh?" Shaili felt a little out of place.

"New to the city?" asked the woman.

"How do you know?" Shaili sounded cautious.

"I have seen you in the neighborhood. Walking past and peering into the café five days in a row." She said with a smile.

Shaili felt sheepish. "Yes. I have just come."

Leila sniggered, but Shaili didn't catch the unintended double entendre implied in her answer.

"Welcome to the neighborhood. Come in for some coffee, won't you?" The woman insisted, her voice friendly.

Shaili was pleased that someone had befriended her in a new country when she was least expecting it.

Leila shook Shaili's hand. "Hi. I am Leila Makhmalbaf. And you are?"

"Shaili. My name is Shaili Ka…Se…Call me Shaili. Pleased to meet you too." Shaili extended her hand.

"Newly wed?"

"Yes. How did you know?"

"The fumbling and discomfort with letting go of your maiden name and accepting your married last name."

"Haan?"

"Been there. Done that."

Shaili was fascinated by Leila's mannerisms, her accent, and her diction. Her ease with her own self was obvious.

While wiping a mug with a dry rag, Leila asked, "By the way, you have a beautiful name. What is it?"

"What do you mean?"

"Which country is it from?"

"Oh. India."

"What does it mean?"

"Tradition."

"Hmm. Would you call yourself traditional?"

Shaili's answer was shy and factual but not conceited. Leila was mesmerized by Shaili's ensemble.

"What's that design on your hands?"

"It's henna tattoo."

"Beautiful!"

"Thank you."

"Why do you wear it?"

"Because brides wear them."

"Significance?"

"In India they say that the darker the color of the tattoo, the more the mother-in-law likes you."

"Yeah, right!" Leila blew a raspberry. She pointed towards Shaili's chuda and continued, "I don't mean to give you the third degree, but what are those red and white bangles for?"

"A bride wears these bangles for at least forty days. It is to remind people that she is newly wed and basically should be treated like a princess, meaning minimal housework."

"No house chores? That's a pretty sweet deal!" Leila winked.

Shaili explained the symbolism of her other ornaments as well to Leila. She became aware how patient she was about answering Leila's questions. There was no toxicity in her explanations. For instance, she would always tell Supriya that to her the chuda was an indication that marriage meant death of the individual inside a woman—the red represented the color of the bride but white denoted the widowhood of her desires. But with Leila, she delved into relevance from a perspective of traditions.

Shaili would describe this moment as a turning point in her book. She had a similar conversation when she met Sadhil for the first time—about names and meanings. But she had rebuked him and insinuated that his query had a negative connotation. But when Leila asked the same questions, Shaili had felt no vexation. She had disparaged Supriya when she'd admired Sadhil's faultless inflection; but here she stood, gawking at every short question and concise sentence that flowed out of Leila's mouth. Shaili had wanted to claw out Mrs. Sethi's frog-like eyes when she'd commented on her chuda and henna tattoo, but with Leila, she acted different. What Shaili did feel was a little conscious of her self. She tried to distract herself from further self-interrogation.

"You work here?" Shaili asked Leila out of inquisitiveness and in an effort to make her fascination a little less obvious. She had heard that women in the West worked as bartenders and waitresses too. She speculated how her father would have reacted if she'd suggested taking up a job in a bar or as a server. Ma, though less judgmental of the two, didn't want to understand the difference between the work responsibilities of a stewardess and a *bai,* the maid-servant. In her world, they both cleaned up after people.

"Oh no. This coffee shop is my friend Ariana's. I just help when not doing my real gig."

"Very nice place."

"I know." Leila handed Shaili a copy of the menu and asked, "What can I get you?"

"Maybe coffee."

"What kind?"

"Umm. Cappuccino please." Shaili said self-assuredly. She had learnt her lesson the hard way and would never order espresso again. She thanked Sadhil, under her breath, for introducing her to coffees that her palate could bear.

"How much is it?"

"Don't worry about it. It's on the house."

Shaili looked at Leila blankly. Leila realized Shaili didn't understand the slang.

"Consider it my 'Welcome to New York' gift."

"Why are you treating me? I don't even know you," said Shaili in a simpering voice.

"No biggie. You can buy me a cup next time."

"But…"

"We can get to know each other that way. What say?"

"Okay. Thank you." Shaili clearly liked the idea of making a new friend. She admired the artwork in the store. That's what had caught her eye the first time she walked down Sadhil's neighborhood.

"All this art is beautiful."

"Thanks."

"Who made it?"

"I did."

"How?

"Ummm. Let's see, I started with my hands and…"

Shaili felt unintelligent. Leila sensed her quirky sense of humor might have been a little cruel for a first meeting. She quickly said, "I am an artist. This is what I do."

"It's all very lovely."

"Why, thank you, missy."

"What do you do?" Leila asked Shaili.

"I was doing an MBA from Pune but then I got married and here I am now." Shaili opened up to Leila, but she held back the gory details of her past. For the first time in her life, Shaili felt emancipated saying what was in her heart, to a complete stranger.

"Classic victim of arranged marriage?" Leila shook her head.

Shaili avoided eye contact with Leila. Leila interpreted Shaili's response from her expressive body language. Shaili looked at the curving staircase leading to an upper level and enquired about it. Leila mentioned that the two levels in the café catered to different crowds and hence the disparate interior. The first level was the lounge area where people relaxed and chatted, over coffee and Arab American snacks, while the second level had a scholarly ambience. It was a writers' lounge where they had regular readings by both established and emerging wordsmiths. That's why, the second level came with contemporary furniture, Internet access, a wine bar, and a podium placed on a wooden plank that was hung by four ropes, so readers and performers felt like part of a literary theatre production. Shaili was mystified with the offerings at *Khubz* and New York altogether.

"Leila, where are you from?" queried Shaili.

"Iran. But I have lived here for eons now, so I think of myself as American. Persian American." True to her name and heritage, Leila had distinct Persian features.

The two got talking and Shaili was befuddled by how open Leila was about her life. Leila had moved to New York with her then-husband, Soroush Firozi, from Tehran. Leila was almost the same age as Sadhil but a divorcée. Shaili gaped at Leila as she shared personal, pivotal information with her. Shaili's mind went to Pune, where her father would have locked her up in a room if he found out that Shaili was talking to a divorced woman. Her mother too wouldn't have been thrilled. They would have thought of Leila as "terrible company." But this was New York, and no one could tell her what to do. She felt alive and was thinking of her own free will—talking to someone without caring about their background. Shaili liked her new independence. Her mind, for a second, went to Sadhil and the time when he'd said that New York allowed him to be what Delhi didn't. For a second, or thirty gala seconds, she gave him the benefit of doubt and almost understood what he meant.

"Here you go." Leila handed over a cup of cappuccino to Shaili. They both sat down at one of the corner tables.

"You know, I have never met an artist before." Shaili said in excitement.

"Really?"

"Ya. All my friends in Pune are studying to be MBAs or doctors or engineers." She added five sachets of sugar to her coffee. Shaili had noticed that both sugar and salt in New York were blander than Pune; but she felt the other way about life.

"Did they want to?" Leila arched her left eyebrow.

Shaili ignored Leila's question. In a fervent tone, she asked her, "Is all the art in this shop yours? Or other artists also?"

"Yup. All mine." Leila beamed.

"I would like to see all your work. Only if it is okay with you." Shaili couldn't believe how outspoken she was with Leila.

"Sure. I normally don't say this to people I've met for the first time, but if you'd like to see my work, you can show up unannounced at my studio. I can you give you the address and the directions to the place. It's in Chelsea." Leila wrote down her address on a piece of paper and gave it to Shaili, but per habit, Shaili didn't think of jotting it down in her diary.

Shaili put the paper inside her wallet and said, "I don't know New York well. I have barely been here a few days. Would you mind taking me?"

"It would be my pleasure."

They chatted for a little while longer and Leila made a fresh mozzarella, tomato, and basil sandwich to complement the second cup of cappuccino.

"Oh my God! It's 9 o'clock. I should go home."

"Howcome?"

"My husband will..." Shaili bit her lip and said nothing further. She didn't know what to say. She wasn't sure why she had used Sadhil's name as a pretext to leave *Khubz.* He had never behaved like a traditional

Indian man—one with a scroll of expectations. Shaili had no idea why she needed an excuse, at all, to leave *Khubz.*

"Or your husband will…"

Shaili didn't address Leila's enquiry. She stood up and straightened the crease in her clothes. As Shaili picked up her bag, she asked Leila, "Will you be here tomorrow?"

"Sure thing." Leila nodded and picked up the dirty dishes as she wiped the table.

"Okay. Good night." Shaili started to leave and then turned around, "Oh. I forgot. How much is the total?"

"Zilch."

"What?"

"C'mon. Nothing."

"Why?"

"Remember, we've done this before. My gift to you."

"Let me pay for the sandwich at least, no."

"Nah! Forget about it. Like I said, you can treat me next time." Leila shrugged her shoulders.

When Shaili got home, Sadhil was waiting for her. He said, "Where were you? I was getting worried."

"I was out. I get bored sitting at home all day." Shaili was back to being obnoxious because she, once again, misinterpreted Sadhil's tone as being meddling.

Sadhil ignored her curtness. He was happy to be home and to be able to eat dinner with his wife. "Anyway, you must be hungry, right? I got some Chinese takeaway." He went into the kitchen and started warming up dinner. "There is some kung pao and chicken, lo mein, and egg rolls. I thought I'd introduce you to American Chinese. I have a feeling you'll like it."

As he laid out the plates, he said, "Maybe over dinner, we can plan what you want to do over the weekend."

Shaili was full with the day's occurrences. Moreover, she had completely forgotten that next day was a Saturday—her first weekend with Sadhil. What would she do if he wanted to come close to her? He hadn't really tried anything until now, but what if this was the weekend he was waiting for? Was the gentle kiss on the cheek a hint? Shaili felt anguish replace logic in her head. More than anything, she wanted to meet her new friend, Leila. She'd promised herself that she would see her.

"I am tired. I am going to sleep." She announced but not rudely. "He didn't even ask me what I would like to eat and got Chinese food. Thank God Leila made me fresh sandwiches," she muttered to herself.

Sadhil was taken aback by Shaili's abruptness. He called out to her in an assertive yet calm voice and asked if everything was okay. She nodded and reiterated that she was jetlagged and exhausted. He mouthed an "okay," but Sadhil felt perturbed by Shaili's unwarranted behavior. He thought she was probably lonely and missed Pune. He felt guilty about not being there for her. He had been working late because he wanted to take time off over the next few weeks and take Shaili to Paris. He was hopeful that the weekend might change Shaili's mood. He would take her out and show her around the city. Tell her about Paris. Talk to her about what she wanted to do with her life. She didn't have to pursue an MBA if she didn't want to. In Pune, she had showed interest in studying journalism.

Sadhil put the food back into the containers. He had lost his appetite. He changed into his lounge pants, watched mindless television, and passed out on the couch. When Shaili went to bed that night, alone in the master bedroom, she didn't realize that the coming weeks would whisper a secret into her ears that would change life as she knew it.

Shaili slept in late. When she woke up, Sadhil was sipping coffee and reading the *New York Times* while the television was tuned to BBC

America. Just the sight of him reading the paper got Shaili assessing him. She conceded to herself that he perpetually looked handsome. He wished her a good morning and enquired if she had slept well. Shaili gestured a "yes" with her head. Sadhil then recommended that Shaili freshen up; he had cooked up a feast for brunch. There was toast, scrambled eggs, bacon, pancakes, and orange juice. But the biggest surprise was when Sadhil handed her a cup of Pune-style coffee. While showering, Shaili cried. She shed tears of repentance and abashment. Sadhil had taken pains to plan a thoughtful brunch for her and all she had done was been spiteful towards him. She hadn't even made tea for him, like a good Indian wife. And he had actually taken the initiative to call up her mother and learnt to make her favorite beverage. She almost reviled him for being so nice.

After indulging in scrumptious food accompanied by minimal conversation, Sadhil asked Shaili what she'd wanted to do that day. It was, after all, their first weekend together as a couple without the two families. Sadhil liked the sound of those words; Shaili felt jittery. She asked him about Chelsea. Sadhil was startled, as Chelsea wasn't a touristy neighborhood. He told her about it but made nothing more of it.

They decided to spend the day touring the Empire State Building and the Statue of Liberty. An old, Indian woman near the Empire State Building had randomly asked them, looking at Shaili's chudas, how long they'd been married and gone on to pronounce that the two would have good-looking children—given how attractive they were. Sadhil had gone red in the face just thinking about it. He hadn't yet made any moves on Shaili because he wanted to give her time to accept her new life, new city, new relationships; but Shaili felt aggravated when the woman decided to bless them both, in Hindi, like a dialogue out of a Bollywood movie.

Sadhil didn't quite understand Shaili's reaction to the woman's remark. Shaili wasn't embarrassed; she was irate. He recognized the look of provocation on Shaili's face and decided to take her out for coffee to distract her from the uncanny interaction. Shaili loved the baroque coffee shop. It served gourmet variety of hot beverages along with scones and clotted crème. A bite into the English decadence helped put the arbitrary comment out of Shaili's mind. She wore a smile again. Sadhil wasn't sure if it was the coffee that made his wife glad or perhaps his company. He tried to decode her actions. Though he enjoyed her presence—his wife's companionship, Sadhil began to question Shaili's mood swings. The reason she avoided him and intimacy like they were the plague. Feeling shy as a newly wed was one thing; consciously staying celibate and creating a distance from him, was another issue.

After an indulgent trip through Strand Bookstore, where Shaili had jumped with joy and accidentally hugged Sadhil, Shaili and Sadhil got home exhausted at seven thirty in the evening. Shaili was in a good mood and offered to warm up the leftover Chinese food from the night before. Sadhil felt an ounce of hope. He took a hot water shower and changed into his pajamas. He played a Jazz CD by Louis Armstrong and turned towards Shaili to confirm if the volume was okay with her. She responded using a monosyllablic, "Yes." He then decided to open a bottle of Reisling to accompany the mood. To him, the ambience was perfect for a romantic evening. Shaili's back was facing him when Sadhil entered the kitchen to help her. He couldn't avert his eyes from her unblemished skin glistening against the dim light. Shaili had worn a sleeveless blouse with a deep back. The satiny skin on her back beseeched him. Sadhil wanted to gently run his fingers across it and hold her. He wanted to caress her naked shoulder blade. Just as he was about to pick her up in his arms and kiss her all over, Shaili turned around and read his mind or at least it seemed that way. Neither of them said anything; Sadhil's throat felt dry.

After dinner, Shaili announced that she was exhausted and wanted to call it a day. Sadhil requested her to hang around for a little bit and ran his fingers on her hand. Shaili had dreaded this instance, especially after the kitchen encounter. Weeknights were so much better and safer. Sadhil left home early and worked late. Shaili made it a point to be asleep in the morning and bushed in the evening.

Contrary to Shaili's hypothesis, Sadhil didn't make any moves on her. He suggested that he would make her favorite coffee and they could talk about what she wanted to do—study, work, or volunteer. Sadhil had picked up a graduate program catalogue from both New York University and Columbia University for masters in business administration, journalism, and creative writing. He told her about the places from where she could get her degree evaluated if she wanted to join a graduate program. He talked about GMAT, GRE, and TOEFL. He made it clear to Shaili that he wasn't trying to coerce her into making a career choice. At the end of the day, it was her call. He just wanted her to know that the sky was the limit, if she wanted. And that he was there to support her the whole way.

Shaili was overwhelmed with Sadhil's gentleness. She thanked him for it and excused herself midway through the conversation. Sadhil's desire, to smooch his wife, was buried that night, again. He hoped the situation would change. He strived to make the marriage work.

On Sunday morning, Sadhil asked Shaili if she wanted to try the New York special breakfast—bagel with crème cheese and coffee. After a local breakfast, which Shaili enjoyed, they decided to spend the day at the Museum of Modern Art. There was a new exhibit in town. Shaili enjoyed the museum. Of course, it reminded her of Leila's work. And thinking about her new friend made her feel a lot calmer.

During the course of the day, a few of Sadhil's close friends had called to see if the Sethis wanted to meet up for drinks in the evening.

They were all looking forward to meeting the woman who had stolen Sadhil's heart. She could hear one of his friends ask, "How is the baby making coming along?" Sadhil ignored the question the first time. But when his friend couldn't take a hint, he had used a question to work as decoy. He responded with "How is the money making coming along?" Sadhil didn't sound rude, but his tone conveyed the apt message, and his friend apologized for his egregious query. Shaili wanted to know if that's what Sadhil was thinking of as well—baby making, but she didn't know how to approach the subject. What she did know was how to avoid it. That evening too, she had used her rehearsed excuse to get out of the commitment by saying that she wasn't feeling too well and wanted to head back home from the museum. But she insisted Sadhil met up with them. Sadhil wasn't that keen. He got the feeling that Shaili wanted to be left all alone, which irked him. She was by herself all week yet didn't want to spend time with him over the weekend. He confronted her. Shaili insisted she was still getting used to the weather and the new time zone. And that she would make for terrible company, but at the same time, she didn't want him to not socialize. He did listen to her for the sake of their so-called marriage. After all, that's what he'd seen growing up. One person learnt to strangle their thoughts to keep the peace in the family. So, Sadhil went out on a Sunday night just so his wife could be happy.

When Sadhil returned after meeting his friends, with dinner in his hands, Shaili was already asleep. He sunk on the sofa. Sadhil felt disenchanted. Every time he thought he had made a breakthrough with his wife, things went back to square one. He wasn't stupid. He had begun to sense that Shaili wasn't just missing home. There was something more to it. If only he could put his finger on it.

Often, Shaili had seemed annoyed around him. If only there was a way he could help her. He wondered if she was coerced to marry him.

Sadhil longed for her, but she didn't respond. Did she have a boyfriend in Pune? His subconscious mind nudged him about his unusual marital arrangement, but his heart assured him to not give up. Not yet. Before Sadhil knew it, he was asleep on the couch, condoning patience.

Shaili pushed Sadhil away, increasingly, as the days went by. Though he remained patient, what other option did he have, he did scrutinize the probable outcome of their abnormal alliance. He knew sooner than later he would have to talk to Shaili about what was bothering him. He felt Paris would be the ideal place for such conversations, so he had to be patient, a little longer.

Amidst all the confusion engulfing Sadhil, Shaili swam steadily towards Leila, her world, and their new friendship. The one place she was never irate.

9

"Did you like Leila from the start?" Supriya pulled Shaili out from her whirlpool of flashbacks.

"Yes, I did, but only as a friend." Shaili smiled.

"Were you close friends?"

"In my first book, if you remember, I described the beginning of my friendship, with Leila, by using a William Arthur Ward quote: *"When we seek to discover the best in others, we somehow bring out the best in ourselves."* She had a positive influence on me. According to Sadhil, I sounded more focused on my career and less agitated. I decided to pursue masters in journalism from Columbia University. I started studying for the GMAT and taking bridge-up classes. Leila helped me with all of it, with no strings attached. On the side, I would attend readings at *Khubz* by emerging and established poets and writers, which she would accompany me to."

"Did you know she was lesbian?" Supriya was known for being upfront. Shyness eluded her.

"Who, Leila?"

"No, Raakhi Sawant. Pay attention, Shails." Supriya made a face while Shaili grinned.

"Not in the beginning. Quite honestly, I wasn't completely scandalized when Leila disclosed that she was gay. It's not like I had an inclination, but for some inscrutable reason, I wasn't taken aback either with her disclosure. When Leila said, "Don't worry; I am not going to hit on you," I didn't know how to react or what to feel. I wasn't sure what to make of such personal information. You know the family I grew up with, right? Ma had taught me to keep 'the dirty laundry at home.' I wholeheartedly admired Leila's strength of character, but I had never met anyone who was not in a relationship in the traditional sense. I hadn't even seen a television show that catered to just the homosexual lifestyle. I didn't say much to Leila that evening but kept a watchful distance from her. We went out for coffee in the neighborhood and talked about my school prospects and life in New York. I thought of calling you that night, Su. You would have marveled at my afternoon and addressed it as an episode from *Sex & The City*.

"Is there a specific locality in New York where all the gay people live?"

Shaili burst out laughing. "Why are you laughing? I am serious." Supriya poked Shaili's third eye. "Here, in Pune, we have localities where Konkanastha Brahmins live. And new out-of-town people reside in different parts of Pune. The same for all the army and airforce people. Everybody has their 'unofficial' fixed place."

"Only you could have asked that." Shaili's facial muscles appreciated the bout of laughter more than Shaili could have ever imagined. "Leila had taken me down to her studio one afternoon, within weeks of my move. The variety and message in her artistic endeavors was overwhelming. Her studio was in a huge loft. She didn't share the space with anyone, so it had several personal touches. When I asked Leila how she got involved with art, she opened up to me without any qualms and told me about herself. I was astonished at the area and..."

"Why? What was so different about the place?" Supriya ignored Shaili's incomplete sentence.

"Hello, may I complete my sentence?" Shaili smiled at Supriya's impatient impetuosity, and raised her eyebrows.

"Sorry. Yes, yes." Supriya shook her head like a pendulum.

"For the first time in my life, I saw an area where different people lived together—men with men and women with women, holding hands, openly expressing their love for each other. I felt like a village idiot, gaping at them with my mouth open! I couldn't even openly utter the word *gay*. I felt morally corrupt even looking at posters suggesting that lifestyle. I had nothing against them, but even after all those weeks, despite living oceans across from my parents, I could feel a slap across my face and Dad's abuses in Punjabi. I was sure he would lynch me to death if he found out I was in such an area. I was convinced Ma would emotionally blackmail me and make me promise that I would never go back to such an area again. 'The devil resides in such places', would have been her reaction."

"Leila must have felt offended by your reaction, no?"

"Leila discerned I was unusually quiet. She later told me that she had wanted to ask me if the discommodiousness was because of who she was. She wasn't insulted. According to her, my reaction was comprehensible since a lot of people felt that way. Thankfully, she didn't take my behavior personally. But after meeting her that evening and listening to her stories, I was dumbfounded."

"We have gays in Pune too, you know. But people here aren't open about it even today. Actually, you and Leila are the first couple I have ever met."

"Really? Do we make you uneasy? If that's the case, we can check into a hotel."

"Idiot, stop being so obnoxiously sensitive. It's not like that. I like

Leila. You know that. It's just different. Like unusual. I mean, I was able to pull Sadhil's leg, but I don't know how to behave around you both as a couple. It's a matter of getting used to. I am telling you all this because if I was speechless, think of what Uncle must have felt. He's a generation older. Be kind to the Old Man. It's your life and your choices, but my advice to you is don't rush him. Don't expect him to come to terms with it right away."

"Right away? For the longest time, I could not bring myself to address Leila as my girlfriend or partner. She was always a friend. In the confines of our four walls, I was pleasant, but the minute we had company, I would denounce her. Was I self-conscious, I don't know? Borderline prude? I mean, even after all these years, for some inexplicable reason, I can't call myself a lesbian." As Shaili tried to say something further, Supriya cut her off.

"It's a taboo here." Supriya tapped the steering wheel.

"I beg your pardon."

"Homosexuality."

"I know."

"People say mindsets are changing, but I don't think so." Supriya shook her head from left to right.

"You aren't convinced. Why so?"

"I think a lot of them continue to suppress their identity. Remain 'closeted' as they say on your American television channels. One of Mhatre's colleague's brothers was gay, but his family thought that he had lost his direction in life. I don't think they even understood what he wanted. They were bothered about their neighbors gossiping about their son. When he tried explaining, they locked up the boy and called a priest to conduct prayers for him. No college, no classes, no friends, Shails. Can you imagine? Guess what happened?"

"What?"

"One day, that nineteen-year old committed suicide. On the pretext of hanging clothes, he went to the terrace of his own society's building and jumped off."

"That's awful! But I can well imagine. I have heard such stories too, in fact from all over."

Supriya was visibly disgusted. "I say two hoots to the damned general public. Why do we fear the repercussions of the judgmental society? Why do we give it such sanctions? When we were kids, Hindu-Muslims couldn't get married and now this. I mean, why does the populace get to decide who can spend their life with whom? You are lucky that Uncle is willing to at least talk to you."

"Lucky? Huh. You, of all the people, are saying that about Old Man Suresh? Leila and I have been through our share of hell, so believe me; I don't expect any of you guys to understand my quandary in twenty four hours."

"Shails, don't be angry, yaar. You know what I mean."

Shaili felt bad about her tone. All Supriya was doing, was trying to be a good friend. Shaili apologized to Supriya. Supriya told her that all was well between the two of them and proceeded to ask more questions.

"Did you tell Sadhil about Leila?"

"Yes and no."

"Meaning?"

"He knew about Leila, but I didn't tell him about what Leila had told me—that she was gay. Not because I didn't want to. It was a lot for me to handle. Or maybe I did want to hide Leila's identity from him, lest he would judge me. And perhaps speculate the real reason for my indifference. I don't know. God, I was so confused. And I wasn't like close to Sadhil or anything though he tried. I think he was pleased I had found a friend. It made him feel less awful because he knew how much I ached for my Supriya." Supriya happily wore a gloated smile on her face, so Shaili paused and hugged Supriya, again. "My friendship with Leila, to him, meant that I was making an effort to settle into his city and our new life."

What Shaili remained oblivious to was with her gradually changing attitude, somewhere, Sadhil nurtured a hope that the missing elements, from their relationship, would find a suitable home and everything would fall into place. It was matter of time.

"Did you introduce the two of them?"

"Who? Sadhil and Leila?"

"No. Mahatma Gandhi and Nehru. What Shaili?"

"Sorry, baba. No, I didn't. Sadhil later told me that he had always pondered why I never introduced Leila to him if she and I were such good friends. He had wondered if it was another sign, of rejection, from his wife."

"But what about those readings you went for at Leila's coffee shop? Not even there?"

"*Khubz*? Sadhil expressed his interest in joining me, for the readings at *Khubz*, but I disregarded them. Weekdays were easy; he kept late hours, and *Khubz* closed before he got back home. I made sure we didn't go to *Khubz* over the weekend. It helped that sometimes Leila had her plans, or Sadhil and I went out. Even when Sadhil tried to talk about it, I would avoid the conversation. He respected my feelings, even if unjustified and stayed out of *Khubz* and my newly formed friendship with Leila."

"Why did you not want him to meet Leila?"

"I don't know. Maybe I was conscious that my girl-crush would become visible. Or that he would notice that I could be a happy person and expect me to be that way at home. Or maybe I just didn't know how to manage traditional relationships given I grew up on poison ivy. I don't know. I never could really decipher my unwillingness."

"How were things between you and Sadhil otherwise?"

"How do you mean?"

"You know. You were getting closer with Leila. Not allowing him to be a part of your life. Did that make a difference how you behaved with each other as a couple? Was he jealous?"

"As time went by, Leila and I met every morning at *Khubz*. Leila's emotions, contrary to mine, were rarely obvious to the world. We would discuss a lot of cerebral and artsy topics. I was intrigued by the commonality between Farsi and Hindi language especially in the words that meant a lot to me; like friend—it was dost in both Hindi and Farsi. A book was ketaab in Persian and kitaab in Hindi. I had fun researching and finding out that both the languages had an Indo-European origin. Leila indulged my interests. I spoke about my family and you, but I was discreet with personal information."

"Really? What about me? All good things I hope?" Supriya said with a smile.

"Sadhil was the sweetest man. Anybody else in his place would have thrown a tantrum. But he was a gem. You know, the closer I grew to Leila, the more my abhorrence of Sadhil increased. I couldn't understand why. It's not like we fought. I barely spent time with him. We had incompatible weekday schedules, and I deliberately chose to keep my schoolwork for the weekend or we went out with his friends. The lack of togetherness made all those sensual desires come out alive, in me, but he wouldn't touch me. Actually, I didn't let him. He was all harmlessly flirty, but I was cold. This one time he picked me up in his arms, and I chewed his head off. Sometimes I could tell that he was angry with me, but he rarely expressed his annoyance. Could I blame him? I never even gave him a flying kiss or a hug. I wondered if I misread my inner desires—if they were directed towards someone other than Sadhil, but I was chicken to admit that. God, I had such mixed feelings. Neighbors making comments like, 'Are you pregnant yet?' reminded me of what was lacking in my life, which I didn't welcome."

Shaili's mind wandered, again, to the last few days before her marriage broke up.

Every time Sadhil suggested they meet his friends, Shaili went out but barely interacted with anyone. It seemed she wasn't willing to accept anyone who was a part of Sadhil's life. Eventually, to get out of social commitments, she used the pretext of being worn-out or buried under school-related work. It bothered Sadhil a little because even when making plans with his friends, he'd always recommended doing things that he knew Shaili would like. Once he'd bought tickets to a newly released Shah Rukh Khan movie and decided to surprise Shaili with it. He'd planned to take her to *Kathi Roll and Chaat* afterwards. Shaili had said a conceited thank you but didn't go out, again. The reason of the day was a backache.

Sadhil couldn't help but continue to be baffled over Shaili's unfriendliness around him. He didn't know who to discuss his problems with about the lack of normalcy in his life. All his friends teased him about his three-week trip to India where he married the first woman he saw. Was that a mistake? He liked Shaili but was that enough? They had seemed compatible when they first met, but was he hasty in his decision? He didn't want his friends to think any less of his wife. Or call him any less of a man. Jokingly he'd asked Supriya about the guys in her and Shaili's life given how gorgeous both of them were. But when Supriya, unsuspectingly, told him, forget dating, Shaili wasn't allowed to keep male friends, he felt guilty about doubting his wife. He chose to believe that Shaili was probably just uncomfortable around men. Or maybe the path of denial worked for him.

Sadhil's crumbling Utopia made him conscious of his own personality. In his reflective, doleful moments, Sadhil wondered if he had encouraged Shaili's behavior, just like his father had supported his mother's asininity. Like his father, Sadhil had always been a solicitous husband, but Shaili continued to behave like a spoilt child, just like his mother. Sadhil was at his wits' end.

Shaili's brain and heart were at that fuzzy point where she couldn't distinguish between illusion and reality. She was irrational. Somewhere, deep inside her soul, she knew she was in the wrong. Or did she? When Sadhil tried doing something nice, she didn't want him around. Shaili couldn't deduce what she wanted, or was she afraid to express it? She never cooked a meal or planned anything around what Sadhil liked. Sadhil left her caring notes without being controlling, but she remained apathetic to them. He cooked over the weekends and they ate out during the week. Sadhil's non-complaining nature, in some ways, gnawed at her. She couldn't fight the thought that he was trying to guilt her into sleeping with him by being so unselfish, and the thought of sleeping with him didn't excite her one bit. Her contradictions perplexed her.

Over a period of time, even when Sadhil offered to take her sightseeing, she said that she wasn't much of a "walker." The demanding preparatory tests and assignments were her crutches when she ran out of excuses. The harder he tried, the more irascible her responses became. The only place she felt in control and at peace with herself was in Leila's company.

When Shaili returned home, after the studio visit in Chelsea, Sadhil was taking out a suitcase from the storage space. She felt nauseous. She was convinced that he was planning to walk away. Or maybe he was throwing her out. That's what men did. "Weak bastards." She didn't know where she would go or what she would do. Now she didn't have the option to move in with Leila either, even temporarily. She was gay. Her thoughts engulfed the warm hello said by Sadhil.

"Shaili, I am going to Chicago on work tomorrow," Sadhil screamed from the second bedroom.

Shaili walked into the kitchen, drank a glass of water, and said, "Okay." She was relieved more than anything.

Sadhil couldn't hear her as the mouthful of water ate up her words. He repeated himself. Shaili rolled her eyes. "He thinks I am uneducated and deaf. Like I couldn't hear the first time." She walked towards the living room and stood near the mystical windows, gaping at the vast expanse of water. Sadhil emerged from the second bedroom looking a little agitated. Shaili was beginning to push his buttons. He had always indulged her eccentricity, but her indifferent behavior tonight, especially, was uncalled for.

"Did you hear what I said?" He asked, in a mildly irritable tone.

"Yup."

"It was a sudden trip that came up."

"Okay."

"But it's just a five-day trip, so I will be back before you know it. And then…"

"Okay." She cut him off as she took another sip of water.

"Will you be alright?"

"Uh-huh."

"Shaili, is all well?" Sadhil's patience was visibly beginning to give away and his voice was edgy.

"Yes. Why?" Shaili gave him a bewildered look like he was the one asking an outrageous question.

Sadhil tried to stay unruffled but Shaili made it tricky for him with her coldness. Her mind was still obsessing about the afternoon and Leila's admission. But Sadhil didn't know that. Not that she divulged anything to him, in any case. Sadhil just knew she was not participating in the conversation like most times. And he rightfully felt provoked.

"Because all I ever hear from you is 'okay.' Nothing else." Sadhil's tone was curt.

"What do you want me to say?" Shaili retorted. "You are going. So you are going. What should I do? Celebrate? Or cry?" She slammed the glass on the corner table and started to walk towards the master bedroom. Shaili's indignation was like her father's. Like him, she had misdirected her infuriation.

"Where is this coming from Shaili?"

"What?"

"Your attitude?"

"What attitude?"

"C'mon. You know what I am talking about."

"No, I don't!" Shaili folded her arms across her chest.

Sadhil looked out the window and continued, "Shaili, we have barely eaten meals together unless I suggested we did. We have rarely spoken about anything. We have hardly spent any quality time together. Come on yaar. We've been married for a frickin' month! Isn't that odd? Is something bothering you? Maybe I can help?" Shaili stood impassively.

Sadhil walked towards Shaili. "I want to get to know you. I really do, but I need your help for it because I am not into mind games. If you need more time, just tell me that. But this speculation is getting unbearable now."

"You are the one sleeping on the couch!" Shaili darted back like a boomerang. The apartment felt oddly cold at just that instant.

"Whoa! Where did that come from?" Sadhil stood baffled. Shaili folded her shoulders and raised her eyebrows. "Every night you tell me that you are too tired. What am I supposed to do?" He raised his voice.

"Whatever married people do!" Shaili yelled and came back near the corner table to pick up her glass of water. She took a few sips.

"And what do you think they do?" Sadhil stood in Shaili's face.

"Like you don't know." Shaili averted her face.

Sadhil, with disgust in his eyes, walked up to Shaili. He pushed her against the wall and brought his face close to hers. She could feel his hot breath burn her cheeks. His lips were almost on hers. Almost. Shaili stood still with her lips parted and they quivered. Sadhil lifted her blouse slightly and touched the button on her jeans for a few seconds. He then ran his fingers over her bare midriff almost tickling Shaili but she stood unmoved and emotionally unfelt. He ran his fingers down to her sculpted hips that fit perfectly in his manly palms and gently stroked them. In an instant, he then pushed her away. Sadhil pounded his fist into the wall. He moved away and sank on the sofa with his face buried in his hands. He caught his breath and then turned towards Shaili. She was still standing pinned against the wall. He addressed her in a calmer tone, "Is that what you want? Huh? That I should force myself on you? Assault you? Tell me Shaili."

Shaili didn't answer back. She was tongue-tied. This was the first time a guy had touched her, but she hadn't felt what she thought she should have. Or what Supriya had sensed when she kissed Mhatre for the first time. Shaili had felt queasy.

"What do you think of me, Shaili? That I married the first thing I saw in India?" Shaili's silence irked him further. She stared at him blankly but couldn't utter a word. The self-realization was paving its way through her being.

"Say something." Sadhil said unrelentingly.

"Don't all you men want the same thing?" Shaili hissed back without thinking.

"Is that what you think? That…that…all men are sexual deviants and heartless creeps? Who are you, Shaili?" Sadhil paced up and down the living room with disbelief.

"Did it ever occur to you that I might actually like you and that I didn't want you to feel compelled to sleep with me? Huh? That I was making sure you took your own time? That I actually love you. That I am not a beast waiting to tear at my wife?"

Sadhil's eyes were wet. He had never seen himself so heated. Not even when Simran had cheated on him. There was something about Shaili. She had compared him to a rapist. He couldn't bear it. His voice cracked when he said, "You are my wife, and I was respecting our relationship, your wish, and your desires, so I waited until you were ready. Ready to talk to me and include me in your life, not just fuck! I want you to think of me as your husband and a friend and not some animal who tore you away from your family."

Sadhil went inside the second bedroom and brought back a brown envelope with him. As he handed the envelope to Shaili, he said, "You know what, I can't talk to you. I am out of here."

He slammed the door behind him and went out for a long walk to clear his head and determine where his marriage was headed. What bothered him most was that he still didn't know what was bugging Shaili. He ran his fingers through his thick mane of hair and hoped a solution would nudge at him. Shaili had sounded like she hated men because of their stereotypical expectation from marriage and women. But that didn't explain why she expected him to sexually assault her. Sadhil knew he hadn't violated her, so what was it? What had she been exposed to? He didn't want to think it, but he wondered if Shaili's father had hurt her. Supriya had mentioned casually that Shaili wasn't allowed to interact with men while growing up, so who else could it be? Sadhil devised ways of asking Shaili about her past without upsetting her. He thought of taking her to a therapist. Sadhil was convinced that Shaili's yesterday was affecting their today and would continue to influence their tomorrow if nothing was done about it.

He walked around Central Park and hoped the windy roads would unveil an answer and make his convoluted life simpler. He saw couples in the park, holding hands. Few of them were kissing passionately. It made him think of his actions from an hour ago. He felt horrible, and he somewhat missed his wife. It wasn't like him to get belligerent. "I should have known better."

He wanted to make it up to Shaili. And he knew one of them had to be an adult about their issues. He grabbed two coffees at the *Starbucks* close to home, which had only recently reopened. The chilled coffee comforted him, and he hoped it would play the same magic on Shaili. He wanted to give his marriage another try. He really wanted to be with Shaili. And coffee was a good start if he had to please her. But when he came back home, Shaili didn't speak with him. She had locked herself inside the master bedroom. He apologized; she remained mute. He beseeched; she didn't budge. Sadhil felt dejected.

He noticed Shaili hadn't opened the envelope he had handed her. He deliberated hiding it but then just left it there. Maybe the content inside the brown envelope would help—at least temporarily. He added a note to it and with hope in his heart, Sadhil slept on the sofa, again.

When Shaili woke up the next morning, her eyes were puffy. She had sobbed all night. There was used facial tissue strewn on the nightstand and kohl smudged on her face. She felt drained out as her head continued to throb persistently. She wore her robe and walked towards the kitchen to make some coffee. Sadhil had left her a mug of coffee on the kitchen counter with a note that read, "Happy anniversary. I am sorry. That's not how I intended to spend our first month anniversary. Forgive me. Once I am back from Chicago, we'll sort everything out. Please look at the contents inside the brown envelope. The one I gave you yesterday. It's on the coffee table."

Shaili's heart skipped a beat. She didn't have the energy to weep anymore. She doubted if Sadhil had left the divorce papers for her. After all, she had been nasty. She couldn't blame him if he wanted to walk away from their marriage. Her hands were shaking as she picked up the packet. There was Post-it stuck on it, "I owe you this." As Shaili pulled out the content, she broke down. She didn't know her tear ducts were still active after flooding her eyes the night before. She clung to the envelope and wailed loudly until she couldn't breathe.

Shaili picked up the phone and dialed. "Can you come?" She was still howling. The voice at the other end enquired something to which Shaili responded "Now."

"What happened?" The person enquired.

"I'll tell you when you are here."

"You are scaring me. Just don't do anything stupid. I'll be there in a few, for sure."

Twenty minutes later, the intercom rang.

Shaili's eyes, even after all those years, were moist with pain and guilt reminiscing about that fateful day.

10

"Was this your first big fight with Sadhil?" Supriya probed.

"Yes, it was."

"You called someone after your fight, right?"

"Yes."

"Was it Aunty?"

"No, I couldn't burden her. I had no idea what I was doing."

"Who was it?"

"Leila." Shaili sighed.

"Like I suspected."

"What do you mean? Your first guess was Ma."

"Oh, that was just to throw you off. Tell me, even until that day you didn't know you liked her."

"Whom?"

"Anarkali! Idiot! Of course I mean Leila."

"Oh. No, not the way you think."

"That's interesting."

"What is?"

"All your actions, in hindsight, seem indicative of your true persona, don't you think?"

"I think about that a lot too. I wish Ma was around that day. She would have understood. I was so dense, right?"

"Don't be so hard on yourself, Shails."

"You know, in those days, I always thought of all my unexpected interactions with Leila as fortuitous encounters." Shaili stared at the water. "I wish Ma were alive. I hope she's looking over us right now. The place she took her last breath is where I am trying to start breathing a new relationship with my father. I just wish she'd told me the truth about herself. Maybe I could have alleviated her pain. I don't know…"

"Sorry to interrupt." Supriya tried to brighten Shaili's mood with her self-deprecatory humor. "You are so right. I can't keep my trap shut." Supriya tapped her temples and dramatically swung her arms towards Shaili. She continued, "My tongue always functions in an overactive mode. I talk too much!" It worked. Shaili flaunted a tender smile and tapped Supriya, gently, on her wrists. Supriya brought her arms to her chin and asked, "What happened then?"

Shaili closed her eyes. She remembered every scene vividly. As she thought about those moments, she missed her mother more than ever.

"Leila is here," said the doorman.

"Send her up," Shaili said wiping her tears.

When Leila showed up at her door, Shaili ran to her and clung to her like a baby. She was inconsolable. Leila noticed the envelope in Shaili's hands.

"What happened, Shaili?" Leila asked. Shaili was still trembling. She handed her the envelope and wiped her stream of tears.

"So? These are tickets to Paris. Why are you crying? Man, I wish someone would get me tickets to Paris. You got yourself a good man there, woman." Leila tried to lighten up Shaili's mood.

Shaili looked up at Leila as if she were stupid but didn't verbalize her thoughts. She narrated the happenings of the prior evening. For the first time, she discussed her marital troubles with anyone. Shaili accepted that the fight had started because of her. And that Sadhil was faultless.

"Don't worry. Sadhil sounds like a nice guy. It'll be fine. Let me make you some tea. Where is everything?"

"What is wrong with me, Leila?" Shaili sniffled. She wanted an answer. She had been searching for it for an eternity and not just a month.

"Nothing. You look healthy." Leila joked again. She had a notion where this was headed.

"Can you, for once, have a serious conversation?" Shaili's eyes looked desperate. They sought help.

"Sure. Go ahead." Leila didn't want to be a part of this exchange, but she cared for Shaili, so she indulged her.

"I have been horrible to Sadhil for reasons I don't understand. A complete bitch as Supriya would say. I don't know, but I am tired of figuring it all out." She walked Leila to the kitchen to show her where all the ingredients for tea and coffee were kept. "Sadhil, he has been such a gentleman. He puts up with me. He gets me tickets to Paris for our honeymoon. I don't spend sixty minutes in a day with him over a meal. I don't deserve him. I don't deserve myself, Leila."

Shaili was bawling with guilt. Leila hugged her to calm her down. Leila looked around for some facial tissue, but she couldn't find any. She tore a piece of paper towel and handed it to Shaili. Just as Leila turned around to switch off the kettle, her elbow hit Shaili's right eye. Leila felt awful and came close to Shaili's face to blow some cool air into her eye. Their eyes met. Shaili liked Leila's touch and inadvertently kissed her on the lips. She then pushed Leila away, and then kissed her back. It felt weird but appropriate in the same breath. Before Shaili could wrap her brains around the moment, Leila reciprocated her hungry touch.

After about twenty minutes of them kissing, the doorman called, "Delivery for you."

Shaili asked the doorman to send the delivery guy upstairs. She said to Leila while fumbling for the right words, "I am sorry. I don't know what I was thinking." Leila assured Shaili that there was no need to apologize. And that she was caught in a weak moment because her husband was away and they had recently fought. Leila didn't want to bear the responsibility of a broken marriage on her soul, yet again. She said bye and excused herself.

Shaili tried to come to terms with her actions. She felt sick to her stomach, but in some ways, she knew she hadn't felt this good when Sadhil had touched her. Not even remotely close. She accepted Supriya's theory on first kiss. She wondered how could something so wrong, by societal standards, feel so right. She wanted to talk to someone, but she knew both Ma and Supriya wouldn't understand. Her actions were probably beyond the realm of her mother's comprehension.

The deliveryman rang the bell and broke Shaili's trance. As she signed the courier receipt and unwrapped the package, hot tears flushed her face, again. Shaili tried not to cry, but she couldn't convince her conscience to listen to pragmatism. Sadhil had ordered Kaplan books and guides for Shaili so she could prepare better for her standardized tests. He'd remembered the challenges he'd faced, as a new student, in America, with American spellings. She held the books close to her heart and felt dreadful. Sadhil genuinely cared for her. She'd thrown a tantrum and put him through misery even though he was the nicest man she would ever meet. She missed the friend in him.

For Sadhil's sake, she decided to give her nuptials another chance. After all, he had forgiven every single mistake of hers. She went to the bedroom and pulled out one of her unpacked bags—the one containing risqué garments. She fondled the lingerie her mother had bought her for the wedding or rather asked Supriya to pick up. Shaili ran her hand over the material. She found it coarse and decided that this wouldn't be up to standard. She needed to buy something Sadhil would like.

The next day, Shaili decided to contact Leila; she was staying in her marriage. It was the normal thing to do. Remain married to a man. But Leila avoided Shaili. She didn't answer or return any of her calls. She wasn't even at *Khubz*. Shaili took a cab down to her studio only to find a lock outside the main door. Shaili waited for about ninety minutes and then walked around for hours looking for Leila in the maze of New York with no luck.

The morning after, Shaili tried a little trick. She had used the public phone, so Leila wouldn't recognize the caller ID and answer the phone, to contact Leila. When Shaili managed to speak with her, Leila gave incredulous reasons for being unreachable. Shaili knew that Leila was lying when she mumbled about how busy she had been at her studio. Shaili had wanted to clear the air. After all, she was the one, who had made the first move. She didn't want to ruin her friendship with Leila. Not seeing Supriya was bad enough. She couldn't lose another friend. She thought it was amazing that in such a short span, she and Leila had found so many things in common. But most importantly, Shaili didn't want to agonize Sadhil. Moreover, she definitely couldn't afford to brew up trouble for Ma back home. She kept telling herself that Sadhil was her husband. A natural relationship. So, Shaili decided to be the perfect Indian woman that everyone expected her to be—a daughter, a wife, and a friend. Life had paved an upheaval in her conduit, but she was determined to straighten everything out.

Shaili requested Leila to join her for lunch. Leila initially declined, but Shaili was persistent. Shaili clarified that she wanted to ask for forgiveness in person. Shaili ordered lunch specials from the Chinese take-away close to home. Her home. She repeated it to herself. It wasn't Sadhil's apartment, but their home. Sadhil liked a particular restaurant and that's why she'd ordered from there. She asked for all the dishes he liked.

Leila showed up sharp at 12:30 p.m. She was wearing orange capris with a blue sleeveless top. Instead of hugging, Shaili shook hands with Leila and welcomed her into her house. Leila was bewildered by Shaili's behavior but went along. Shaili accepted the cheesecake Leila had brought for dessert. She remarked that it was Sadhil's favorite dessert. It was a lie or maybe not. Shaili didn't know. She'd never bothered to find out Sadhil's tastes. Even when Leila praised the Sethi apartment, Shaili sneaked in Sadhil's name and how he was a stupendous man with exquisite tastes.

There was an aura of formality surrounding the afternoon. Not much had changed in the past thirty-six to forty hours, the time when they last saw each other, but in some ways, a lot had altered. While biting onto her spring roll, Leila told Shaili about the new reading at *Khubz* that week by a renowned Asian poet. Shaili heard with great interest, but she informed Leila that she wouldn't be able to join her as Sadhil was expected to be home the same evening. And she wanted to be there for him. "I want to do right by him." She tried hard to prove to Leila that the earlier incident was an aberration—nothing that would happen ever again because she was a happily married woman.

After lunch, like two good friends, Shaili and Leila watched *When Harry Met Sally*. Neither of them said a word. Not even when the infamous scene came up—the one where Meg Ryan moans in the restaurant. Shaili realized how much she missed Supriya. Supriya would emulate the scene, word for word, in hush tones. Shaili thought Supriya's impersonation of Meg Ryan was hilarious with a hint of Pune accent. But with Leila, she discerned her reaction had to be socially appropriate.

Shaili decided to fill the quietude in the living room with words. Insipid utterances. Hedonic words. Reckless expressions. She asked Leila for suggestions for a good lingerie store. Supriya had raved about *Victoria's Secret*, but Shaili didn't know if there was a branch close to where she lived. She wanted to surprise Sadhil with a black, sheer, silk negligee with a plunging neckline. She had it all planned. Leila just needed to give her the name of the store. Leila squirmed as she shared the store details with Shaili because Shaili was willingly pouring out more information than Leila would have liked to hear. But she allowed her out of amenity. Internally, Leila wanted to run away from Sadhil's apartment. To change the topic, Leila suggested they eat some cheesecake.

As they both entered the kitchen, Shaili showed Leila where the plates were kept. Lost in her thoughts, Shaili forgot she had a cheesecake server at home. She took out a butter knife and a big spoon and scooped into the cheesecake. Before she realized, the crème squirted out of the dessert and onto her shirt. Leila smirked. That's when it dawned on Shaili that she had forgotten to put the cheesecake inside the refrigerator. Leila had bought a fresh piece, and with the high temperatures that day, the filling had melted. Slowly, Leila burst into laughter. It was like a sprinkle of ingenuous gurgles. In trying to wipe away the crème from her shirt, Shaili had managed to squirt and pour more crème on her face and hands. Shaili wanted payback for her mockery. She took a handful of the gooey decadence and smudged it onto Leila's face. Leila retaliated. They were like frivolous six-year-olds on a sugar high. Leila had declared a cheesecake war and they were holding each other tight, trying to slap the cake on each other.

One thing led to another. No one remembered who made the first move, but before they knew it, they were kissing, moaning, and tearing at each other's clothes in the unused nuptial bed Sadhil had bought—the same bed where Shaili had never sat with Sadhil let alone make love.

Neither of them was thinking consciously. Shaili had never felt such ecstasy. She wasn't shy or infuriated any longer. For the first time in her life, she felt content.

The following evening, Leila had invited Shaili over for dinner. She had cooked authentic Persian cuisine and made several rounds of *cosmopolitans* (because Supriya couldn't wait for Shaili to try the real drink) and vodka martinis. Leila had asked Shaili to bring a change of clothes. It was implied that Shaili would spend the night. Though neither woman ever brought it up, they were both uncomfortable with hanging out at Sadhil's apartment. It felt like they would be cheating on a decent guy.

Shaili was in a different zone. She had never felt more complete, but she felt awkward about the intimate moments. Spending the night was one thing; waking up the next morning and placing her arms around Leila was another. She felt exposed. It didn't come easily to her and Leila didn't push her either. Shaili did think about Sadhil. How would he react to the scenario? She felt like a contrite sinner when she thought of him. It seemed as though the two women had slinked into Sadhil's heart and stolen his wishes. They solved crossword puzzles and read the newspaper, together, over coffee, toast and eggs the next morning. Shaili was surprised by how comfortable she felt in such an uncomfortable arrangement.

Around midnight, the day before Sadhil was to return, Shaili woke up to realize that life wasn't as it seemed to be. She struggled to interpret the happenings of the past couple of days. She looked at Leila sleeping peacefully and established that however much she tried, she couldn't stop being who she was. It had taken her twenty plus years to come to terms with her identity, and she couldn't go back to denying the truth about herself. Not any longer. Did she really like Leila or was Leila just assisting her in figuring out herself? Shaili couldn't distract herself from exploring the reasons behind the "new" her. Was she born this way? Was her father responsible?

The only man she knew growing up was Suresh Kapoor. He was an egotistical fool, who had turned Shaili into a man-hater. She believed he was an uncompassionate man who laid out everyone's life plans. She just assumed that's what all men did. So, all her life, she believed men were animals who wanted to exploit and repress women. There was a reason she hated them. That's why she could never give Sadhil a chance even though he continued to put up with her. Shaili cried, for the first time, for Sadhil. She felt responsible for ruining his life even though it wasn't premeditated. Shaili realized that she didn't love Sadhil or any other man. The revelation brought her a blend of tranquility and tribulation. She decided it was time she spoke with Sadhil.

Sadhil returned, per his promise, by the end of the week. He had tried to call Shaili from Chicago, but she didn't answer her phone. He thought she was probably still angry with him and that's why hadn't taken his calls. Sadhil couldn't wait to be home and end the row between him and Shaili. He had bought two tickets to a dinner cruise for the following Saturday. He hoped the stars in the sky along with champagne and soft music might alter Shaili's mood.

Shaili didn't contact Sadhil the entire week for different reasons. She had spent most of her time at Leila's. Even though Shaili saw his missed calls when she got home, she didn't know what to say. Nothing could stop the storm that was going to shake up their lives.

Much to Sadhil's shock, Shaili was home when he reached the apartment. It was pouring outside and he figured the torrential rains had kept Shaili indoors. But he saw the table was laid with his favorite food, and Shaili was standing in the hallway with a half a smile on her face accentuating her trembling lips. Shaili had wanted to talk to him as soon as he returned. But she knew that he would be home around dinnertime and probably be hungry. That is why she was waiting for Sadhil near the entrance. She wanted to ask him—food first or conversation. She wasn't trying to be cruel by raising his hopes and then dashing them to the ground. But Sadhil misinterpreted her actions. He felt butterflies at the pit of his stomach. He couldn't hide the hope discharging out of his dimple. It was finally beginning to feel like he was married and that someone cared for him. Shaili was the person he had fallen in love with. He felt like a giddy-headed teenager after his first kiss.

Shaili gave him a tight hug. He was pleasantly shocked. He loved the fragrance of her deodorant mixed with her own smell. Her skin was pressed against his shirt. He hugged her back. He wanted to say so many things. Ask her so many questions. Kiss her. Sadhil wasn't a loud romantic, but today, he wanted to stand on his patio and fawn over his beloved and sing a ballad for the moon. He wanted to announce to the world that he was mirthful—a happily married man. But his thoughts were interrupted when he felt Shaili shuddering. His shirt felt a little wet. Then he heard a soft, suppressed whimper. He withdrew himself from Shaili. She had large droplets of tears streaming down her cheeks. Before Sadhil could ask anything, Shaili said, "I am sorry." She couldn't look him in the eye.

"Baby, don't cry. I am sorry too." Sadhil couldn't believe the words leaving his lips. He had always wanted to call Shaili "Baby," "Pumpkin," "Sweetheart," "Shailu," and so many other nicknames.

"I have done you wrong." Shaili couldn't look at Sadhil. The veil of remorse hindered her vision.

"Don't worry about it. I was harsh too. I shouldn't have done..."

"You don't understand." Shaili didn't wait for Sadhil to finish his sentence.

"I do, sweetheart. We both said things in the heat of the moment. You shouldn't take those words seriously."

"It's not just that, Sadhil."

"Let's put all this behind us. Please Shailu."

"I can't."

"But, Shails. We aren't the first couple to argue."

"I know."

"Darling, fights between a husband-wife happen in every marriage. They are practically mandatory for relationships to last." Sadhil wiped Shaili's cheeks. He stroked her mole with affection. There was a yearning in his eyes to kiss it and run his hands through Shaili's bountiful hair. He wanted to feel her soft lips against his clean-shaven chin.

Shaili, slowly, removed his hand. She paused for a second and took a deep breath.

"Sadhil, what if someone doesn't want to be husband-wife?"

"What? What do you mean?"

"What if one of us is not meant to be a part of this?"

"You can't take an isolated incident from last week and…"

"I am not. I am just saying."

"Shailu, sweetie. Think with a cool head."

"I am Sadhil. It might…"

"What happened?"

"I've had time to think. It might be best for both of us if we go our separate ways."

"What has changed in the last week? I thought we were getting along, not two badly at that."

"It's …umm…it's just that…"

"I love you. Right from the moment we met. You know why?"

"Sadhil, I…"

"Tell me what I can do differently. I don't want to lose you."

"I don't love you!" Shaili said it out unexpectedly. She knew there was no easy way to express it, especially when Sadhil was determined to not listen to her. Sadhil was dismayed. He looked vacantly at Shaili. He wasn't expecting to hear that, not in the least.

"I am sorry. I truly am. You can hate me. Hit me. Abuse me. Kill me. I have done you wrong, but I don't love you."

"I heard that the first time." Sadhil's body language had changed. Shaili felt intimidated. He wasn't trying to scare her, but her guilt misinterpreted the tone of his sentence. The equation was altered. All of a sudden, Sadhil had the upper hand in the conversation.

"Are you in love with someone else?"

Shaili stared at the floor.

"I asked you something. Are you in love with someone else?"

"Maybe. I don't know."

"Don't know? What the fuck is wrong with you?"

"I…I…I am not sure."

"Not sure? Really!"

"I mean. Not yet. Like, I don't know yet."

"How many people's life will you ruin, Shaili?"

Shaili remained silent and guiltily stared at the floor.

"Do I know this person?"

"A little."

"Do you have a straight answer for anything?"

"It's com…complicated."

"Well, I am not going anywhere, so tell me."

"Sadhil, I can't…Can we please talk about it later? First…first eat your favorite food. I got kung pao chicken for you." Shaili realized the idiocy of her words as soon as they left her mouth. She pined for her mother and Supriya.

"Let's see. You just told me that our marriage is over. But that's not important because you want me to stuff my face with food! What kind of a sick, rotten person are you?"

Sadhil asked Shaili to look into his eyes and tell him the truth. Shaili was quiet as the night. She was coming to terms with the truth herself. Sometimes, when with Leila, she'd pinched herself to confirm all this was happening to her. She still could not comprehend it all.

"Does this person live in the U.S.?"

"Sadhil don't do this."

"Don't pretend like you care about me. Answer my question!"

"Yes."

"Did you marry me just so you could be near this person?"

"No!"

"Because your parents forced you to marry me?"

"No."

"You married me because I was your passport to be near your lover? Huh?"

"No. God. No. I would never do that to you."

"Well, we have both seen what you are capable of doing so let's not go down that road."

Shaili knew she had earned Sadhil's sternness. His intonation was curt like the rain hitting the windowpane that evening. He sounded like an ogre, and she was responsible for it.

"Where did you meet this person?"

"In New York."

"How? When?"

"When you were at work."

"Nice! When I was keeping long hours, slogging my ass off and earning money to fulfill your needs. So I could give you a comfortable life, take you to Paris on our honeymoon. And you were shacking up."

"Sadhil…please…"

Sadhil was almost scared to verbalize the thoughts he'd internalized. But he couldn't not know. Not today.

"Has this person touched you?"

"Sadh…"

"Oh My God! You fucking wouldn't let me come near you all these weeks while you were whoring yourself out. I feel disgusted just talking to you."

"It's not like that."

"Sure! You jerked your hand away when I touched your ring finger. Or what about the time when you were crossing the street near Central Park? You didn't see the 'Don't Walk' sign, and you were going to be run over by a bus had I not stopped you. What was my fault? I'd held your shoulder to stop you from crossing. But you, in your sanctimonious tone, had berated me for 'being an opportunist.' You had screamed your guts out in public like I was raping you. When I asked you about your over-reaction, you'd apologized unattachedly like I was in the wrong. Every single time I tried getting close to you, you built a fortress around yourself. I thought you squirmed at the newness of our marriage. I gave you fucking space because I believed your aloofness would go away with time. Given your issues with intimacy, I even considered if you were molested as a child. But it was none of that, was it?? You deliberately closed all doors to any discussions. Now I know why. You have a man, someone you met less than two weeks ago, fucking you! Aren't you a hypocrite?!?!

"I can explain."

"Explain what? Why every single night I crashed on the sofa while you locked yourself in the bedroom? Our conversations were monologues of me asking about your day. Why I ate dinner alone, night after night? Or why you didn't want to be a part of my life or meet my friends? Or why you made me feel like a criminal for marrying you. Not once did I wake up to a smile from you. I tried and tried and couldn't figure out what the problem was. I drove myself crazy looking for a reason. What

I could do to welcome you into my life and to be able to see you happy for twenty four hours at a stretch."

"Sadhil…the problem was me…is me…"

"Tell me something. Have you two been together in this apartment, in my house, our house?"

"You are making this harder on yourself."

"Don't patronize me!" Sadhil had blood in his eyes. Shaili thought he was going to hit her. But she couldn't have been more wrong about him, yet again. Sadhil had to restrain his emotions, so he wouldn't break down.

"Yes, we have."

"Where? Where did you? Huh?"

"Please don't make me."

"In the bed? *Our* bed? The places you and I had moments? The jacuzzi? This bloody sofa where I longed for you? I want to know the truth."

"Sadhil, I am sorry. I swear I hadn't planned it this way."

"Shaili. I hate lies! And I abhor liars!"

"I feel bad, Sadhil."

"Don't pity me!"

"Sadhil, I have hurt you. I know. You have every right to feel the way you do. I have failed miserably as a human being. But you have no idea how dreadful I feel. I didn't plan to wreck your life or mine. I promise you, I never lied to you. When I met you in Pune, I was clouded. And maybe I agreed to marry you to get out of my parents' abusive home, but it wasn't with the purpose of betraying you. I was struggling with my feelings for you. I wasn't sure what was obscuring my judgment. Maybe it was my resentment towards my father or being pushed into getting married at such a young age or the phobia of moving to a new country leaving behind the familiar. So I was mean. But you were so empathetic towards me. Ironically, your compassion made everything more complex. See, I had grown up to despise men. It was easier that way. But I admired and liked you—a man—something I wasn't used to."

Shaili sobbed loudly. She allowed her anguish to overflow veraciously, like the flooded Ganges; she had held it back, with a societal barrier, for twenty-two years. She told Sadhil about her family and the circumstances at the Kapoor household. Sadhil had calmed down a little by now. He hadn't exonerated Shaili, but he felt a lot less vengeful. He almost pitied her after listening to her story about her life.

But his mind went back to Shaili's deeds. A broken family didn't justify her actions. It was still no excuse to cheat on her husband and demolish her chances of establishing a home. Before Sadhil could say anything, Shaili looked at him.

"Sadhil, I think, you deserve the truth more than anyone."

"You think?"

"Sadhil I…I…"

"What now? Are you pregnant with this bastard's child?"

"Please stop."

"Don't you dare tell me what to do!"

"I am not expecting."

She drew a deep breath and said, "I am a lesbian."

"Yeah. You are les… What?"

"I am gay, Sadhil."

"No! Can't…We are married…I would have…But…You didn't…"

"I am sorry, but it's true. I've denied it for too long."

"Sure. Whatever."

"Sadhil, are you okay?"

Sadhil didn't acknowledge Shaili's confession. He didn't know what to think. He tried but couldn't come to terms with what Shaili had to say. Here he had wanted to beat his competitor to a pulp for messing up his marriage, but what would he do or say to another woman. He felt stupid for not noticing any signs sooner. Shaili being gay was never a reason he'd considered for their dysfunctional relationship. He asked himself if he was in denial. He was instantly reminded of his friend Mike, whose wife had left him for another woman. The friends had teased him saying, "Dude, were you so bad that you completely turned her off men?" or "Dude, you can't even ask her what she has that you don't? I mean, we all know what she has is a whole lot different." All of a sudden, the clichéd humor stung him. Sadhil wasn't prepared for this news. He didn't know whether to feel more or less infuriated. He wasn't sure if he could even address Shaili as an infidel. He would always wonder, like Shaili, if her father was responsible.

"Since when have you known? That you were, you know…that… you…" Sadhil couldn't even form a lucid sentence.

"I didn't know, until recently. It was an accident. I was fragile after our fight. Right after you left for Chicago. And one thing led to another. I know my actions are unpardonable. You might think of me as covetous. But I honestly tried to be like the others—the traditional, Indian girl Ma wanted me to be. I swear I did. Cook alu gobhi for you. Give you children. But I couldn't pretend, Sadhil. I just couldn't. Not any longer. I felt suffocated in my own body."

"And is Leila your girlfr…partn…lover…whatever the term is?"

Shaili froze. She said, "How did you know it was her?"

"I am so stupid!" Sadhil's right hand cupped his head while his left hand rested awkwardly on his hip. "It was obvious to a blind man if I didn't have my trust blinder on. I mean, the only time you seemed happy in New York was after you'd spent the day with Leila. And, you never once let me meet her! As if you were hiding something and that I might actually derive a conclusion. Here I thought you'd finally made a friend as close as Supriya, and you didn't want me intruding on your girl-time. Men have their poker buddies whom they never introduce to their families. I should have seen it. I feel like a fucking retard!" Sadhil clenched his teeth and right hand.

"Sadhil…but…" Shaili was still wrapping her brains around Sadhil's guess.

"Are you two together?"

"NO! I mean, I don't know. It's all too new."

"God, Shaili. You are something else."

There was a moment of silence. Sadhil collected his thoughts. A lot had to be done. All the lives needed to be rearranged. His throat screamed for mercy. He turned to Shaili and said, "I will speak with the lawyers on Monday to draw up the divorce papers." He choked a little.

"I don't want anything."

"Just because you failed in your duties as a wife doesn't mean I have to reciprocate with the same pettiness. What's yours is yours." Sadhil wasn't trying to be despicable, but he couldn't hide his raw wounds. "I want you to be happy. I am trying. But I can't have you around for long. It's hard. I want you to look for another arrangement. The alimony should help you get on your feet sooner than later. If you'd prefer, we don't have to tell your parents or mine the reason behind the divorce. It might be too soon, and they won't probably get it anyway." Sadhil didn't want Shaili to know that he feared what the families would tell him. That he was a weak man who couldn't control his wife.

"Why are you so kind to me?" Shaili was overwhelmed with Sadhil's thoughtfulness.

"I am trying to prove that Lolita had betrayed Humbert even before he had abducted her. The truth about her came to light when it was too late." Sadhil said in a solemn pitch.

Shaili didn't want to retort. Sadhil hadn't made an erroneous comment. She had always thought of herself as the victim, like Lolita and of Sadhil as Humbert. But how was she different from Lolita, the seductress who played Humbert and made the world commiserate with her? In the new light, she too wanted to sympathize with Humbert.

"Do you forgive me?"

"You are kidding, right? It's too soon."

"I understand. But will you ever absolve me?"

"I am not sure if I ever will completely. Maybe with time. Who knows?"

"Will you at least try?"

"Don't push it, Shaili. I know what it feels like to not be with the person you love. I guess, in a strange way, I understand. But just don't push it."

"Do you hate me, Sadhil?"

"I don't. I don't think I ever can. But in all honesty, you have killed my competence to trust."

Shaili hugged Sadhil and wept. He didn't hold her back or say anything. Sadhil quietly mourned the death of his love. It was pouring and gurgling outside, but the combined downpour in all of the New York City boroughs couldn't have compared to the tears shed in the Kapoor-Sethi household that night—some visible and others unseen.

Over a period, the divorce proceedings took place, but there was no drama involved. Shaili and Sadhil parted on amiable terms, but Sadhil expressed his apathy about staying in touch with Shaili. He sold his apartment on the Upper East Side and moved to Tribeca, closer to work. As fate would have it, Tribeca was the neighborhood where Shaili would eventually settle down as well. Sadhil's old apartment had too many bad memories in it. The good ones were created by Shaili and Leila, which he couldn't get out of his mind. Every item in his apartment mocked him. Sadhil immersed himself in work. Several women expressed interest in being with him. After all, he was the perfect man. He dated a few women, eventually, but he never married again. He knew Shaili took away with her the side of him that could implicitly trust another woman.

Sadhil and Shaili decided not to clarify the reason for their separation to either side of the families. He didn't want society bemoaning his ex-wife or judging their failed relationship. Sadhil had been cautiously stingy with his words and told everyone, "It just didn't work out." Even without him disclosing any facts, his mother had spread calumnies and believed Shaili must have been the problem. She'd said, "You can never trust Pune girls and Pune weather." He'd muttered to her if that were the case, why was he introduced to one?

From the alimony Sadhil paid Shaili, she moved into her own place, a studio apartment on 125th Street and Broadway. Her apartment was close to her graduate school. After finishing her bridge-up classes, Shaili pursued masters in journalism. She won partial scholarship to the two-year program and worked a night job at a radio station. She interned with a local newspaper to get an insight into the world of journalism and to network with her peers. Shaili barely slept or ate for those couple of years but she didn't mind the struggle. It got her mind off whatever had happened. But she was finally happy, doing what her heart had desired all along, but her brain had chosen to shun.

After graduating from school, a reputed New York newspaper hired her. She earned a name for herself and gradually won awards. Over the years, she would rise above the ranks and become the editor-in-chief at this publication. Shaili also wrote two books that delved into her personal journey from an honest perspective.

Leila had asked Shaili to move in with her, but Shaili had declined. She had an undeniable pride. She appreciated Leila's offer, but she didn't want to depend on anyone ever again or use anyone's support, even if emotionally. She had taken enough from Sadhil. And her father had taken enough from her. She needed to know that she could survive on her own.

But she eventually dated Leila and promised to live with her once she was financially independent. That was the timeline she had in mind about informing Ma of her unconventional decision about Leila. Leila would then make a trip to India because Shaili was forbidden. But until then, it was living on a tight budget and burning the midnight oil. She ate *Top Ramen* noodles for years. And it tasted divine. It was bought from her own sweat and blood. Not her father's arrogant charity or Sadhil's kind paycheck.

She often thought about Sadhil and the little things he did for her. He'd remembered that the semi-colon was her favorite punctuation mark because it intrigued the reader with its incomplete thought. It was kind of like her life, she'd believed at the time. She felt indebted to him. She wondered what he was up to now. Was he dating anyone? Maybe married and had kids? He was suitable husband material—competent in every way. She hoped and prayed he was settled because she knew he was a great guy and that it would be a tragedy if a perfect man like Sadhil was dealt an imperfect ending. In her prayers, she wished him well always.

"I am sorry for everything you have been through, Shails. I didn't want to point fingers, but my gut instinct told me that you had initiated the breakup. Not that you ever told me. I asked you several times, but you never said anything. That is how you get when you believe you're guilty. I told Mhatre it must have been you. I said the same to Aunty too. Even before I guessed you'd left Sadhil for another woman."

"What made you so sure?"

"You seemed antsy about the wedding all along. Like something was eating you up from the inside. From whatever interaction I had with Sadhil, he'd seemed mature and caring. When he was still married to you, without your knowledge, he would call your mother and me and ask us about your likes and dislikes. The day after your wedding, he'd driven down to your parents' place and picked up a thermos of Pune-style coffee, so you would wake up to at least something recognizable."

"Sadhil did that?"

"Not that it would change anything today, but yes, he did. Most men don't care as much, Shails. I told you marriage was a commitment of a lifetime that needed to be made with the head and heart and not by rebelliousness. Your hatred was for your father, but you spat venom on an innocent bystander."

Before Shaili could respond, Suresh Kapoor and Leila showed up with four cups of coffee—two per person. Suresh Kapoor handed one of the cups to Shaili and the other to Supriya. Shaili stepped out of the car while Leila gave Suresh Kapoor a cup, which he generously accepted. It would remain a mystery to Shaili and Supriya why Suresh Kapoor looked much more relaxed around Leila after their trip to the teastall. The dynamics changed, and Shaili followed Suresh Kapoor to the water, so they could finish their conversation.

11

As the Kapoor family walked back towards the lake, Shaili thanked him for the coffee. He nodded and took a sip of the hot beverage. The rain had seemed to diminish by now. As Shaili cupped her hands with her soul drink, Suresh Kapoor looked at her.

"Tell me something."

"Ask away."

"Why did you marry Sadhil?"

"Again? Are we not done yet with that chapter of my life?"

"I thought we are here today because you wanted to talk."

"Fine. I don't know. Maybe to get out, escape." Shaili didn't sound irate, just factual.

Suresh Kapoor looked bewildered. Shaili unfolded what was stored in her memory for all these years. "The toxicity of your words corroded me like sulfuric acid every day that I lived there. I tried so hard to appease you, but nothing was ever enough. Just nothing. I know it sounds melodramatic, but it hurt to even breathe around you because you would find fault with everything I did.

"I was mystified by your neuroticism. After spending hours in the garage, helping you with your business, you never once verbally thanked me. But without asking for it, you had bought me a *Kinetic Honda* when I started college. I was given the go-ahead to drive the petite car, the *Maruti 800*, if Ma needed to get somewhere but not even talk to the parking attendant if he was a man.

"As a child, I couldn't comprehend that the problem lay with you and not me. Your moodiness had me convinced that I wasn't good enough for anything, and it broke my heart. A second place in track events would embarrass you and you would publicly announce, '*Bloody Goan blood she has. That's why she doesn't do well in sports.*' In my third grade, when I got ninety five percent marks overall in my final exams and topped all the three sections, you'd screamed, 'Where did you lose the other five percent? You're not focusing enough!' I withdrew myself into a shell.

"I felt incompetent and decided to win your approval at any cost. I thought maybe partaking in the *non-girly* activities would make you proud of me. So, unlike other girls my age, who played with dolls all day, I started to help you out in your garage. I had grease on my face instead of makeup and bruises on my knees instead of bangles around my wrists. I played sports and was soon addicted to cricket.

"I remember it like it was yesterday. In 1983, when India won the World Cup, remember the pair of us was listening to the scores in the garage when the victory was announced? You had hugged me and picked me and twirled me around, for the first time, and maybe the last as far as I could remember. In my mind, your conduct that day was a testament that you would accept me if I acted like a boy.

"After that episode, I took it upon myself to update you on cricket scores especially when India was playing Pakistan and winning, in the hope that you would shower a half-smile recognition for my efforts, if not hold me in your arms. But you continued to act impassive. I had heard that many men preferred having sons to carry on their family name. I had kept trying to be the son you didn't have. 'Maybe he doesn't like me because I am a girl,' I had confessed to Ma. But Ma had shushed me like all the other times. I wish she hadn't. She should have spoken with me. At least made me believe I wasn't the reason for the unhappiness in the house. Covering up her family's filth didn't help anyone including herself.

"The difference between you both is that you never stopped blaming me, and she didn't stop you from blaming me. In the end, I suffered. I was confounded, scared, angry, and miserable. Eventually, there was a blurry line between what you, maybe, desired and what I had become." Shaili's eyes welled up.

"You probably don't recall, but I had bawled my eyes out when you forgot my seventh birthday. Ma, Supriya, Tanisha and I had eaten a gourmet meal of aloo parathas, prawn vindaloo, alu gobhi, peas pulao, and kheer, at home, after having waited for you for a few hours. Ma had consoled me, but no words were comforting enough. Maybe because her only words were, 'Don't cry my child. Your father loves you.' If she'd taught me to deal with problems instead of denying them, maybe the Sadhil chapter would never have been written." Shaili paused for a second. "You came home sloshed that night, again, ready to pass out. On seeing the left over meal, you scolded Ma for spending all that money on a lavish, weekday dinner. You derided her by yelling that she didn't know the value of money. You called her names, including squanderer, which was the biggest misrepresentation of Ma's traits. I heard the entire conversation and felt terrible about my birthday falling on a weeknight. I was confident that had my birthday fallen on a Sunday, you, my father, would have acted differently. After all, Sunday lunches and dinners, the day you were home from work, were five-course meals."

"I do remember the incident. What you didn't know was that I was filled with regret the next day. Though I had intentionally skipped your birthday, I hadn't intended to rebuke Meena, in front of you on your birthday, for the extravagant celebration. It wasn't about the money, and your ma knew it. I was strict with you because I wanted you to be realistic—life isn't a bed of roses." Suresh Kapoor sighed at the lake.

"So, you agree? You hated me even before you found out I was gay. Even when I was a child, you were cold to me. Why?" There was a creepy silence for a few minutes. Shaili looked adamantly into Suresh Kapoor's eyes beseeching him to answer the most important question of her life. That one unanswered query had altered Shaili's views on relationships, love, and trust.

Suresh Kapoor drew a deep breath, as if unleashing a sinister secret from his emotional chamber, and said, "I didn't hate you; it was who and what you reminded me of."

"And that would be? What? What? Tell me. What did I remind you of?" Shaili searched for lucidity in her moment of madness.

"*Betrayal*!" The minute Suresh Kapoor said those words, the dormant rage in his eyes oozed out like angry lava from the crater of an active volcano, but he didn't tell Shaili about his wife's tales. To Suresh Kapoor, Shaili was a constant memento of Suresh Kapoor's failures. She embodied his lack of control over his wife. No one knew that he would rape and hit Mrs. Kapoor only when drunk, never otherwise. It was his way of establishing his manhood and forgetting the cruel truth about his own life. The woman he had fought the world for was impure. In his eyes, his wife had deliberately belittled him.

"Your problems were with Ma! I am not arguing about them any longer. I can imagine how difficult it must have been for you. But what was my fault? I was punished my entire life because I was symbolic of something you despised? Something I had no control over or even had a hand in? How mature!"

"Who said anything about your mother? Nothing like that. Watch your mouth!"

"Stop defending her! I know everything." The certainty in Shaili's voice was inimitable. "Were you going to tell me about it at all today?" She sounded as if the secret service, of personal relationships, had made "indubitable disclosure," on her mother's past, into her ears.

Suresh Kapoor realized that Shaili knew the truth he and his wife, Meena Kapoor, had denied their entire lives. He turned to her, "I was trying to protect you. But how did you find out?"

"Ma told Leila about it."

"Meena spoke with Leila? When?"

"When Leila met her."

"When did they meet?"

"It was on one of Leila's business trips to India."

"They met each other? Even if I tried, I couldn't compete with your dead mother, now could I?" Suresh Kapoor shook his head at another secret his wife kept from him. But he didn't seem angry. He turned to Shaili, "Did they get along?"

"Who?"

"Meena and Leila?"

"Of course they did! Like a house on fire!"

"How did they meet?"

"Leila first met Ma about ten or eleven years ago in Mumbai. As an artist, Leila was on a tour exhibiting her art in several cities in India. When Leila was working on an exhibit in Mumbai, around the same time, Ma was in the city attending Nisha Mirchandani's wedding."

"Where was I?" Suresh Kapoor asked loudly as he tried to remember his whereabouts from over a decade ago.

"You couldn't make it to that wedding. You had some work-related deadlines. It worked out well because that's how I could plan the *Meet the Mom trip,*" added Shaili sheepishly. "I had managed to convince Leila to help execute it."

"Ma, my friend Leila is going to Mumbai. I am sending a Mother's Day gift for you."

"You didn't have to, beta. Being able to talk to you is the biggest gift for me."

"Ma, no clichéd dialogues please. Accha listen, it's a diamond pendant that symbolizes us. It has a woman surrounding her child in a circle of love."

"Why are you wasting money, beta? My days of wearing jewelry are gone. Where will an old woman like me wear jewelry to anyway?"

"Stop your melodrama. It comes with a nice, thin chain so Hitler… umm…sorry, Old Man Suresh won't be able to see it. You won't have to answer his questions about 'Who gave it to you?' 'Where you find the money?' and other blah-blah-blah."

In their first meeting, Leila and Mrs. Kapoor didn't have much to say to each other. There was an awkward silence when Leila handed over the jewelry and the packet, containing a letter and money, from Shaili. It read, "Ma, I am sending you a thousand dollars. Leave that wretched old man. Just walk away. I will send you more if you need it. Why don't you move here with me?"

"Shaili is such a silly girl," she grinned while wiping her moist eyes. "She wants me to leave Pune. She knows I can't." Leila didn't know what to make of those confessions, so she stood quietly through them all.

"Laie-la." Mrs. Kapoor mispronounced Leila's name, but Leila didn't say anything.

"Yes."

"Laie-la, how is Shailu? It's just that I have not seen her in years. Not after her marriage or you know." Mrs. Kapoor tried not to cry. "Has she put on some weight or not? I hope so. I am not there to cook for her, no. She tells me she eats almonds and takes care of herself, but I don't know if that's enough." Mrs. Kapoor rambled on for a few more minutes.

It was obvious to Leila Mrs. Kapoor yearned for her daughter. The maternal rawness in her personality appealed to the abandoned child in Leila. "She misses you too." Leila assured Mrs. Kapoor. She said what Mrs. Kapoor wanted to ask and longed to hear.

"You know, Shaili likes the laddoos I make. She also likes my prawn vindaloo, but she told me non-vegetarian items aren't permissible through U.S. Customs. But will you take some laddoos for her on your way back? I'll make them fresh and pack them nicely. Please."

"Sure, Mrs. Kapoor." Leila liked the refreshing simplicity in Mrs. Kapoor's personality.

Mrs. Kapoor reciprocated Leila's kindness with a loving smile and a request, "Call me Aunty. Not Mrs. Kapoor. You are my Shailu's friend. You're like a daughter to me." Mrs. Kapoor's appeal didn't come as a shock to Leila. Shaili had told her that in the Indian culture, everyone from the parents' generation qualified to be addressed as Aunty and Uncle. Leila said, "Sure."

As time went by, Leila's trips to Bombay and Pune became more frequent. Her work earned her fabulous reviews, which brought along global opportunities. Eventually, J'Studio Art Gallery in Pune and Guild Art Gallery in Mumbai partnered up with the Asian Arab Association in New York to work on art relating to the Indus Valley civilization and the ancient civilization of Mesopotamia and Leila was commissioned to create a variety of pieces for this project.

Leila had met with Mrs. Kapoor on all her business trips to India. She saw Supriya too a few times. Supriya had wanted to meet Leila more often, but given her personal commitments, she couldn't always spend a lot of time with Leila. Supriya, in her humorous and vivacious tone, would say to Leila, "My life these days is focused on three Cs: cooking for my husband, caring for my two children, and companionship for my aging in-laws."

"You shouldn't talk like that, beta." Mrs. Kapoor would say to Supriya.

"True, no, Aunty?" Supriya would elbow Mrs. Kapoor's arm.

Leila would smile but not say much.

Leila tried to stay a few extra days in Pune so she could see more of Mrs. Kapoor. She knew how much it meant to Shaili that she and her mother spend time together. But what Leila didn't share with anyone was that she was grateful for Mrs. Kapoor's company. It was around Mrs. Kapoor that her general, indifferent attitude would dissipate. The hungry orphan in her revered every embrace and all the pampering.

Mrs. Kapoor felt contented around Leila. The mother in her, who pined for her older daughter, liked hearing stories about Shaili. She would cook Leila Shaili's favorite dishes. In some ways, it brought her closer to Shaili. She would sneak into the gallery, with a small container of homemade Indian food like prawn vindaloo with pilaf and sabudaana khichdi, when her husband was at work. She would cup Leila's cheeks with her hands and say, "Laie-la, don't eat restaurant food all the time. It's not good for you. I'll bring you freshly cooked food from home. Shailu mentioned that you don't like very spicy food, so I won't put any chilli. Okay?"

Little did Leila know that she would find a mother in Mrs. Kapoor after having lost her own. She eventually got used to being overfed. Her cheeks filled out a little. She remembered Shaili's tip: Indian mothers express their love through food. If you don't eat, they think you didn't like their cooking. "No" is not an option.

"Ma taught Leila a lot of Indian recipes." Shaili told Suresh Kapoor casually.

"No wonder she was telling the coffee boy how to brew the coffee." Suresh Kapoor spoke with a straight face. Shaili sniggered.

"How did your mother find out about you…as in, you and her…Leila?"

"She had suspected it for a while, I guess. Then one time, on one of Leila's Pune trips, when Leila met up with Ma, she shared the coffee recipe with Leila as if she were a family member. Leila found it odd but didn't make much of it. As Ma shared the guidelines for her coffee, she'd said in a very unruffled tone, *'I know you are not just Shaili's friend, are you?'* Leila was taken aback by Ma's bluntness. She was unsure how to handle her question. She tried to form a lucid response but words evaded her. Supriya, who was supposed to be the designated buffer for such a situation, was at her daughter's school play that afternoon. Leila wanted to walk away from the awkwardness, but the desperation in Ma's voice manacled her pragmatism. Ma searched for an answer in Leila's eyes. *'Tell me no, Laie-la. I need to know my daughter is doing fine. That she is living happily. I didn't mean to, but I took happiness away from her.'* Leila later told me that Ma was choking on her words while wiping her anxiety with her dupatta. Leila, however hard she tried, couldn't deny that the conversation was getting uncomfortable. In her quest to minimize the discommodiousness, the straight shooter in Leila said to Ma, *Aunty, Shaili and I are in a committed relationship.*"

"How did Meena respond?" Suresh Kapoor was trying to find ways of understanding his daughter's choices. He wondered if his dead wife's reaction would help him get a cue.

"Interestingly, Ma had said, *'I have no problems, beta. No need to explain. Sometimes love sees no reasons. It happens. I want my Shailu to be happy. If this is how it is then so be it.'* Ma genuinely surprised Leila. I had prepared her for hullabaloo. It did happen; the mayhem and the what-will-people-say derision eventually came from you and Tanisha, but Ma accepted our relationship without a hitch."

Suresh Kapoor continued to battle his thoughts when Shaili said, "Leila was overwhelmed with Ma's reaction. Her own family had wished her death, but Ma had understood. She had held Ma's hands and thanked her—her forehead bowed to Ma's palms. Ma and Leila had so much to say to each other, but they chose to savor the newly formed perfect but untraditional relationship in tranquility. Leila didn't show her tears but a part of her felt disconcerted—if only her own mother could comprehend why her daughter had selected this course in her life; if only she would accept her with open arms like my mother. Leila hadn't heard from her since the time she had openly admitted the truth about her identity. Her rigid parents, still based in Tehran, had blamed her irreverent actions on America. They didn't want to know that their daughter didn't choose to be different; she was born that way."

"What was your reaction?" Suresh Kapoor had a suspicious look on his face.

"Honestly, I was surprised with the way Ma reacted. I still remember when Leila mentioned her talk with Ma to me; I was carrying a pile of laundered clothes to my closet. The stack slipped from my hands onto the floor, in bafflement. I always speculated why Ma wouldn't emotionally blackmail me."

"What? What do you mean?"

"You know what I mean. Indian moms are incredible at inducing guilt and saying things like, '*I will end my life,*' and inane drama like that. I had expected Ma to be furious or sad or something. But not so amenable, you know. When I pestered Leila, she remained tight-lipped and said, '*Maybe she loves you unreservedly and wants you to be happy.*' I should have known right then that the two women shared something even I wasn't privy to. I was thrilled that Ma and Leila were so at ease with each other, but Ma's immediate acceptance of my choices bugged me. Always."

"It is not that easy for me, but how much do you know about your mother?" Suresh Kapoor interjected suddenly.

"Enough that I am here today, despite our past, Dad."

"When did you find out?" Suresh Kapoor stared at the ground.

"A little before we left New York for Mumbai and Pune. I had just found out about Ma's death and Leila was trying to organize our tickets."

"Shaili." Leila tapped on Shaili's shoulders. "I spoke with the travel agent."

"Uh-huh."

"We are booked on the *Jet Airways* flight to Mumbai this evening. We can take a pre-paid taxi to Pune directly from the airport."

Shaili was lost in her own world. She looked at Leila with expectant eyes, "You and Ma were close, right L? She must have said something to you."

"How do you mean?"

"Like a hint. If something was bothering her…a reason…

Shaili didn't realize that Leila had dodged her question and started to pack.

"Ma wasn't weak. Come on, she put up with Dad. And a bad marriage. So I can't wrap my mind around her suicide."

"Umm…Sometimes…You never…What…"

"Why do you think she killed herself?"

"Can we talk about it on the flight?" Leila sounded firm.

"Why?"

"Because that would be the appropriate place."

"And what do you mean by that?"

"We really need to get going. That's why."

"Wait. Do you know why Ma…Please look at me. What are you hiding???"

"Nothing."

"Swear on me."

"It's just that we need to pack."

"Packing can wait. You know something, don't you?" Shaili closed the top cover of Leila's bag, so she couldn't add anything inside. "So can the rest of the chores. If you know something, please tell me now." Shaili asserted.

Leila threw up her arms in exasperation. "God, you are adamant."

"I am waiting."

"Fine. I am sorry you had to find out this way. I was hoping we could wait until we reached Pune."

"Find what out?"

"There is no easy way to say this, but…"

"But what?" Shaili interrupted.

"Mr. Suresh Kapoor isn't your biological father," Leila confessed softly, fully aware this would upset Shaili immensely.

Shaili dropped to the floor. Leila's words echoed in her ears. She had lost the verve to deal with more surprises today. "Tell me you are lying. L, tell me that Old Man Suresh is my goddamn father." Shaili cried softly.

Leila stood quietly.

She looked at Leila and asked, "Am I adopted?"

"No."

"You are telling me that Ma was a fucking whore? My own mother? That she didn't know who my father was."

"Shaili…listen to me…"

"She was nice to me because she had her own dirty little secret? Didn't she?" Shaili shrieked with incredulity.

Leila didn't know how to calm Shaili down. She didn't think and before she knew it, she slapped Shaili. "Stop it. Don't say another word. You have no idea what your mother went through—just to have you. To protect you, your mother didn't tell you her entire life story."

"What story?"

"Your mother didn't care whom she married. She was a living corpse. She sacrificed her own life for others. True, she never told Mr. Kapoor about her affair and the level of her involvement. She didn't think sharing details of her ex-lover would have any positive effects on her future. She requested Suresh Kapoor that they relocate to Pune. She just wanted to be closer to her heart. In any case the families wouldn't have accepted their inter-caste marriage. They would have had to elope. Might as well have been Pune. When Suresh Kapoor agreed on Pune, Mrs. Kapoor felt indebted. But she paid for that obligation until the day she died."

"Stop talking to me in riddles. Who did she want to be closer to in Pune? What kind of retribution are you talking about?"

Before Leila could have said another word, Shaili asked, "Who was my *father*?"

"Om Khanna." Leila responded calmly.

"Om? Om? Where does he live? What does he do? And why did he break up with Ma?"

"He died before you were born. He was one of Mr. Kapoor's best friends."

Shaili felt the ground beneath her feet slip away. She bewailed the loss of the people she loved and the ones she never met, or would ever get to know. Her heart throbbed with pain when she realized that she was now an orphan. The loss of a parent at any stage for a child is always devastating. But to lose them both, on the same day when cosmically they died over three decades apart, is excruciatingly mindboggling.

"What happened to Om Khanna?"

Leila shared with Shaili what Mrs. Kapoor had told her about Om Khanna. "Mrs. Kapoor and Om Khanna were childhood sweethearts. They knew each other since high school, but it wasn't just puppy love. Om was a few years older than your mother. They were compatible in every which way. Both were good-looking scholars with an astute mind. They were liberals at heart, so when Om asked your mother out, she said a yes right away. But for fear of scandal they never told anyone about their relationship."

"Not even Om Khanna's friends?"

"No. Not even Om's friends."

"Why? That's so bizarre. I tell Supriya everything."

"Firstly, not true. Secondly, those times were different. Your mother and Om Khanna were from dissimilar backgrounds. Inter-caste marriages weren't acceptable. Om knew his friends' shallow mentality. The two couldn't take any chance especially when Om Khanna knew Mr. Kapoor was in love with your mother. Perhaps he didn't trust his friend's young heart."

Mr. Kapoor intervened, "I never told anyone how I felt about your mother. She was way out of my league. She would never have fallen in love with me, a *Bhaloo*. How could Om know? If I knew she was in love with Om, I would have stepped aside. I would have helped them." Mr. Kapoor took off his glasses and pressed the corner of his eyes.

Shaili stood quietly. She believed him. Before she could say anything, he urged her to continue. Shaili repeated Leila's words.

"Time flew. Mrs. Kapoor joined Indraprastha College in Delhi. Om Khanna graduated from the National Defence Academy in Pune. Om and your mother had access to the Delhi Gymkhana Club. When he was in town, they would hang out there. Om introduced her to the world of squash and badminton. He was different from other men who ogled at your mother. Om stimulated her. He liked Meena for the person she was, not the short dresses she wore."

Leila got up to drink a glass of water. It was an insidious effort to ensure Shaili was doing all right. She continued, "The long distance relationship was tough on them. They met when Om was in town on vacation—a few times a year. But they stuck together. Om introduced your mother to Coffee Home. It was the rendezvous for liberal writers in those days. Your mother once told me that she taught Om to dance. Jive was in vogue in India. And she also taught him ballroom dancing. Om needed to be a proficient dancer given his professional background. At the National Defence Academy they had formal black tie events that demanded good hand and eye coordination movements. Om had promised your mother a romantic dance at the Academy once they were married. To practice, they would meet at *Volga* in Connaught Place."

Shaili sat stupefied. All her life, she had known her mother was suffering. But she didn't know all she had given up. There were traits in Ma's character that she wasn't familiar with. Sports? But when Shaili asked her to play tennis, she would make excuses that she could either hold a cooking spoon or a racquet and since food kept their family together, she'd rather stick with that. What else about her mother was hidden from her?

"You are such a prototype of your parents."

"Huh?"

"You get your athletic body and sporty mindset from Om Khanna. Tall like your father. Delicate features like your mother, Mrs. Kapoor always said that you stood out from other babies. You reminded Mr.

Suresh Kapoor of Om Khanna, especially the mole on your cheek. It stood out. The way it did on Om's face. That's why he felt spiteful just looking at you. Your mole taunted him. When you were born, he thought it was a blemish. He tried scrubbing it away.

"Your mother never told you, but she always wanted to be a writer. It was great that Om was stationed in Pune. Pune University had a good program in journalism which your mother had planned to pursue after marriage. It would give her the flexibility to work even with Om's transferable job. Most Air Force bases had a community newspaper."

Shaili stood still for a moment. "What happened then?"

"Your parents had planned to get married. They were just waiting for your mother to complete her undergrad degree."

Then the fateful day happened. Suresh Kapoor and his four close friends Afzal, Om, Kapil, and Aurobind were passing by *Lala's*, the community grocery store. Om Khanna was a Punjabi boy from Chandigarh. Mrs. Kapoor was purchasing besan bhujiya and talking to the owner. She put her high-pitched transistor next to her ears and leapt with exhilaration when England's team lost their key batsman to an Indian bowler, an anomaly those days. Her skirt just about touched her knees and moved capriciously every time she jumped.

"Hey look. It's Meena. Poetry in motion," whispered Aurobind the poet.

"*Kitthey*?" asked Kapil, while loutishly bending his knees slightly to adjust his crotch.

In broken Punjabi, Aurobind replied, "*Utthey.*" He pointed in Mrs. Kapoor's direction. Her back was now facing them.

"Oy yaar, kya soni lag rahi hai." Kapil licked his lips and smacked them after making the raucous comment.

Afzal, Om, and Suresh looked discomposed with Kapil's remarks, but Kapil couldn't be bothered. He continued with his prattling. "*Arrey waah*! I like how spicy she looks. Just like that besan bhujiya packet in her hand." Kapil ran his hands through his hair and made moaning sounds. Om urged him to stop, several times, politely. But the aggravation on Suresh's face was apparent. His eyebrows were furrowed. He tried to control his sentiments but Kapil wouldn't stop hooting. Thankfully Meena couldn't hear him from the distance. Aurobind smiled awkwardly; Afzal looked away and began to walk towards the street end; Om asked Kapil, once again, to end the nonsense; but Suresh had a meltdown. He walked up to Kapil.

"Enough! How dare you?" Suresh clenched his fist and brought it close to Kapil's face, an inch away from his nose.

Kapil tapped Suresh's chest and said, "Or what? Haan? What will you do Bhaloo? Just chill."

"Just don't! It won't be pretty!" Suresh was stern.

Kapil was genuinely surprised. "After all these years, our friendship means nothing? You'll break our friendship for that Goan slut? Waah, bhai, waah. You motherf..."

"Enough. Stop fighting, you two!" Om intervened. Om had always known that Suresh liked Meena. Just the way he looked at her spoke volumes of his crush. Om often teased Meena about her secret admirer. Meena Kapoor, Meena D'souza before marriage, was the modern girl every guy liked. She was sweet, petite, and completely poised. Her wheatish complexion accentuated the dimple on her chin, which was noticeable from almost five hundred metres. Forget braids; Meena boasted short hair, wore lipstick, dressed in bellbottoms and floral skirts, and was confident talking to boys. And she loved cricket. There was a transistor stuck to her ear at all times if there was a cricket series on. Her unconventional, almost Western upbringing made her the most sought after girl in north and west Delhi. But she didn't have many friends; women were resentful of her and men were intimidated by her.

"Stay out of this, Om," Suresh stretched out his left arm in Om's direction indicating him to stop. Om wasn't sure what Suresh's unrequited love would make him do to impress Meena.

"I am sure it's uncomfortable for that lady." Om asserted himself without making it obvious that Meena D'souza was his girlfriend, and he couldn't stand any man talk dirty about her.

"I will do what I want." Kapil was adamant. He darted back at Suresh "And Bhaloo, what was I saying? Haan, so for that frock-wearing whore, you will hit your best friend! Tell me? Huh! Come on. Take a shot. I dare you!"

That was it. Before Om could do or say anything further, the obsessed lover in Suresh punched Kapil in the face really hard. Kapil's nose started bleeding. Suresh punched Kapil, again. This time, Kapil plummeted to the ground. Suresh was out of control. He kicked Kapil on his thigh and knees. He then bent down and slapped Kapil. "Didn't I tell you to shut up??" Suresh stood up and kicked Kapil in the groin—once, twice, thrice until he lost count. Kapil let out a loud cry that broke Meena's reverie and Om's armor of denial. No one had ever seen this side of Suresh. It scared them a little. Afzal and Aurobind stood frozen for a few minutes. Finally, Om physically restrained Suresh until he calmed down. Om knew that instant Suresh Kapoor wasn't just infatuated with Meena D'souza; he loved her. He was concerned.

Mrs. Kapoor witnessed the drama but didn't know she was the reason behind the chaos. Brawl in her colony was a common occurrence amongst boys of her age. In addition, she was distracted by the scorekeeping of the India-England cricket match. The deal was that the owner would give her free besan bhujiya in return for score updates. On her way out, she bent her head down and walked away but not without a slight, absent-minded grin on her face. Suresh Kapoor assumed she was smiling at him for defending her honor. His friendship with Kapil might have ended that evening but Suresh didn't care. He was ecstatic about new beginnings. He dreamt of spending his life with his beloved, Meena.

But Meena D'souza had actually smiled at Om Khanna. Earlier that day, Mrs. Kapoor had found out that she could graduate a semester early from college. She had given the good news to Om, who had suggested they get married next month. He was scheduled to leave for Pune the next day and he would send the train tickets for your mother. In the meantime, he planned to look for a bigger place and arrange for their wedding. Though nervous and untrained, both Om and Meena were jubilant about their new life.

Om had told Meena about the fight and Suresh's feelings towards her. He was afraid what Suresh would do when he found about their affair. He was especially concerned for her safety because he was going to be away.

Leila sighed. "That was the night you were conceived. Mrs. Kapoor could barely wait for those weeks to pass. She had every detail taken care of. The tickets were bought. University forms filled. A 'sorry' letter addressed to her parents. But the night your mother was scheduled to leave for Pune, Om's plane crashed into Pashan Lake. He and his co-pilot were believed to have been burnt to ashes in the crash. Your mother was devastated. There was no one she could talk to. No one knew about their affair. A little after Om's death, Mr. Kapoor proposed to your mother. She quietly accepted it, his abuse, a life of torment. You know the rest."

"Pashan Lake? My dream. Mom and my trips to the lake when I was a child." Shaili soaked in the revelation.

"How did Dad…Mr. Suresh Kapoor react when Ma told him about me?"

"He was enraged. He hit her until her lip bled. 'Who is the father? Tell me *Kanjari*' he cursed, using the Punjabi word for whore. When confronted, she told him the truth. She loved your real father. She wasn't looking into conning Mr. Kapoor. Her pregnancy was unanticipated. But Mr. Kapoor didn't believe her. He was furious to find out that his wife had slept with one of his closest friends. And now wanted him to raise their illegitimate child. His ego created a self-fulfilling prophecy. He believed that your mother loved him. But her pruriency clouded her judgment, and she got impregnated." Leila unzipped her bag.

"He blamed her for playing him. Mrs. Kapoor offered to walk away but Mr. Kapoor didn't agree. Something inside of him didn't allow him to dump her. Was it the dutiful friend? Or a good human being underneath those layers of menace? Or just immeasurable love for his wife? Or maybe it was societal consciousness. That was the time when he asked Mrs. Kapoor to quit her job. He forbade her from interacting with men. She was told to wear clothes that covered her body from top to toe. But one thing was sure: the news of your arrival made Mr. Kapoor extremely insecure. He changed. He went from being a considerate, romantic to a beast."

12

"Did you ever love Ma after you found out about her past?"

"Why do you think I chose you over Tanisha today?"

"I am not sure I get what you're saying."

"Reconnecting with you meant ending everything with Tanisha, Shaili. You know how your sister feels about you…what you are…"

"I can't believe you would do that for me."

"That answers your question, right?"

Shaili nodded. "Did you forgive her?"

"I have been trying all these years. A little by little every day."

"Then, why did you not leave Ma if you couldn't completely absolve her?"

"Because in our culture, marriage is a commitment of a lifetime. Plus, love and loyalty make us do unthinkable things." Thinking about the days of his youth, the nerves on Suresh Kapoor's hands stiffened. The time he defended Meena's honor or the time when he fought his parents so he could marry her or when he eloped with Meena to Pune only to find out that she was pregnant with one of his best friend's child. And this best friend hadn't had the courtesy to tell Suresh about his relationship with Meena despite knowing how he felt about her, after the fight. But instead of revisiting the hurtful, bookmarked pages from his life, he chose to listen to his daughter today.

Out of nowhere, Shaili screamed, "You couldn't make up your mind, could you? On the one hand you wouldn't leave Ma; on the other, you wouldn't let her live." Suresh Kapoor look startled with Shaili's sudden change of mood. She continued, "You judge me for being indecisive. How are you any different? At least I walked away the minute I learnt the truth. But you, no. God, you are such a fake!"

A little after Shaili blabbered those words, she realized the conversation was headed towards a blackhole if she let the past overpower her, again. She reminded herself that she was here today, out of her own free will, to mend her relationship with the person she grew up calling "Daddy." She bit her lower lip and tapped it with her left index finger. She thought of other ways of connecting with Suresh Kapoor. Her mother would have wanted the same. And anyone who knew Shaili understood that Meena Kapoor and Supriya Mhatre meant the world to her.

Shaili gently stroked her father's right wrist and said, "Dad, I am not here to fight with you. But the fact is that you and I are so disconnected that I needed a few hours at Supriya's to figure out what I was going to say to you. And how I would do it. I practiced my dialogues, but no one tells you the true difference between rehearsal and the real show. The former offers your words solitude to ferment and the mirror is your audience; the latter is accompanied by listeners with pre-conceived notions."

"Don't beat around the bush!"

Shaili looked away from him and sat down, so Mother Earth could embrace her exhausted existence. "I reached Pune earlier this morning and not this afternoon. I had to pinch myself to confirm that I was really in Supriya's, parents' place along with Supriya and Leila. To me, time stood still in the Agarkar manor. The rusted grill outside the windows, peeling beige walls, Supriya and her parents' photographs in old frames, and the smell of coconut were familiar to me, but my world has changed since the last time I stepped into that house."

It felt like it was only yesterday that Shaili and Supriya had sneaked in spicy savories like vada pao and kachi dabeli along with *Wills* cigarettes, and forbidden magazines into this mansion. With Supriya's bedroom door locked, the girls had become slaves to the obsessions of the young adults. Ace of Base's album, *The Sign*, would be playing in the background. With their heads bopping and hips shaking, the girls decided to indulge in a few experimental puffs of cigarettes while giggling at debauche confessions in *Debonair,* a men's magazine, which was originally modeled after *Playboy*. Of course, their inexpertness with cigarettes was accompanied by bouts of coughing and incense burning. One time, the quizzes in another "Mummy-can't-see-magazine" revealed that Shaili would be a tigress "in bed" and Supriya a tigress "in life." With their heads rested on the same pillow and faces turned towards the ceiling fan, they had both laughed so hard, at what they believed to be the absurdity of the words that the cigarette slipped from Supriya's hands and almost burnt the bed sheet.

The more expressive of the two friends, Supriya, was a prankster. When they were sixteen, Supriya had stolen her mother's copy of *Femina* and written a false letter to agony-aunt, Pearl Padamsee, who was a columnist for the magazine. The note read, *"My name is Sheila Sampat. I am an overweight nineteen-year-old woman madly in love with our milkman, Gokul. My parents refuse to accept our love, but I can't live without him. Gokul says if I elope with him, he will keep me happy. What should I do?"* Supriya heard back from Padamsee and was thrilled to see her question answered even though it was accompanied by admonishment: *"All foolish people make such statements. Please grow up and finish your studies first. Lose weight, exercise, and look good. Perhaps, life will change."*

On several occasions, mostly based on Supriya's suggestion, the girls flipped through the zodiac sign and horoscope section of other saucy publications. One of them had predicted that Supriya would be the "Queen of Hearts" in her relationships and that Shaili's life would be defined as an "Atypical journey." The giggles of their youth mocked the prophecies then. But did it all come true?

As Shaili continued to gaze at the reminiscences and the time lost, her eyes went to one of her favorite quotes, laminated and decorated on the dresser, "When a relationship dies do we ever really give up the ghost or are we forever haunted by the spirits of relationship's past?" The brevity of the words nudged Shaili and her mind went to her mother. Before Shaili could process any more sorrow and console her eyes, Supriya's parents' maid's freckled fingers poked her. The old lady, with tobacco stained teeth, had brought a tray of steaming hot tea and asked Shaili, with a river of curiosity in her eyes, if the noise pollution in Pune bothered her, assuming that she probably wasn't used to cars honking and autorickshaw drivers playing deafening music any longer. She offered to close the windows in the house, but Shaili stopped her. Strangely, the blaring of the car horns didn't hassle her. It used to when she lived in Pune, along with the other suppressed voices of her soul; but in New York, where she'd accepted her inner tone, her frame of mind had changed. Today, the smog of automobiles created a trail of memoirs that prodded her. The uninhibited vehicles, almost colliding into each other and creating a bubble of traffic jam, persuaded her to mentally compare her own persona in the two cities.

A part of Shaili had yearned for Pune all these years. She missed the layers of dust bathing her skin after riding the *Kinetic Honda* in the middle of the day. The long scarf draped tightly around her face prevented filth, and sometimes reality, from permeating her skin. Later in life, Shaili wondered if she wrapped her face, mummy-like, so no one could detect the unfamiliar choices printed on it.

As she continued to evaluate her transformation, all of a sudden, the windowpane creaked and then flung open. Shaili's hair rebelled and acted as a veil for her comely face. The curtains fluttered with ecstasy. The voluptuous rain was beating against the cobblestone streets as if trying to erode every bitter remembrance Shaili had left behind; the tempestuous wind was blowing as if trying to cleanse her state of mind. The universe had come together to remind her of the sum total of gain and loss over these fifteen years. Shaili stretched both her arms out of the window and collected water in her palm like it was a pail. She knew it was about time she created an oasis of clemency.

"Today, I want to talk to you about how I operate in my new world if you like."

Suresh Kapoor sat down beside Shaili. He didn't say anything. She pulled some of the grass from the soft, wet earth as she articulated her thoughts and spat out remnants of caustic language.

"It has not been easy, you know."

"What hasn't?"

"My journey. And don't you dare make an excuse for bringing coffee while I am talking, okay?" Suresh Kapoor sat with an indecipherable gaze. Shaili continued, "I wish I had my family with me."

"We were all there with you." He interrupted Shaili.

"Of course you all were there, but just physically. When I was struggling with defining my own identity, I was completely lonely. I was so tired from feeling upset. My skin cringed looking at its own reflection in the mirror. Not knowing what I wanted or who I wanted was excruciating. Like being breathless underwater. Questions, that I had no answers for, decided to build a hive on my soul. Thoughts that no one would want to hear about started leaking out of every untainted cell in my brain. Geez, I had to get used to being someone I wasn't even though this new person was the actual me. Does that make sense to you?"

"Somewhat." Suresh Kapoor confessed.

"See, what I was for twenty plus years and then someone else. Like Ma in her salwaar kameez with dupatta, you know. She didn't whine, but anyone with an iota of intelligence could see that she never felt like her true self in those clothes." Shaili stuttered and shivered every now and then. Every emotion was followed by an agonizing, piercing break. She didn't look her father in the eye. Not because she felt shame, because it was undeniably an awkward conversation to have with a parent.

"Your arrangement is unnatural! I said it before, and I am saying it again. The Western world has corrupted you."

"People who live in glass houses shouldn't throw stones at others. You judge me while your marriage was the most dysfunctional alliance in the history of human relationships."

Shaili's bluntness sewed Suresh Kapoor's lips shut. Shaili chuckled at the mundane postulations and her tyrannical world. Her father wasn't the first parent to blame America because their child hadn't followed the social norms. At least Suresh Kapoor was having a dialogue with Shaili. Leila had faced worse. Her parents had ousted her from their lives.

"See, we both know we aren't here to talk about my new career that you disapprove of, so why beat around the bush?"

Suresh Kapoor knew what was coming next. He kept quiet.

"How do I explain this to you in a way you get it? No place has got to do anything with who I am."

"Yes, it has." Suresh Kapoor babbled.

When Shaili said, "Oh, please! Stop living in denial," bellicosely, the obstinacy inside of Suresh Kapoor dipped to a point where his arguments froze. He backed off. She continued, "I am a lesbian and that's a fact. Whether you choose to deal with it or not, it's your volition, but I won't defend my life anymore."

Suresh Kapoor looked ill at ease with Shaili's admission about who she was. Was it his parenting? A part of his brain took responsibility, internally, for being an austere parent with Shaili; but the other part told him that he did the right thing given Shaili was an embodiment of deception. In his head, by being mean and vigilant with her, he had tried to ensure that the man she ended up with didn't have to suffer any lies—the way he had in his marriage. He felt even the breeze and the birds at the lake judged him for his daughter turning out so drastically different from everyone else. Like somehow it was solely his fault because he was the only parent alive. He believed he was a failure as a parent because not only was his daughter a divorcee but also she was someone who loved and lived with another woman and that too without any remorse.

Suresh Kapoor wasn't the type to accept defeat so easily. He said, while twirling his moustache upwards, "You were alright in Pune under my guidance." Shaili was exhausted from dealing with the streaks of monotonous, slanderous, sanctimonious declarations hurled at her. Suresh Kapoor conveniently overlooked the look on Shaili's face and continued, "Did you become…whatever it is you are…to get back at me? For all the times I scolded you when you were a child?"

"Not everything is about you!" Shaili rolled her eyes and stood up. "You know what, I can't be accountable for your happiness. I spent far too many years, consumed with repentance, for reasons unknown to me just so I could please you. Somehow make you proud of me. But this is it."

"Meaning what?"

"I mean, you can't acknowledge my identity even today when I am sincerely trying to tell you about it. Does my beatitude not matter to you at all? Would you rather I spent my life wretchedly pretending to be someone I am not? Are you really that ashamed of who I am?"

Suresh Kapoor sighed loudly. He picked up a pebble from the ground and threw it in the lake. "Both you and your mother had unfathomable secrets. I feel like both of you used me for your own selfish reasons. Your mother chose to end her life when she couldn't face the truth any longer. She chose to marry me, have you, and kill herself all at her own convenience. Fact is, she did what she had to all these years—including visit her dead boyfriend. She was a dutiful wife and a devoted mother, but never a companion. Because her heart was never with me. Even in the end, all she left me was a letter. But that doesn't help me, Shaili."

"What? But. I mean. As in…"

"I know what you are going to say, Shaili. That neither of you did it on purpose. The fact is, I don't know and at this point don't care whether it was intentional or not. What I know is that the history of deception has repeated itself in my very own house. Both the times, I was the idiot at the receiving end. That's what is not easy for me to accept. I am ashamed that I couldn't see what I was getting into when I married your mother. I am ashamed that I didn't know, you, my own child was so drastically unusual. I am ashamed I didn't see the signs in either of you." Suresh Kapoor couldn't control the tears flooding his eyes. He wiped them with the corner of his kurta.

Shaili was speechless. Suresh Kapoor lowered his eyes and tugged at Shaili's *dupatta* like an obstinate child who wants to be heard in a room crowded with boisterous adults. She poked her left cheek with her tongue. He eventually looked into her eyes and said, "But I can't be ashamed of your decision when, frankly, I just don't understand who you are."

"You…" Shaili tried to interrupt him, but he continued to speak boldly. "Let me finish, Shaili. See, I somewhat understood you when we lived in the same house. Even if a little bit. I might have kept my distance from you, but I had a sense of involvement. I provided for you. And then you moved away which brought with it a wave of changes. The physical distance created a barrier that kept increasing with time."

"I moved away? You got me married and sent me away! Like I was a burden! I still remember the day you made up your mind and the happenings afterwards. I spent my entire life seeking your approval. Somewhere in that struggle, I lost the key to my own desires. Moving out of Pune gave me a perspective. Because of the distance, I was finally able to think without you or Ma or Supriya or Tanisha trying to convolute my thoughts."

"Now you are saying your mother didn't love you? Will you spare anyone?"

"I would never say that. All I am saying is that the person standing in front of you is the real me—sanguine and successful. Don't you get it that I am finally not petulant because I chose to accept the reality? I needed the untainted revelation, and I couldn't have had that if I was with you all in Pune because I never thought about myself when I lived here. I was too scared to comprehend the possibilities of what you would do to Ma or me if I second-guessed certain aspects of my life."

Suresh Kapoor looked disconcerted and almost waited for Shaili to say something further. Shaili, oblivious to his reaction, threw both her arms out in frustration and said, "In my quest to keep everyone pleased, I subdued my needs for the longest time. I felt my existence was a lie. I couldn't figure out why, but I felt the entire universe was taking advantage of me."

"I don't get you, Shaili. I am trying, but I can't understand."

Shaili knew he sounded earnest. She looked at him and said, "Didn't a wise person once say that you can entertain a thought without accepting it? We can take it one step at a time."

By now Suresh Kapoor's face was doused with salty water. Shaili couldn't decipher all the emotions his tears represented, but in the process of decoding, she felt waterworks in her own eyes. Despite everything she and Suresh Kapoor had been through, he still thought of her as his *own* child.

Suresh Kapoor wiped the pearl-shaped orphan teardrop sitting on Shaili's mole. It flowed and mingled with the other strands of the tear-family residing on her cheek. She smeared his tears with the corner of her dupatta. At that moment, their thoughts chose to remain silent and represent white doves.

Supriya and Leila sat in the car while Shaili and Suresh Kapoor talked. They hadn't been privy to most of the verbal exchange between the father-daughter. But whenever an intense argument roared, like the rains, Supriya and Leila caught snippets. That's when Supriya would suggest that she and Leila intervene. Leila would advise her against it. She implicitly understood the importance of this meeting to Shaili. Shaili had told her that though she couldn't alter the beginning of her own life's story, there was still time to amend the ending.

After a few more minutes of quietude, Shaili shook Suresh Kapoor's right arm and said, "Daddy, I didn't mean to hurt you. I promise. What would do if you were in my place?" She sounded like an eight-year old child seeking atonement after indulging in incopious amounts of candy at a new neighbor's house.

"Well, I stayed with your mother. Despite her reprehensible history, I was with her until the day she died."

"But were you happy?" Shaili pulled away, so she could look into his eyes.

"I…Umm…We had our differences, but we didn't deprive you children of anything. We took good care of you."

"Did you think because of all the materialism you showered on Tanisha and I, we wore a blindfold? Dad, be honest to yourself. I lived with you and Ma for over two decades, and I still remember what happened in the house. So, please answer my question: Were you and Ma ever blissful together?"

Suresh Kapoor looked for the right words. Shaili continued, "Do you want me to exist in an unfulfilling relationship, like you did, or actually grab the joyful experience I have being with Leila?"

Suresh Kapoor touched Shaili's right shoulder and urged her to face him. "I don't get it."

Shaili realized her father looked worn out and powerless. She conceded he was truly remorseful. She cupped both his hands and said, "I am here. Ask me what you want to know, but please don't be contemptuous. I have no patience for it anymore."

"I want to know one thing."

"Sure."

"Why Leila?"

Suresh Kapoor didn't take her warning seriously. Or that's what Shaili thought when she widened her pupils and brusquely reminded him, "Again with your fatuous investigation."

"Calm down, Shaili! I am not being nasty much as you'd like to believe. I am inquisitive." Suresh Kapoor stopped Shaili before she could accuse him of misdemeanor. Contrary to what Shaili thought, he had no plans of getting into a heated debate again. As a father, he wanted to know why his daughter thought of Leila as the person she wanted to spend the rest of her life with.

"Well, okay. Here is the thing. Leila is a person of minimal pretensions. She allowed me to be myself at the time when even I didn't know who I was. You must have realized by now that she is extremely non-meddlesome and has abiding faith in her decisions. Her attitude made my voyage, into the new world, much easier." Shaili smiled and tossed her head. "Leila is laidback, so even though she is there, she isn't really, you know. When I met her, I was disturbed, and my life was in disarray. I was en route to annihilate my very own existence. I needed someone with strong convictions to snap me out of my bubble of denial. But someone who was not impatient, overprotective, pushy, possessive, or calculating. I had had all of those." Shaili bit her tongue herself before it rolled out any crude comparisons. She said, "End of the day, Leila and I carried similar scars."

"What scars?"

"As if Erida, the Greek Goddess of Hate, had whispered vileness into the ears of our dear ones, so they would resent us until the day we died. We were both family loving, but castaways. In our own ways, we were both prototypes of unflinching defiance."

Suresh Kapoor confessed, "I am not following you."

Shaili deduced she needed to lessen her intimacy with language if she wanted to have a dialogue with Suresh Kapoor. She said, "Culturally, we were similar. I didn't have to explain myself to Leila or my equation with you or Tanisha. She was in a comparable boat or maybe worse. At least I had Ma and Supriya. Leila had no family looking out for her—an orphan with both parents alive. But most importantly, at least for me, what clicked was that our core values were in sync. Family meant a lot to both of us despite the sprinkles of dogmatism."

"I have asked you this question before, but you started fuming. As a father, don't I have the right to know if she broke up your marriage?" Suresh Kapoor didn't shy from repeating his question.

Shaili scoffed irony. "You can't break a broken person, Dad. You should know that better than anyone!"

"And Leila is the only person you ever liked?"

"Why does that come as a surprise to you?"

"It's just that, I thought, since you found out, did you not want to know, to meet others?"

"As in, research if there were other fishes in the sea? Is that what you are trying to ask?" Shaili completed Suresh Kapoor's thought. It's like she had X-rayed his brain.

"Yes." He looked unperturbed.

"You think just because I am gay, I must be a slut?" Shaili's face turned an unpleasant crimson.

She was incoherent with rage, at least in Suresh Kapoor's books. Astounded by her impudence, he let out a high-pitched, authoritative, wail, "Mind your language!"

"Sorry." Shaili pouted her lips and blew out a gallon of incensed energy. She immediately recognized that her remark was superfluous. Her speech veered towards an approachable direction. "It's just that I am tired of explaining myself to others. The misconceptions and prejudices revolving around homosexuality are sickening. Why don't you all get it that we are humans too? Same flesh and blood. Same friggin' organs!"

"Whenever we choose to take an unusual route, we have to be geared up for questioning. Not everyone enquires with the intention of being interfering. If you want to live in the society, either abide by their rules or be ready for a flood of curiosity. People get conscious around unfamiliarity." Suresh Kapoor paused to catch a breath. "I speak from experience."

"I guess." She thought of trying a different approach to connect with him. She entwined her index fingers and patted her lips with her fingertips. The rhythmic tapping seemed to magically nourish her thoughts. She excitedly snapped her fingers and in an energized voice asked, "Ma was the only one you loved your entire life, right?"

"What does this have to do with her?"

"Answer me, will ya?"

"Yes."

"How did you know she was the one for you?"

"I just knew it."

"It was the same way for me. My gut told me. Dad, I have the same senses and sensibilities like a straight person." Shaili touched Suresh Kapoor's right wrist, "Some people go through life searching that one person who can make them exultant; luckily for me, I found it in the only person I dated. Ma and you taught me too well."

Suresh Kapoor nodded, as if in agreement with Shaili's lexis of appreciation. He said, "How does it work?"

"What does?

"Between you two."

The ground beneath Shaili's feet shifted. She had made a conscientious effort to bond with her father, but this is where she drew the line. She didn't want to chat about the personal details of her life with anyone. She said uneasily, "I am not sure I quite comprehend your dilemma."

"You both are women."

"Ya, the last time I checked." Shaili realized how she'd never thought of Suresh Kapoor as an able orator. Ambiguity, even if unpremeditated, was one of his strengths.

"Is there a husband in your what you have? In your community? One of you has to be the wife, no? How else do you decide who cooks and cleans and takes care of the family?"

"There are no right or wrong rules. It would be pretentious of me if I spoke for everyone. But what I can tell you is that Leila and I don't believe in any kind of stereotypes. I guess, since we both came from male dominated societies, which we frown upon, neither of us wanted to bury ourselves with being the "husband" so to speak. We are both content doing our own stuff without actually assigning gender-specificity to our roles. It works for us. Does that answer your question?"

Suresh Kapoor gestured his head in agreement. He waited for a few seconds, as if catching his breath, and then remarked. "I have never seen you like this—so confident and alert. It is good." Shaili's ears rang with disbelief. Did Suresh Kapoor actually openly compliment her? Before Shaili could part her lips so her inquiring mind could form questions, Suresh Kapoor suddenly voiced a guilt-laden question, "Did I make you who you are?"

"Could you be specific what you mean by that?"

"You know. What you are now."

"You mean, gay?"

"Oh, you get your obstinacy from me. Yes, gay! There you go, I said it." Both Suresh Kapoor and Shaili shared a smile.

"I don't think I have an answer to that question. I don't know if the onus is on nature or nurture. But one thing I can tell you is that both Sadhil and Supriya too speculated that."

"So, you do blame me?"

"If you are asking me whether or not I am irate about who I turned out to be, then my answer is: I am happy finding out a key fact about myself. I do blame you for not letting me live my life when I was younger. It would have saved us all a lot of heartache, especially Sadhil."

"And here I thought I was being a good father by limiting your interaction with boys. Guiding your career choices, taking care of you."

"Becoming a parent and actually mastering parenting skills are two different points, but we will talk about it another time."

"Why not now?"

"In this moment of distress, when you are trying to cope with plentiful amount of inconceivable information, I can't fathom burdening you with any new theories."

Shaili's allegations weren't wasted on Suresh Kapoor. He tried to channelize the order of his thoughts. "Can I ask you another question? Don't get mad, again."

"Shoot away."

"Since the only friend you had growing up was Supriya, were you two also what you and Leila are?"

"Eew! Gross! That is the most outrageous, yet valiant question you have asked! But please stop before I pull out a barf bag."

"What bag??"

"I might have to puke." Shaili cringed her nose at her father's question. "Let me ask you something instead. Were you friends with any other woman aside from Ma when you were younger?"

"A few of them in our colony."

"Did you date them too?"

"What kind of stupid question is that?"

"The same kind you asked me."

"No manners you have left in you!"

"Well, did you, Dad?"

"Of course not. We were just friends! I only loved your mother." Suresh Kapoor was horrified by his daughter's outspokenness.

"So, what makes you think that I would obscure boundaries? Why, because I am gay? Dad, Supriya was and will always be my best friend and that's about it." Shaili tried to clear the fog of ignorance from the mind of her disbelieving father.

"Okay, okay. I understand. Do you think everything is perfect in your life—now that you know?"

"Dad, haven't you heard: *Being happy doesn't mean that everything is perfect. It means that you've decided to look beyond the imperfections.* Life is only as perfect as you make it out to be. I am older and hopefully wiser, so I have learnt to take the bad with the good. But why did you ask such a loaded question?"

"Because, Shaili, I am a conventional man. I don't think I will ever openly approve of the path you have decided to tread upon. I grew up in times when men married women. They earned the money and women managed the house. All our religious texts say the same."

"That's not entirely true. *Kama Sutra* states otherwise." Shaili felt odd about bringing up the *Kama Sutra* with her father. But the analogy flowed from her mouth subconsciously. Suresh Kapoor pretended that his oldest child didn't refer to *the Manual* of sensual pleasures. He couldn't deny the confabulation all afternoon had been everything short of traditional.

"I am too old and tired to unlearn what I know." He told Shaili plainly, but the candor in his voice was irrefutable.

Shaili started weeping. She hadn't expected Suresh Kapoor to applaud her preferences, but somewhere she'd hoped the ending would be different. They had both suffered prodigiously. Suresh Kapoor's eyes fell to the ground, as if he'd appraised the situation and reached a conclusion.

He said, "But I am also an old-fashioned father and my child's happiness is of utmost importance to me. I won't condone your decision, but I will support you. You can count on me. I'll be there for you whenever you need me. That's what parents do—support their children's choices even though they might not understand them."

"Dad, don't you get it? That's what I have sought my entire life—your acceptance. I am fine until you aren't aversed to me. We don't have to always agree, but it would be nice if we could cordially disagree. You are the only family I have left, and I wouldn't want to lose you."

Suresh Kapoor knew that Shaili had sounded realistic in her expectations. With his palms folded, he bent his head. Shaili held his hands and pressed them softly. Mr. Kapoor pulled the diamond pendant, Shaili had sent for her mother the first time Leila had met her, out of his pocket.

"Where did you find this?" Shaili clung to the pendant. It was redolent of her mother.

"Your mother left it for you before she died. She said you would understand, in the letter she left for me."

Shaili stared at the lake for a few moments and wailed loudly. "Ma might be dead, but her end hasn't gone a waste, Dad." Shaili moved towards Suresh Kapoor and hugged him tightly, like a child scared of standing alone in a dark room on a stormy night.

The pendant was symbolic of new relationships. The circle of love represented Suresh Kapoor and Shaili.

Shaili understood why the lake was like a cloister to her mother.